Where are the Children?

MARY HIGGINS CLARK

Original English language edition
Where are the Children?

Simon & Schuster, New York

Simon & Schuster, Inc.
1230 Avenue of the Americas
New York
New York 10020
U.S.A.

This edition published by arrangement with the original publisher Simon and Schuster, Inc., New York.

This book is a work of fiction. Names, characters, places, organizations, and incidents are either products of the author's imagination or used fictitiously. Any resemblance to actual events, places, organizations, or persons, living or dead, is entirely coincidental.

21, rue du Montparnasse
75283 Paris Cedex 06

HARRAP's® est une marque de Larousse SAS.
www.harrap.com

ISBN 978 2 81 870324 3

About the author

Mary Higgins Clark is the author of thirty-two worldwide bestsellers. There are more than seventy million copies[1] of her books in print. She lives in Saddle River, New Jersey.

1. exemplaires

DIRECTION DE LA PUBLICATION : Carine Girac-Marinier

DIRECTION ÉDITORIALE : Claude Nimmo

NOTES EN MARGE : Étienne Leyris

RÉVISION DES NOTES : Marianne Mouchot

INFORMATIQUE ÉDITORIALE : Philippe Cazabet, Marie-Noëlle Tilliette

CONCEPTION GRAPHIQUE : Uli Meindl

MISE EN PAGES : Cynthia Savage

FABRICATION : Rebecca Dubois

Mot de l'Éditeur

Vous aimeriez lire en langue originale, mais le vocabulaire, les expressions figurées ou la syntaxe vous arrêtent parfois ?

Cette collection est faite pour vous !

Vous trouverez en effet, en note dans la marge, une traduction de certains mots et expressions qui vous permettra d'avancer facilement dans votre lecture.

Nous n'avons pas cherché à vous donner une traduction littéraire de l'ouvrage et nous nous sommes parfois écartés du sens littéral pour vous fournir celui qui convient le mieux à l'histoire. Aussi les mots sont-ils traduits dans le contexte du texte original.

Les expressions figées anglaises sont, bien entendu, rendues par une expression équivalente en français.

Les allusions à des réalités culturelles du monde anglo-saxon sont expliquées également dans la marge, pour vous aider à mieux comprendre la trame de l'histoire.

Vous aurez ainsi, en regard du texte original, tout le savoir-faire d'un dictionnaire rien que pour vous et adapté à ce livre !

Notre objectif est de vous mener jusqu'au mot FIN en vous donnant les clés nécessaires à la compréhension du récit.

Laissez-vous gagner par l'angoisse, l'humour et le suspense qui règnent chez les maîtres de la littérature anglo-saxonne.

Lire en VO ? You can indeed!

A note from Mary Higgins Clark...

It is hard to believe that thirty years have passed since the magical day when *Where Are the Children?*[1] was published[2]. It seems like only yesterday.

On this special anniversary, I look at my bookshelves[3] and read the titles of all the novels[4] I have written since then[5]. They are all, for different reasons, very special to me. Nevertheless, *Where Are the Children?* has its own unique place[6]. It launched me[7] on the career I love. One of the definitions of happiness is "to love what you do" and I've been blessed because that gift was given to me[8].

Over these years I have enjoyed telling stories and meeting so many of the wonderful people who are my readers, and I thank you for that.

And now, Happy Reading!

Mary Higgins Clark

1. [« la Maison du guet » dans la version française]
2. [en 1975]
3. rayonnages
4. romans
5. que j'ai écrits depuis
6. occupe une place à part
7. Il m'a donné accès
8. ce bonheur m'a été accordé

To the memory of my mother,
NORA C. HIGGINS,
with love, admiration and gratitude

Introduction

Where Are the Children? was my first suspense novel[1] and the book that really changed my life.

I had written before and actually made a living[2] for a time doing scripts for radio shows. I had also published some short stories[3], but while they were fun and gratifying[4], they didn't pay the bills[5], so I decided to try my hand[6] at a real book.

My first effort was a biographical novel about George Washington; it took three years to write[7], was published invisibly, and went directly to the remainder tables as it came off press[8]. That didn't faze me[9]—I considered it a triumph. After all, it *was* published. Triumph or no, however, I sincerely wanted my next book to sell.

It was at that point that I studied my bookshelves and realized that from the time I was first able to read[10], whenever possible I had chosen to curl up with[11] suspense stories. Clearly they were my favorite kind of fiction. I had begun with books featuring[12] girl detectives like Judy Bolton and Nancy Drew[13]; from them I had moved on to Agatha Christie, Josephine Tey, Ngaio Marsh, Charlotte Armstrong, Mignon Eberhart and Daphne du Maurier, to name just a few[14].

1. roman à suspense
2. avais de fait gagné ma vie
3. nouvelles
4. si elles me procuraient plaisir et satisfaction
5. factures
6. m'essayer
7. il me demanda trois années d'écriture
8. passa directement de l'imprimerie chez les revendeurs
9. Je ne me laissai pas démonter
10. pris conscience que dès que j'avais su lire
11. m'installer dans un coin pour savourer
12. dont les héroïnes étaient
13. [de la série des Alice]
14. pour n'en citer que quelques-uns

Whenever I read these books, I always tried to keep up with the author[1], to spot the bad guy[2], to solve[3] the crime early on[4]. Those writers were wonderful teachers, and gradually I absorbed some of the techniques they used.

I'll use an old and familiar story to illustrate what I mean. One version of the Hansel and Gretel legend[5] is that Hansel dropped smooth stones[6] to mark the path back out of[7] the forest, while Gretel dropped breadcrumbs[8]. When they wanted to find their way back home, they discovered that while the stones were still there, the breadcrumbs had been eaten by the birds.

In the same sense[9], suspense writers drop their own different versions of smooth stones and breadcrumbs, and invite the reader to follow them on their journey[10]. The breadcrumbs, so quickly gobbled up[11], turn out not to be the clues they seemed[12], while the stones, which blend in[13] so well with the landscape[14], often prove to be the true guide to finding the solution to the crime. Over the years, I became quite good at separating the two.

As a reader, I loved suspense. I thought I understood it. So I decided to see if I could *write* it.

Some advice[15] I had heard in a writing class came back to me[16]: Take a true case[17] or situation, one that interests you; ask yourself two questions: "Suppose...?[18]" and "What if...?[19]"; then turn it into fiction.

At that time in New York there was a celebrated[20] murder case, covered daily in the newspapers and on television[21]. A beautiful twenty-six-year-old mother—her name was Alice Crimmins—was accused of killing her five-year-old son and her three-year-old daughter. As it turned out[22], covered constantly by the press, she was convicted[23] of both deaths, then both convictions were thrown out on technicalities[24]. Eventually,[25] she was released from[26] prison, having spent only a very short time there. Once she was out, she remarried and disappeared from the public eye.

1. suivre le fil de l'histoire
2. repérer le méchant
3. résoudre
4. assez tôt
5. conte
6. laissait tomber des galets
7. jalonner le chemin du retour à travers
8. des miettes de pain
9. manière
10. voyage
11. avalées
12. se révèlent ne pas être les indices qu'elles semblaient être
13. se fondent
14. dans le paysage
15. conseil
16. me revint
17. une affaire réelle
18. Supposons que... ?
19. Et si... ?
20. célèbre
21. dont la presse et la télévision rendaient compte quotidiennement
22. En fin de compte
23. reconnue coupable
24. les deux condamnations furent annulées pour vice de forme
25. Finalement,
26. libérée de

The case dragged on for years.[1] It got so much media attention at the time that it was virtually[2] impossible not to hear about it and to have an opinion as to Alice Crimmins's guilt[3] or innocence. Any mention of her name was sure to start a lively debate[4]. So I asked myself the two questions: "Suppose...?" and "What if...?"

Suppose a beautiful young mother is accused and later convicted of the deliberate murder of her two young children? *Suppose* she gets out of prison because the conviction is overturned[5] on a technicality? *Suppose* she remarries and starts a new life, then seven years to the day her two children died[6], the two children from her *second* marriage disappear?

I decided it was a strong premise[7], and so I began to plan my book. The setting[8] was my first consideration[9]. At that time I had just started renting[10] a summer cottage on Cape Cod[11] in Massachusetts and had fallen in love with the area. The Cape has lonely beaches[12] to walk on and brilliant sunsets that offer a promise of joyous times to come. It also has terrifying nor'easters[13] that lash[14] the ocean savagely and send torrents of windswept rain across the Cape's narrow, sandy width[15]. In short, it has atmosphere.[16]

It is, therefore[17], the perfect place for a young woman with a wounded spirit[18] to flee to[19]. Cape people are reticent[20]. They respect privacy[21] and would never intrude upon[22] or question a person who is a loner[23].

As I began to outline[24] the book, I could visualize the young woman—whom I called Nancy Harmon—leaving San Francisco and getting on a bus that would take her across the country to the Cape, which she had visited as a child and remembered as a place of peace—a place where she could heal[25].

My working[26] title for the book was *Die a Little Death*[27] a phrase I had read in a memoir[28] written by a mistress of Louis XIV of France. She had borne him a child[29], and it lived only eight months. In the mem-

1. L'affaire avait duré des années.
2. pratiquement
3. culpabilité
4. discussion animée
5. jugement a été cassé
6. jour pour jour après la mort de ses deux enfants
7. bon point de départ
8. cadre
9. préoccupation
10. je venais de louer
11. [presqu'île sur la côte nord-est des États-Unis]
12. plages peu fréquentées
13. vents de nord-est
14. fouettent
15. de fortes averses sur la bande sablonneuse qu'est Cape Cod
16. Bref, une atmosphère se dégage du lieu.
17. donc
18. à l'âme blessée
19. où venir se réfugier
20. réservés
21. la vie privée
22. importuner
23. personne solitaire
24. À mesure que j'ébauchais
25. guérir de ses blessures
26. provisoire
27. Un avant-goût de la mort
28. des mémoires
29. eu un enfant de lui

oir she wrote, "And I with my baby died a little death." I thought it was an appropriate[1] title because in my story, part of Nancy, in essence[2], died with her first two children. Since that time she had managed to blot out[3] all memories of her life with them, but now she must suddenly try to recall[4] every detail of the events leading up to[5] their disappearance if she is to save[6] her second family.

At the time I was writing the novel, I had a fulltime[7] job in radio, so the book took me three years to finish[8]. When I was finally satisfied and knew I could add nothing more to it, I wrote in my journal, "I have finished the book, and it is GOOD!!!"

I still remember the black-and-white suit[9] I was wearing when I dropped off[10] the manuscript with my agent's secretary[11]—it was a very important day for me. Then six weeks passed without any word from my agent. Timidly I phoned her: "Pat," I said, "by any chance have you had time to look at my book?"

Pat Myrer had been a senior editor[12] before becoming an agent, and usually she ripped my short stories apart[13] and had me rewrite them before she would send them out[14]. When she told me that this time she felt no rewriting was necessary, that my novel was already out on submission with publishers[15], I realized I was on my way[16] because I was sure in my heart that the book would sell.

The world was a slightly[17] different place thirty years ago, and when I wrote that book, child molestation[18] was pretty much[19] a taboo subject. While there were no explicit scenes dealing with[20] that, it was clear enough[21] to the reader that the kidnapper was also a molester[22]. As a result,[23] two of the publishers to whom my manuscript was submitted turned it down[24]. They feared the subject of children in that kind of jeopardy[25] might upset[26] their women readers. Fortunately for me, however, Simon & Schuster decided to take a chance, and they bought the book.

1. approprié
2. surtout
3. s'effacer de la tête
4. se rappeler
5. menant à
6. si elle veut avoir quelque espoir de sauver
7. à plein temps
8. il me fallut trois ans pour finir le livre
9. tailleur
10. déposai
11. à la secrétaire de mon agent [littéraire]
12. rédactrice en chef
13. d'habitude, elle éreintait mes nouvelles
14. de les faire publier
15. qu'elle avait déjà proposé mon roman à des éditeurs
16. que ça y est, j'étais lancée
17. un peu
18. la pédophilie
19. pratiquement
20. traitant de
21. très clair
22. pédophile
23. En conséquence,
24. le refusèrent
25. péril
26. ne mette très mal à l'aise

At the suggestion of Phyllis Grann, then an editor at Simon & Schuster, it was given a new title. The concern she expressed was that[1] *Die a Little Death* might sound too much like a hard-edged crime story[2], so the title was changed to the more descriptive—and compelling[3]—*Where Are the Children?*

The publication of that book marked the turning point[4] in my life, and began a long and happy marriage with Simon & Schuster that has lasted to this day[5].

MHC

1. Elle craignait que
2. un roman policier sanglant
3. accrocheur
4. tournant
5. dure encore

Coup de pouce pour vous aider à bien comprendre le début de l'histoire...

Il fait un terrible temps de novembre à Cape Cod, une presqu'île de la côte Est des États-Unis, très prisée des touristes l'été.

Un homme erre dans la grande maison ventée où il vit en ermite. Il lui faut nuire à cette femme qui surveille si bien ses enfants. La tempête menace...

Prologue

He could feel the chill[1] coming in through the cracks[2] around the windowpanes[3]. Clumsily he got up[4] and lumbered over to[5] the window. Reaching for[6] one of the thick towels he kept handy[7] he stuffed it[8] around the rotting frame[9].

The incoming draft[10] made a soft, hissing[11] sound in the towel, a sound that vaguely pleased him. He looked out at the mist-filled[12] sky and studied the whitecaps churning in the water[13]. From this side of the house it was often possible to see Province-town, on the opposite shore[14] of Cape Cod Bay.

He hated the Cape. He hated the bleakness of it[15] on a November day like this; the stark grayness[16] of the water; the stolid[17] people who didn't say much but studied you with their eyes. He had hated it the one summer he'd been here—waves of tourists sprawling[18] on the beaches; climbing up the steep embankment[19] to this house; gawking in[20] the downstairs windows, cupping their hands over their eyes to peer[21] inside.

He hated the large for sale sign[22] that Ray Eldredge had posted on the front and back of the big house and the fact that now Ray and that woman who worked for him had begun bringing people in to see the house.

1. froid
2. fissures
3. carreaux
4. Il se leva tant bien que mal
5. marcha pesamment jusqu'à
6. Se saisissant de
7. qu'il gardait à portée de main
8. l'enfonça
9. châssis vermoulu
10. courant d'air
11. sifflant
12. embrumé
13. remous d'écume sur l'eau
14. rivage opposé
15. son aspect désolé
16. grisaille uniforme
17. impassible
18. vautrés
19. talus escarpé
20. regardant, bouche bée, par
21. mettant leurs mains en visière pour lorgner
22. écriteau « à vendre »

Last month it had been only a matter of luck[1] that he'd come along as they'd started through[2]; only luck that he'd gotten to the top floor before they had[3] and been able to put away[4] the telescope.

Time was running out.[5] Somebody would buy this house and he wouldn't be able to rent it again. That was why he'd sent the article to the paper[6]. He wanted to still be here to enjoy seeing her exposed for what she was[7] in front of these people... now, when she must have started to feel safe.

There was something else that he had to do, but the chance had never come. She kept such a close watch on[8] the children. But he couldn't afford[9] to wait anymore. Tomorrow...

He moved restlessly[10] around the room. The bedroom of the top-floor apartment was large. The whole house was large. It was a bastardized evolution[11] of an old captain's house. Begun in the seventeenth century on a rocky crest that commanded a view of the whole bay, it was a pretentious monument to man's need to be forever on guard[12].

Life wasn't like that. It was bits and pieces.[13] Icebergs that showed in tips[14]. He knew. He rubbed his hand over his face, feeling warm and uncomfortable even though the room was chilly. For six years now he'd rented this house in the late summer and fall[15]. It was almost exactly as it had been when he had first come into it. Only a few things were different: the telescope in the front room; the clothes that he kept for the special times; the peaked cap[16] that he pulled over his face, which shaded it[17] so well.

Otherwise[18] the apartment was the same: the old-fashioned sofa and pine tables and hooked rug[19] in the living room; the rock maple bedroom set[20]. This house and apartment had been ideal for his purpose until this fall, when Ray Eldredge had told him they were actively trying to sell the place for a restaurant

1. coup de chance
2. au moment où ils entamaient la visite
3. avant eux
4. ranger
5. Il ne restait plus beaucoup de temps.
6. journal
7. savourer le moment où elle apparaîtrait sous son vrai jour
8. surveillait de si près
9. se permettre
10. s'agitait
11. rénovation médiocre
12. répondant au besoin de l'homme d'être toujours sur ses gardes
13. Elle était faite de bric et de broc.
14. dont on ne voyait que des bouts
15. en automne
16. casquette à visière
17. la cachait
18. Pour le reste,
19. tapis au crochet
20. chambre à coucher en érable

and it could be rented only with the understanding it could be shown on telephoned notice[1].

Raynor Eldredge. The thought of the man brought a smile[2]. What would Ray think tomorrow when he saw the story? Had Nancy ever told Ray who she was? Maybe not. Women could be sly[3]. If Ray didn't know, it would be even better. How wonderful it would be to actually see Ray's expression when he opened the paper! It was delivered[4] a little after ten in the morning. Ray would be in his office. He might not even look at it for a while[5].

Impatiently he turned from[6] the window. His thick, trunklike legs were tight[7] in shiny black trousers. He'd be glad when he could lose some of this weight[8]. It would mean that awful business of starving himself again[9], but he could do it. When it had been necessary he'd done it before. Restlessly[10] he rubbed a hand over his vaguely itchy scalp[11]. He'd be glad when he could let his hair grow back in its natural lines[12] again. The sides had always been thick and would probably be mostly gray now.

He ran[13] one hand slowly down his trouser leg, then impatiently paced around[14] the apartment, finally stopping at the telescope in the living room. The telescope was especially powerful—the kind of equipment that wasn't available for general sale[15]. Even many police departments didn't have it yet[16]. But there were always ways to get things you wanted. He bent over and peered into it, squinting one eye[17].

Because of the darkness of the day, the kitchen light was on, so it was easy to see Nancy clearly. She was standing in front of the kitchen window, the one that was over the sink[18]. Maybe she was about to get something ready to put into the oven[19] for dinner. But she had a warm jacket on, so she was probably going out. She was standing quietly, just looking in the direction of the water. What was she thinking of? Whom

1. louée qu'à la condition qu'elle puisse être visitée sur simple appel téléphonique
2. le fit sourire
3. faire des cachotteries
4. livré
5. avant un certain temps
6. se détourna de
7. Ses jambes grosses comme des troncs étaient trop serrées
8. maigrir un peu
9. Il allait devoir – quelle corvée – s'affamer à nouveau
10. Par nervosité,
11. crâne qui le démangeait un peu
12. de façon naturelle
13. passa
14. arpenta
15. qu'on ne trouvait pas dans le commerce
16. n'en disposaient pas encore
17. Il se pencha et regarda dans le viseur en plissant un œil
18. évier
19. allait-elle préparer un plat à mettre au four

was she thinking of? The children—Peter... Lisa...? He'd like to know.

He could feel his mouth go dry and licked his lips[1] nervously. She looked very young today. Her hair was pulled back from her face. She kept it dark brown. Someone would surely have recognized her if she'd left it the natural red-gold shade[2]. Tomorrow she'd be thirty-two. But she still didn't look her age[3]. She had an intriguing young quality[4], soft and fresh and silky[5].

He swallowed[6] nervously. He could feel the feverish dryness of his mouth[7], even while his hands and armpits[8] were wet and warm. He gulped[9], then swallowed again, and the sound evolved into a deep chuckle[10]. His whole body began to shake with mirth[11] and jarred[12] the telescope. Nancy's image blurred[13], but he didn't bother refocusing the lens[14]. He wasn't interested in watching her anymore today.

Tomorrow! He could just see the expression she'd have at this time tomorrow. Exposed to the world for what she was; numbed with worry and fear[15]; trying to answer the question... the same question the police had thrown at her over and over[16] seven years ago.

"Come on, Nancy," the police would be saying again. "Come clean with us.[17] Tell the truth. You should know you can't get away with this. Tell us, Nancy—where are the children?"

1. s'humecta les lèvres
2. les avait gardés roux doré, sa couleur naturelle
3. ne faisait toujours pas son âge
4. un côté étonnamment jeune
5. soyeux
6. avala sa salive
7. Sa bouche était sèche, fiévreuse
8. aisselles
9. Sa gorge se serra
10. se transforma en un rire étranglé
11. hilarité
12. ébranla
13. se brouilla
14. ne prit pas la peine de régler à nouveau l'objectif
15. paralysée par l'anxiété et la peur
16. lui avait assénée, encore et encore
17. Avouez !

1

Ray came down the stairs pulling the knot closed on his tie[1]. Nancy was sitting at the table with a still-sleepy Missy on her lap[2]. Michael was eating his breakfast in his poised, reflective way[3].

Ray tousled[4] Mike's head and leaned over to kiss Missy. Nancy smiled up at him. She was so darn pretty[5]. There were fine lines[6] around those blue eyes, but you'd still never take her for thirty-two[7]. Ray was only a few years older himself, but always felt infinitely her senior[8]. Maybe it was that awful[9] vulnerability. He noticed the traces of red at the roots[10] of her dark hair. A dozen times in the last year he'd wanted to ask her to let it grow out, but hadn't dared[11].

"Happy birthday, honey[12]," he said quietly.

He watched as the color drained from her face[13].

Michael looked surprised. "Is it Mommy's birthday? You didn't tell me that."

Missy sat upright[14]. "Mommy's birthday?" She sounded pleased.

"Yes," Ray told them. Nancy was staring down at the table[15]. "And tonight we're going to celebrate[16]. Tonight I'm going to bring home a big birthday cake and

1. en remontant son nœud de cravate
2. sur les genoux, une Missy encore endormie
3. à sa manière posée, réfléchie
4. ébouriffa
5. tellement belle
6. rides
7. on ne lui donnait certainement pas 32 ans
8. plus âgé qu'elle
9. terrible
10. racines
11. osé
12. chérie
13. la vit blêmir
14. se redressa
15. fixait la table
16. fêter ça

a present[1], and we'll have Aunt Dorothy come to dinner. Right, Mommy?"

"Ray... no." Nancy's voice was low and pleading[2].

"Yes. Remember, last year you promised that this year we'd..."

Celebrate was the wrong word. He couldn't say it. But for a long time he'd known that they would someday have to start changing the pattern[3] of her birthdays. At first she'd withdrawn[4] completely from him and gone around the house or walked the beach like a silent ghost[5] in a world of her own[6].

But last year she'd finally begun to talk about them... the two other children. She'd said, "They'd be so big now... ten and eleven. I try to think how they would look[7] now, but can't seem to even imagine.... Everything about that time is so blurred. Like a nightmare[8] that I only dreamed."

"It's supposed to be like that," Ray told her. "Put it all behind you[9], honey. Don't even wonder what happened anymore[10]."

The memory strengthened[11] his decision. He bent over Nancy and patted[12] her hair with a gesture that was at once[13] protective and gentle.

Nancy looked up at him. The appeal on her face changed to uncertainty.[14] "I don't think—"

Michael interrupted her. "How old are you, Mommy?" he asked practically[15].

Nancy smiled—a real smile that miraculously eased[16] the tension. "None of your business[17]," she told him.

Ray took a quick gulp[18] of her coffee. "Good girl," he said. "Tell you what, Mike. I'll pick you up[19] after school this afternoon and we'll go get a present for Mommy. Now I'd better get out of here.[20] Some guy is coming up to see the Hunt place. I want to get the file together.[21]"

"Isn't it rented?[22]" Nancy asked.

1. cadeau
2. implorante
3. à modifier le déroulement
4. elle s'était éloignée
5. fantôme
6. à elle
7. à quoi ils pourraient ressembler
8. cauchemar
9. Oublie tout ça
10. Ne cherche même plus à savoir ce qui s'est passé
11. renforça
12. tapota
13. à la fois
14. Son regard implorant laissa place à l'incertitude.
15. de façon très concrète
16. apaisa
17. Ça ne te regarde pas
18. gorgée
19. viendrai te chercher
20. Il faut que j'y aille.
21. Je veux rassembler les pièces du dossier.
22. Ce n'est pas déjà loué ?

"Yes. That Parrish fellow[1] who's taken the apartment on and off[2] has it again. But he knows we have the right to show it anytime. It's a great spot[3] for a restaurant and wouldn't take much to convert[4]. It'll make a nice commission if I sell it."

Nancy put Missy down and walked with him to the door. He kissed her lightly and felt her lips tremble under his. How much had he upset her[5] by starting this birthday talk? Some instinct made him want to say[6], *Let's not wait for tonight. I'll stay home and we'll take the kids and go to Boston for the day.*

Instead[7] he got into his car, waved[8], backed up[9] and drove onto the narrow dirt lane that wound[10] through an acre[11] of woods until it terminated on the cross-Cape road that led to the center of Adams Port and his office.

Ray was right, Nancy thought as she walked slowly back to the table. There was a time to stop following the patterns of yesterday[12]—a time to stop remembering and look only to the future. She knew that a part of her was still frozen[13]. She knew that the mind dropped a protective curtain over painful[14] memories—but it was more than that.

It was as though her life with Carl were a blur[15]... the entire time. It was hard to remember the faculty[16] house on the campus, Carl's modulated voice[17]... Peter and Lisa. What had they looked like? Dark hair, both of them, like Carl's, and too quiet... too subdued[18]... affected by her uncertainty[19]... and then lost—both of them.

"Mommy, why do you look so sad?" Michael gazed at her[20] with Ray's candid[21] expression, spoke with Ray's directness[22].

Seven years, Nancy thought. Life was a series of seven-year cycles. Carl used to say that your whole body changed in that time. Every cell renewed itself[23]. It was time for her to really look ahead[24]... to forget.

1. Ce type, là, Parrish
2. de temps en temps
3. Ce serait très bien
4. ne serait pas difficile à aménager
5. L'avait-il secouée
6. Poussé par une sorte d'instinct, il faillit dire
7. Au lieu de quoi,
8. fit au revoir de la main
9. fit une marche arrière
10. chemin de terre qui serpentait
11. env. 4 000 m²
12. habitudes du passé
13. restée bloquée
14. douloureux
15. était brouillée
16. pour enseignants
17. voix modulée
18. éteints
19. gagnés par son indécision
20. la regardait
21. franche
22. adoptait le franc-parler de Ray
23. se régénérait
24. regarder vers l'avenir

She glanced around[1] the large, cheerful kitchen with the old brick fireplace, the wide oak floors[2], the red curtains and valances[3] that didn't obstruct the view over the harbor[4]. And then she looked at Michael and Missy....

"I'm not sad, darling," she said. "I'm really not."

She scooped Missy up[5] in her arms, feeling the warmth and sweet stickiness of her[6]. "I've been thinking about your present," Missy said. Her long strawberry-blond[7] hair curled[8] around her ears and forehead. People sometimes asked where she got that beautiful hair—who had been the redhead[9] in the family?

"Great," Nancy told her. "But think about it outside. You'd better get some fresh air soon. It's supposed to rain later and get very cold."

After the children were dressed, she helped them on with their windbreakers[10] and hats. "There's my dollar," Michael said with satisfaction as he reached into the breast pocket[11] of his jacket. "I was sure I left it here. Now I can buy you a present."

"Me has money too." Missy proudly held up a handful of pennies[12]. "Oh, now, you two shouldn't be carrying your money out[13]," Nancy told them. "You'll only lose it. Let me hold it for you."

Michael shook his head. "If I give it to you, I might forget it when I go shopping with Daddy."

"I promise I won't let you forget it."

"My pocket has a zipper[14]. See? I'll keep it in that, and I'll hold Missy's for her."

"Well..." Nancy shrugged[15] and gave up[16] the discussion. She knew perfectly well that Michael wouldn't lose the dollar. He was like Ray, well organized. "Now, Mike, I'm going to straighten up[17]. You be sure to stay with[18] Missy."

"Okay," Michael said cheerfully. "Come on, Missy. I'll push you on the swing[19] first."

1. parcourut du regard
2. parquet de chêne à larges lattes
3. cantonnières [bandes au-dessus d'une fenêtre]
4. port
5. prit Missy
6. sa chaude et douce moiteur
7. blond vénitien
8. bouclaient
9. rouquin
10. coupe-vent
11. en glissant la main dans la poche intérieure
12. brandit fièrement une poignée de petite monnaie
13. sortir avec vos sous
14. fermeture Éclair
15. haussa les épaules
16. abandonna
17. faire du rangement
18. Promets-moi de rester près de
19. balançoire

Ray had built a swing for the children. It was suspended from a branch of the massive oak tree at the edge[1] of the woods behind their house.

Nancy pulled Missy's mittens[2] over her hands. They were bright red; fuzzy angora stitching formed a smile face on their backs[3]. "Leave these on," she told her; "otherwise your hands will get cold. It's really getting raw.[4] I'm not even sure you should go out at all[5]."

"Oh, please!" Missy's lip began to quiver[6].

"All right, all right, don't go into the act[7]," Nancy said hastily[8]. "But not more than half an hour."

She opened the back door and let them out, then shivered[9] as the chilling breeze enveloped her. She closed the door quickly and started up the staircase[10]. The house was an authentic old Cape[11], and the stairway was almost totally vertical. Ray said that the old settlers must have had a bit of mountain goat in them[12] the way[13] they built their staircases. But Nancy loved everything about this place.

She could still remember the feeling of peace and welcome it had given her when she'd first seen it, over six years ago. She'd come to the Cape after the conviction had been set aside[14]. The District Attorney[15] hadn't pressed for a new trial[16] because Rob Legler, his vital prosecution witness[17], had disappeared.

She'd fled here, completely across the continent—as far away from California as she could get; as far away from the people she'd known and the place she'd lived and the college and the whole academic community[18] there. She never wanted to see them again—the friends who had turned out not to be[19] friends but hostile strangers who spoke of "poor Carl" because they blamed his suicide on her[20] too.

She'd come to Cape Cod because she'd always heard that New Englanders[21] and Cape people were reticent and reserved[22] and wanted nothing to do with strangers, and that was good. She needed a place to hide, to

1. lisière
2. les moufles
3. un visage souriant en angora duveteux était brodé au dos
4. Il commence à faire très froid.
5. que je devrais vous laisser sortir
6. trembloter
7. pas de scène
8. s'empressa de dire
9. frissonna
10. escalier
11. vraie maison traditionnelle
12. colons devaient avoir du sang de chèvre en eux,
13. à voir comment
14. eut été annulée
15. procureur
16. procès
17. principal témoin à charge
18. de l'université, des professeurs et de leurs familles
19. s'étaient révélés, non pas
20. la tenaient pour responsable de son suicide
21. les habitants de Nouvelle-Angleterre
22. réservés et discrets

1. faire le tri dans tout ça
2. réfléchir à
3. se les était teints en châtain
4. à la une des journaux
5. seul le destin
6. l'avoir poussée
7. agence immobilière
8. pris rendez-vous
9. agent immobilier
10. sur un coup de tête
11. enseigne peinte à la main
12. jardinières
13. chrysanthèmes
14. au visage tanné
15. s'accrocher à
16. locataire
17. à faire face aux dépenses
18. ne voulait même pas lui faire visiter la maison du vieux Hunt
19. La Maison du guet
20. isolée
21. exposée au vent
22. location
23. entièrement meublée
24. Elle serait à vendre
25. nom de jeune fille
26. n'était pas indiscret
27. s'isoler
28. On ne se sent pas seul
29. l'ensemble séjour-salle à manger
30. aménagée

find herself, to sort it all out[1], to try to think through[2] what had happened, to try to come back to life.

She'd cut her hair and dyed it sable brown[3], and that was enough to make her look completely different from the pictures that had front-paged newspapers[4] all over the country during the trial.

She guessed that only fate[5] could have prompted her[6] to select Ray's real estate office[7] when she went looking for a house to rent. She'd actually made an appointment[8] with another realtor[9], but on impulse[10] she'd gone in to see him first because she liked his hand-lettered sign[11] and the window boxes[12] that were filled with yellow and champagne mums[13].

She had waited until he finished with another client—a leathery-faced[14] old man with thick, curling hair—and admired the way Ray advised him to hang on to[15] his property, that he'd find a tenant[16] for the apartment in the house to help carry expenses[17].

After the old man left she said, "Maybe I'm here at the right time. I want to rent a house."

But he wouldn't even show her the old Hunt place[18]. "The Lookout[19] is too big, too lonesome[20] and too drafty[21] for you," he said. "But I just got in a rental[22] on an authentic Cape in excellent condition that's fully furnished[23]. It can even be bought eventually[24], if you like it. How much room do you need, Miss... Mrs....?"

"Miss Kiernan," she told him. "Nancy Kiernan." Instinctively she used her mother's maiden name[25]. "Not much, really. I won't be having company or visitors."

She liked the fact that he didn't pry[26] or even look curious. "The Cape is a good place to come when you want to be by yourself[27]," he said. "You can't be lonesome[28] walking on the beach or watching the sunset or just looking out the window in the morning."

Then Ray had brought her up here, and immediately she knew that she would stay. The combination family and dining room[29] had been fashioned[30] from the old keeping room[1] that had once[2] been the heart of the house. She loved the rocking chair in front of the fireplace and the way the table was in front of the windows so that it was possible to eat and look down over the harbor and the bay.

She was able to move in[3] right away[4], and if Ray wondered why she had absolutely nothing except the two suitcases[5] she'd taken off the bus, he didn't show it[6]. She said that her mother had died and she had sold their home in Ohio and decided to come East[7]. She simply omitted talking about the six years that had lapsed in between[8].

That night, for the first time in months[9], she slept through the night[10]—a deep, dreamless[11] sleep in which she didn't hear Peter and Lisa calling her; wasn't in the courtroom[12] listening to Carl condemn her.

That first morning here, she'd made coffee and sat by the window. It had been a clear, brilliant day—the cloudless sky purple-blue[13]; the bay tranquil and still[14]; the only movement the arc of sea gulls hovering[15] near the fishing boats.

With her fingers wrapped around[16] the coffee cup, she'd sipped[17] and watched. The warmth of the coffee had flowed through[18] her body. The sunbeams[19] had warmed her face. The tranquillity of the scene enhanced[20] the calming sense of peace that the long, dreamless sleep had begun.

Peace... give me peace. That had been her prayer during the trial; in prison. *Let me learn to accept.* Seven years ago...

Nancy sighed[21], realizing that she was still standing by the bottom step of the staircase. It was so easy to get lost in remembering[22]. That was why she tried so hard to live each day... not look back or into the future.

She began to go upstairs slowly. How could there ever be peace for her[23], knowing that if Rob Legler

1. salon
2. autrefois
3. emménager
4. tout de suite
5. valises
6. n'en laissa rien paraître
7. sur la côte Est
8. s'étaient écoulées entre-temps
9. depuis des mois
10. toute la nuit
11. sans rêves
12. salle d'audience
13. d'un bleu violacé
14. paisible et sans un mouvement
15. l'arc de cercle des mouettes planant
16. serrant
17. bu tranquillement
18. gagné
19. rayons du soleil
20. renforçait
21. poussa un soupir
22. se perdre dans ses souvenirs
23. trouverait-elle jamais la paix

1. réapparaissait,
2. elle serait de nouveau jugée pour meurtre
3. Cela ne sert à rien.
4. Arrivée en haut de l'escalier,
5. chambre principale
6. ouvrit en grand
7. des moutons se formaient dans la baie
8. baissait
9. connaissait maintenant suffisamment Cape Cod
10. évoluait le plus souvent en tempête
11. laisser les enfants dehors
12. les faire profiter au maximum du grand air
13. faisait la sieste
14. jardin d'enfants
15. reniflait pas mal
16. lui recommander de ne pas ouvrir
17. habitudes
18. se plaignait
19. lui serraient trop le cou
20. hésita
21. portait un col roulé
22. De plus
23. lancer une machine
24. essayer de réprimer l'inquiétude

ever showed up[1] they'd try her again for murder[2]; take her away from Ray and Missy and Michael? For an instant, she dropped her face into her hands. *Don't think about it*, she told herself. *It's no use.*[3]

At the head of the stairs[4] she shook her head determinedly and walked quickly into the master bedroom[5]. She threw open[6] the windows and shivered as the wind blew the curtains back against her. Clouds were starting to form, and the water in the bay had begun to chum with whitecaps[7]. The temperature was dropping[8] rapidly. Nancy was enough of a Cape person now[9] to know that a cold wind like this usually blew in a storm[10].

But it really was still clear enough to have the children out[11]. She liked them to have as much fresh air as possible[12] in the morning. After lunch, Missy napped[13] and Michael went to kindergarten[14].

She started to pull the sheets from the big double bed and hesitated. Missy had been sniffling[15] yesterday. Should she go down and warn her not to unzip[16] the neck of her jacket? It was one of her favorite tricks[17]. Missy always complained[18] that all her clothes felt too tight at the neck[19].

Nancy deliberated[20] an instant, then pulled the sheets completely back and off the bed. Missy had on a turtleneck shirt[21]. Her throat would be covered even if she undid the button. Besides[22], it would take only ten or fifteen minutes to strip and change the beds and turn on a wash[23].

Ten minutes at the most, Nancy promised herself, to quiet the nagging feeling of worry[24] that was insistently telling her to go out to the children *now*.

2

Some mornings Jonathan Knowles walked to the drugstore to pick up his morning paper. Other days he pedaled on his bike. His outing always took him past[1] the old Nickerson house, the one that Ray Eldredge had bought when he married the pretty girl who was renting it.

When old Sam Nickerson had had the place it had begun to be rundown[2], but now it looked snug[3] and solid. Ray had put on a new roof and had painted the trim[4], and his wife certainly had a green thumb[5]. The yellow and orange mums in the window boxes gave a cheerful warmth[6] even to the bleakest day[7].

In nice weather, Nancy Eldredge was often out early in the morning working on her garden. She always had a pleasant greeting[8] for him and then went back to her work. Jonathan admired that trait[9] in a woman. He'd known Ray's folks[10] when they were summer people up here[11]. Of course, the Eldredges had helped settle the Cape[12]. Ray's father had told Jonathan the whole family line right back to the one[13] who had come over on the *Mayflower*[14].

The fact that Ray shared enough love for[15] the Cape to decide to build his business career here was par-

1. Sa promenade le faisait toujours passer devant
2. n'était plus en très bon état
3. confortable
4. boiseries
5. la main verte
6. note de chaleur et de gaieté
7. même les jours les plus maussades
8. un salut aimable
9. qualité
10. les parents de Ray
11. passaient l'été ici
12. joué leur rôle dans la mise en valeur de Cape Cod
13. tout l'arbre généalogique en remontant jusqu'à l'ancêtre
14. [vaisseau qui amena les premiers émigrants anglais, en 1620]
15. ait assez apprécié

1. des étangs
2. assez de grands terrains à occuper
3. passé des vacances
4. attendu avec impatience
5. réussi
6. Emily ne devait pas connaître ça
7. où des bajoues faisaient leur apparition
8. Avocat à la retraite
9. fouiner chez les antiquaires
10. étudiait quelques grandes affaires d'homicide
11. ponctuellement
12. Le vent était mordant.
13. sortit son cache-nez
14. soleil voilé
15. jetait un regard
16. Au travers des arbustes dépouillés, le regard portait jusqu'à la mer.
17. promontoire
18. plissa les yeux
19. avoir à peine remarqué
20. vraiment pénible
21. avait envie de

ticularly exemplary in Jonathan's eyes. The Cape had lakes and ponds[1] and the bay and the ocean. It had woods to walk in, and land for people to spread out on[2]. And it was a good place for a young couple to raise children. It was a good place to retire and live out the end of your life. Jonathan and Emily had always spent vacations[3] here and looked forward to[4] the day when they'd be able to stay here the year around. They'd almost made it[5], too. But for Emily it wasn't to be[6].

Jonathan sighed. He was a big man, with thick white hair and a broad face that was beginning to fold into jowls[7]. A retired lawyer[8], he'd found inactivity depressing. You couldn't do much fishing in the winter. And poking around antique stores[9] and refinishing furniture wasn't the fun it had been when Emily was with him. But in this second year of his permanent residency at the Cape, he'd started to write a book.

Begun as a hobby, it had become an absorbing daily activity. A publisher friend had read a few chapters of it one weekend and promptly sent him a contract. The book was a case study of famous murder trials[10]. Jonathan worked on it five hours every day, seven days a week, starting promptly[11] at nine-thirty in the morning.

The wind bit against him.[12] He pulled out his muffler[13], grateful for the watery sunshine[14] he felt on his face as he glanced[15] in the direction of the bay. With the shrubbery stripped you could see clear to the water.[16] Only the old Hunt house on its high bluff[17] interrupted the view—the house they called The Lookout.

Jonathan always looked at the bay right at this point of his trip. This morning again, he squinted[18] as he turned his head. Irritated, he looked back at the road after barely registering[19] the stormy, churning whitecaps. That fellow who rented the house must have something metallic in the window, he thought. It was a damn nuisance[20]. He felt like[21] asking Ray to mention it to him, then ruefully brushed the thought away[1]. The tenant might just suggest that Jonathan check the bay somewhere else along the way.

He shrugged unconsciously. He was directly in front of the Eldredge house, and Nancy was sitting at the breakfast table by[2] the window talking to the little boy. The little girl was on her lap. Jonathan glanced away[3] quickly, feeling like an intruder[4] and not wanting to catch her eye[5]. Oh, well, he'd get the paper, fix[6] his solitary breakfast and get to his desk[7]. Today he'd begin working on the Harmon murder case—the one that he suspected[8] would make the most interesting chapter of all.

1. à regret abandonna l'idée
2. derrière
3. détourna les yeux
4. intrus
5. croiser son regard
6. préparer
7. s'installer à son bureau
8. d'après lui,

3

Ray pushed open the door of his office, unable to shake[1] the nagging sensation of worry that like an unlocated toothache[2] was throbbing[3] somewhere inside him. What was the matter? It was more than just making Nancy acknowledge[4] her birthday and risking the memories it aroused[5]. Actually, she'd been pretty[6] calm. He knew her well enough to understand when the tension was building[7] about that other life.

It could be triggered[8] by something like the sight[9] of a dark-haired boy and girl together who were the ages of her other children, or a discussion of the murder of that little girl who'd been found dead in Cohasset last year. But Nancy was all right this morning. It was something else—a feeling of foreboding[10].

"Oh, no! What does that mean?"

Ray looked up, startled[11]. Dorothy was at her desk. Her hair, more gray than brown, casually framed[12] her long, pleasant face. Her sensible[13] beige sweater[14] and brown tweed skirt had an almost studied dowdiness[15] and signaled the wearer's indifference to frills[16].

Dorothy had been Ray's first client when he had opened this office. The girl he had hired didn't

1. incapable de se débarrasser
2. telle une rage de dents sourde
3. l'élançait
4. Ce n'était pas seulement faire dire à Nancy que c'était aujourd'hui
5. souvenirs qui allaient avec
6. plutôt
7. montait
8. déclenché
9. vue
10. mauvais pressentiment
11. surpris
12. encadraient avec naturel
13. pratiques
14. pull-over
15. manque d'élégance
16. dénotaient l'indifférence aux chichis de celle qui les portait

show up[1], and Dorothy had volunteered to help him out for a few days. She'd been with him ever since.

"You do realize that you're shaking your head and frowning[2]," she told him.

Ray smiled sheepishly[3]. "Just morning jitters[4], I guess. How are you doing?"

Dorothy immediately became businesslike[5]. "Fine. I have the file all together on The Lookout. What time do you expect[6] that fellow who wants to see it?"

"Around two," Ray told her. He bent over her desk. "Where did you ever dig out[7] those plans?"

"They're on file in the library[8]. Don't forget, that house was begun in sixteen-ninety. It would make a marvelous restaurant. If anyone is willing to[9] spend money renovating it, it could be a showcase[10]. And you can't beat that waterfront location[11]."

"I gather[12] Mr. Kragopoulos and his wife have built up and sold several restaurants and don't mind spending the dollars to do everything the way it should be done."

"I've never yet met a Greek who couldn't make a go of a restaurant[13]," Dorothy commented as she closed the file.

"And all Englishmen are fags[14] and no German has a sense of humor and most Puerto Ricans[15]—I mean Spics[16]—are on welfare[17].... God, I hate labels[18]!" Ray took his pipe from his breast pocket and jammed it[19] into his mouth.

"What?" Dorothy looked up at him bewildered[20]. "I certainly was not labeling—or I guess, maybe I was, but not in the way you took it[21]." She turned her back to him as she put the file away, and Ray stalked into[22] his private office and closed the door.

He had hurt her[23]. Stupidly, unnecessarily. What in the hell was the matter with him? Dorothy was the most decent[24], fair-minded[25], non-biased[26] person he knew. What a lousy thing to say to her.[27] Sighing, he reached for the humidor[28] on his desk and filled his

1. ne s'était pas présentée
2. froncez les sourcils
3. d'un air penaud
4. des angoisses matinales
5. professionnelle
6. attendez
7. Où diable avez-vous déniché
8. bibliothèque
9. prêt à
10. opération magnifique
11. c'est très bien situé sur le front de mer
12. Si j'ai bien compris,
13. faire tourner un restaurant
14. des pédés
15. des Portoricains
16. des Latinos
17. profitent des allocations
18. j'ai horreur des clichés
19. la fourra
20. ébahie
21. pas comme vous l'avez compris
22. entra d'un pas raide
23. l'avait froissée
24. correcte
25. impartiale
26. objective
27. C'était moche, de lui avoir dit ça.
28. humidificateur à tabac

pipe. He puffed thoughtfully on it[1] for fifteen minutes before he dialed Dorothy's extension[2].

"Yes." Her voice was constrained[3] when she picked up the phone.

"Are the girls in yet?[4]"

"Yes."

"Coffee made?"

"Yes." Dorothy did not ask him if he was ready to have some.

"Would you mind bringing yours in here and a cup for me? And ask the girls to hold calls[5] for fifteen minutes."

"All right." Dorothy hung up[6].

Ray got up to open the door for her, and when she came in with the steaming[7] cups he carefully closed it.

"Peace", he said contritely[8]. "I'm terribly sorry."

"I believe that[9]," Dorothy said, "and it's all right, but what's the matter?"

"Sit down, please." Ray gestured to the rust-colored leather chair[10] by his desk. He took his coffee to the window and stared moodily out at the graying landscape[11].

"How would you like to come to our house for dinner tonight?" he asked. "We're celebrating Nancy's birthday."

He heard her sharp intake of breath[12] and spun around[13]. "Do you think it's a mistake?"

Dorothy was the only one on the Cape who knew about Nancy[14]. Nancy herself had told her and asked her advice[15] before she had agreed to marry Ray.

Dorothy's voice and eyes were speculative[16] as she answered. "I don't know, Ray. What's the thinking behind a celebration?[17]"

"The thinking is that you can't pretend that Nancy doesn't have[18] birthdays! Of course, it's more than just that. It's that Nancy has got to break with[19] the past, to stop hiding."

1. tira dessus pensivement
2. d'appeler Dorothy sur son poste
3. forcée
4. Les filles sont-elles arrivées ?
5. prendre les appels
6. raccrocha
7. fumantes
8. d'un air désolé
9. Je veux bien le croire
10. désigna le siège en cuir couleur rouille
11. fixa avec morosité le paysage de grisaille
12. son petit cri de surprise
13. se retourna vivement
14. à connaître l'histoire de Nancy
15. avait demandé son avis
16. songeurs
17. Pourquoi le fêter ?
18. on ne peut pas faire comme si Nancy n'avait pas d'
19. tirer un trait sur

1. menace
2. a témoigné
3. ça fait plus de 6 ans qu'il n'a pas refait surface
4. Dieu seul sait
5. Peut-être même est-il revenu en douce
6. de ne surtout pas relancer tout ça
7. Il risque une peine assez sévère
8. allons plus loin
9. Sincèrement
10. est très réservée
11. C'est gentiment dit.
12. blagues
13. comme quoi ma femme se croyait
14. les gens d'ici
15. je me fais de plus en plus charrier parce que je ne suis inscrit qu'au golf
16. voulait bien participer à un groupe de parents d'élèves
17. Inutile de dire qu'elle a décliné.
18. j'ai réussi à l'emmener
19. de moins en moins probable
20. sosie
21. Un point c'est tout.

"*Can* she break with the past? *Can* she stop hiding with the prospect[1] of another murder trial always hanging over her?"

"But that's just it. The *prospect*. Dorothy, do you realize that that fellow who testified[2] against her hasn't been seen or heard of for over six years[3]? God knows[4] where he is now or if he's even alive. For all we know, he's sneaked back[5] into this country under another name and is just as anxious as Nancy not to start the whole business up[6]. Don't forget, he's officially a deserter from the Army. There's a pretty stiff penalty waiting for him[7] if he's caught."

"That's probably true," Dorothy agreed.

"It is true. And take it one step further[8]. Level with me[9], now. What do people in this town think of Nancy?—and I include the girls in my own office here."

Dorothy hesitated. "They think she's very pretty... they admire the way she wears clothes... they say she's always pleasant... and they think she keeps to herself pretty much[10]."

"That's a nice way of putting it.[11] I've heard cracks[12] about my wife thinking she's[13] 'too good for the folks around here[14].' At the club I'm getting more and more ribbing about why I only have a golf membership[15] and why I don't bring that beautiful wife of mine around. Last week Michael's school called and asked if Nancy would consider working on some committee[16]. Needless to say, she turned them down.[17] Last month I finally got her to go[18] to the realtors' dinner, and when they took the group picture, she was in the ladies' room."

"She's afraid of being recognized."

"I understand that. But don't you see that that possibility gets less likely all the time[19]? And even if someone said to her, 'You're a dead ringer[20] for that girl from California who was accused'... well, you know what I mean, Dorothy. For most people it would end there. A resemblance. Period.[21] God, remember that guy who used to pose for all those whiskey and bank ads[1], the one who was a ringer for Lyndon Johnson? I was in the Army with his nephew. People do look like other people. It's that simple[2]. And if there ever is[3] another trial, I want Nancy to be entrenched with the people[4] here. I want them to feel she's one of them and that they're rooting for her[5]. Because after she's acquitted, she'll have to come here and take up life again[6]. We all will."

"And if there's a trial and she isn't acquitted?"

"I simply won't consider that possibility," Ray said flatly[7]. "How about it? Have we got a date tonight?[8]"

"I'd like very much to come," Dorothy said. "And I agree with most of what you've said."

"Most?"

"Yes." She looked at him steadily[9]. "I think you've got to ask yourself how much of this sudden desire to opt for[10] a more normal life is just for Nancy and how much because of other motives."

"Meaning what?"

"Ray, I was here when the Secretary of State of Massachusetts urged you to go into politics[11] because the Cape needs young men of your caliber[12] to represent it. I heard him say that he'd give you any help and endorsement[13] possible. It's pretty hard not to be able to take him up on that[14]. But as things stand now[15], you can't. And you know it."

Dorothy left the room without giving him a chance to answer. Ray finished the coffee and sat down at his desk. The anger and irritation and tension drained from him[16], and he felt depressed and ashamed of himself. She was right, of course. He did want to pretend that there wasn't any threat[17] hanging over them, that everything was just nifty[18]. And he had a hell of a nerve[19], too. He'd known what he was getting into[20] when he'd married Nancy. If he hadn't, she certainly had pointed it out[21]. She'd done her best to warn[22] him.

1. ces pubs
2. aussi simple que ça
3. Et si jamais il y avait
4. complètement intégrée
5. la soutiennent
6. reprendre le cours de sa vie
7. catégorique
8. Bon, alors ? Viendrez-vous ce soir ?
9. résolument
10. d'adopter
11. vous a incité à entrer en politique
12. envergure
13. soutien
14. accepter sa proposition
15. en l'état actuel des choses
16. l'abandonnèrent
17. menace
18. parfait
19. sacré culot
20. où il mettait les pieds
21. en tout cas, elle avait été très franche
22. prévenir

Ray stared unseeingly at[1] the mail[2] on his desk, thinking of the times in the last few months when he'd blown up unreasonably at[3] Nancy just the way he had this morning at Dorothy. Like the way he had acted when she had shown him the watercolor[4] she'd done of the house. She should study art. Even now she was good enough to exhibit[5] locally. He'd said, "It's very good. Now which closet[6] are you going to hide it in?"

Nancy had looked so stricken, so defenseless[7]. He'd wanted to bite his tongue off[8]. He'd said, "Honey, I'm so sorry. It's just that I'm so proud of you. I want you to show it off."

How many of these flare-ups[9] were being caused because he was tired of the constant constriction on[10] their activities?

He sighed and started going through his mail[11].

At quarter past ten, Dorothy threw open the door of his office. Her usually healthy pink complexion[12] was a sickly grayish white[13]. He jumped up[14] to go to her. But shaking her head, she pushed the door closed[15] behind her and held out[16] the paper she'd been hiding under her arm.

It was the weekly[17] *Cape Cod Community News*. Dorothy had it open to the second section, the one that always featured a human-interest story[18]. She dropped it on his desk.

Together they stared down at the large picture that to anyone was unmistakably[19] Nancy. It was one he'd never seen before, in her tweed suit[20], with her hair pulled back and already darkened[21]. The caption[22] under it said, CAN THIS BE A HAPPY BIRTHDAY FOR NANCY HARMON? Another picture showed Nancy leaving the courtroom during her trial, her face wooden and expressionless[23], her hair cascading down her shoulders. A third picture was a copy of a snapshot[24] of Nancy with her arms around two young children.

1. fixait sans le voir
2. courrier
3. s'était emporté de façon injuste contre
4. aquarelle
5. exposer
6. placard
7. si blessée, si vulnérable
8. s'arracher la langue
9. sautes d'humeur
10. qu'il faille toujours limiter
11. à éplucher son courrier
12. Son teint, d'ordinaire rose et frais,
13. d'un affreux blanc grisâtre
14. se leva d'un bond
15. referma la porte
16. brandit
17. hebdomadaire
18. brossait toujours le portrait de quelqu'un au parcours intéressant
19. indéniablement
20. tailleur en tweed
21. teints en noir
22. légende
23. le visage de marbre
24. cliché

The first line of the story read: "Somewhere today Nancy Harmon is celebrating her 32nd birthday and the seventh anniversary of the death of the children she was found guilty of murdering[1]."

1. pour le meurtre desquels elle a été reconnue coupable

4

IT WAS TIMING[1]. The whole universe existed because of split-second[2] timing. Now his timing would be perfect. Hurriedly, he backed the station wagon out[3] of the garage. It was such a cloudy day it had been hard to see much through the telescope, but he could tell that she'd been putting the children's coats on.

He felt[4] in his pocket and the needles[5] were there—filled, ready to use, to produce instant unconsciousness[6]; dreamless[7], absolute sleep.

He could feel the perspiration[8] starting under his arms and in his groin[9], and great beads of it[10] were forming on his forehead[11] and rolling down his cheeks. That was bad. It was a cold day. Mustn't look excited or nervous.

He took a precious few seconds to dab his face[12] with the old towel he kept on the front seat and glanced over his shoulder[13]. The canvas raincoat[14] was the kind many Cape men kept in their cars, especially around fishing season; so were the rods[15] that showed[16] against the back window. But that coat was big enough to cover two small children. He giggled excitedly[17] and swung the car toward Route 6A.

1. C'était une question de timing
2. quart de seconde
3. À la hâte, il sortit le break en marche arrière
4. tâta
5. seringues
6. inconscience
7. sans rêves
8. transpiration
9. à l'aine
10. perles de sueur
11. front
12. se tamponner le visage
13. jeta un coup d'œil par dessus son épaule
14. imperméable en toile
15. cannes à pêche
16. visibles
17. eut un petit rire ravi

Wiggins' Market was on the corner of this road and Route 6A. Whenever he was at the Cape he shopped there[1]. Of course, he brought most of the staples[2] he needed with him whenever he came to stay. It was too risky to go out much[3]. There was always the chance[4] that he'd run into[5] Nancy and she'd recognize him even with his changed appearance. It had almost happened four years ago. He'd been in a supermarket in Hyannis Port and he'd heard her voice behind him. He was reaching for a jar[6] of coffee, and her hand went right up next to his[7] as she took a jar from the same shelf. She was saying, "Wait a minute, Mike. I want to get something here," and while he froze[8], she brushed against him[9] and murmured "Oh, I'm sorry."

He didn't dare to[10] answer—just stood there—and she moved on. He was positive[11] she hadn't even looked at him. But after that he had never risked a meeting. It was necessary, though, for him to establish a casual routine[12] in Adams Port, because someday it might be important for people to dismiss his comings and goings as routine[13]. That was why he bought milk and bread and meat at Wiggins' Market always about ten in the morning. Nancy never left the house before eleven, and even then she always went to Lowery's Market, down the road a half mile. And the Wigginses had begun to greet him as a customer of long standing[14]. Well, he'd be there in a few minutes, right on schedule[15].

There wasn't anyone out walking at all. The raw wind was probably discouraging any inclination to go outdoors. He was almost to Route 6A and slowed to a full stop[16].

The incredible luck.[17] There wasn't a car in either[18] direction. Quickly he accelerated, and the station wagon shot across[19] the main street and onto[20] the road that ran along the back of the Eldredge property. Audacity—that was all it took[21]. Any fool[22] could try to come up with a foolproof[23] plan. But to have a

1. c'est là qu'il faisait ses courses
2. provisions
3. dangereux de sortir trop souvent
4. risque
5. de tomber sur
6. boîte
7. vint se placer juste à côté de la sienne
8. restait figé sur place
9. le frôla
10. n'avait pas osé
11. certain
12. une routine
13. ne rien voir d'anormal dans ses allées et venues
14. client de longue date
15. pile à l'heure
16. ralentit jusqu'à l'arrêt complet
17. Quel coup de chance.
18. aucune
19. traversa en flèche
20. pour s'engager dans
21. c'est tout ce qu'il fallait
22. N'importe quel imbécile
23. infaillible

plan so simple that it was unbelievable even to call it a plan[1]—a schedule timed to the split second—that was real genius[2]. To willingly leave yourself open to failure[3]—to tightrope-walk[4] across[5] a dozen pits[6] so that when the act was accomplished no one even glanced in your direction—that was the way.

Ten minutes of ten.[7] The children had probably been out one minute now. Oh, he knew the possibilities. One of them might have gone into the house to the bathroom or for a drink of water, but not likely[8], not likely. Every day for a month straight[9] he'd watched them. Unless it was actually raining[10], they came out to play. She never came to check them for ten to fifteen minutes[11]. They never went back into the house for those same ten minutes.

Nine minutes of ten. He steered the car into[12] the dirt road on their property. The community paper would be delivered in a few minutes. That article would be out[13] today. Motivation for[14] Nancy to explode into violence... exposure of her part[15]... all the people in this town talking in shocked tones[16], walking by this house, staring...

He stopped the car halfway into the woods. No one could see it from the road. She couldn't see it from the house. He got out quickly and, keeping close to the protection of the trees[17], hurried to the children's play area. The leaves were off most of the trees, but there were enough pines and other evergreens[18] to shield him[19].

He could hear the children's voices before he saw them. The boy, his voice panting[20] a little—he must be pushing the girl on the swing[21]... "We'll ask Daddy what to buy for Mommy. I'll take both our money."

The girl laughed. "Good, Mike, good. Higher, Mike—push me higher, please."

He stole up[22] behind the boy, who heard him in that last second. He had an impression of startled[23] blue eyes and a mouth that rounded in terror[24] be-

1. même impensable de lui donner ce nom
2. du pur génie
3. S'exposer délibérément à l'échec
4. marcher sur un fil
5. au-dessus d'
6. fosses
7. Dix heures moins dix.
8. c'était peu probable
9. pendant tout un mois
10. s'il pleuvait vraiment
11. Elle ne venait voir si tout allait bien qu'au bout de 10 ou 15 minutes
12. tourna dans
13. allait paraître
14. Ce qui amènerait
15. aux yeux de tous
16. sur un ton scandalisé
17. restant à couvert sous les arbres
18. arbres à feuillage persistant
19. qu'on ne le voie pas
20. haletant
21. balançoire
22. arriva à pas de velours
23. surpris
24. s'arrondit de terreur

fore he covered both with one hand and with the other plunged the needle through the woolen mitten. The boy tried to pull away[1], stiffened[2], then crumpled noiselessly to the ground[3].

The swing was coming back—the girl calling, "Push, Mike—don't stop pushing." He caught the swing by the right side chain, stopped it and encircled the small, uncomprehending wiggly body[4]. Carefully stifling[5] the soft cry, he plunged the other needle through the red mitten that had a smiling kitten face sewn on the back[6]. An instant later, the girl sighed and slumped[7] against him.

He didn't notice that one mitten caught on[8] the swing and was pulled off[9] as he easily lifted both children in his arms and ran to the car.

At five minutes of ten they were crumpled[10] under the canvas raincoat. He backed down the dirt road and onto the paved[11] highway behind Nancy's property. He cursed[12] as he saw a small Dodge sedan[13] coming toward him. It slowed up slightly to let him pull into the right lane and he turned his head away.

Damn the luck.[14] As he passed, he managed a swift sidelong glance[15] at the driver of the other car and got an impression of a sharp nose and thin chin[16] silhouetted[17] from under a shapeless[18] hat. The other driver didn't seem to turn his head at all.

He had a fleeting feeling[19] of familiarity: probably someone from the Cape, but maybe not aware that the station wagon he had slowed up for had come off[20] the narrow dirt road leading from the Eldredge property. Most people weren't observant[21]. In a few minutes this man probably wouldn't even have a recollection[22] of having slowed for an instant to let a car complete a turn[23].

He watched the Dodge through the rearview mirror[24] until it disappeared. With a grunt[25] of satisfaction, he adjusted the mirror so that it reflected the canvas raincoat on the back deck[26]. It was apparent-

1. se dégager
2. se raidit
3. s'effondra sans bruit
4. petit corps qui se tortillait sans comprendre
5. étouffant
6. où était cousue au dos une tête de chaton souriante
7. s'affaissa
8. était restée accrochée
9. avait été arrachée
10. recroquevillés
11. goudronnée
12. jura
13. berline
14. Quelle poisse !
15. parvint à jeter un coup d'œil en coin
16. menton
17. se profilant
18. informe
19. brève impression
20. sortait de
21. observateurs
22. souvenir
23. terminer son virage
24. rétroviseur
25. grognement
26. plage arrière

ly tossed casually[1] over fishing gear[2]. Satisfied, he flipped the mirror back into place[3] without looking into it again. If he had looked into it, he would have seen that the car he had just been watching was slowing, backing up.

At four minutes past ten he walked into Wiggins' Market and grunted a greeting[4] as he reached into the refrigerator section for a quart of milk.

1. jeté négligemment

2. matériel de pêche

3. réajusta le rétro

4. marmonna un bonjour

5

Nancy came down the steep staircase precariously balancing an armful of towels and sheets, pajamas and underwear[1]. On impulse she'd decided to do a wash that could be hung outdoors to dry before the storm broke. Winter was here. It was on the edge of the yard, forcing the last few dead leaves off the trees. It was settling[2] into the dirt road that now was as hardened as concrete[3]. It was changing the color of the bay into a smoky gray-blue.

Outside, the storm was building[4], but now, while there was still some weak[5] sun, she'd take advantage of it[6]. She loved the fresh smell of sheets dried outside; loved to pull them against her face as she drifted off to sleep[7] with the way they captured the faint scent of cranberry bogs[8] and pine and the salty smell of the sea—so different from the coarse, rough, dank smell[9] of prison sheets. She pushed the thought away.

At the foot of the staircase she started to turn in the direction of the back door, then stopped. How foolish.[10] The children were fine. They'd been out only fifteen minutes, and this frantic[11] anxiety that was her constant albatross[12] had to be conquered[13]. Even now she suspected that Missy sensed it[14] and was begin-

1. avec dans les bras, en équilibre instable, une pile de serviettes et de draps, de pyjamas et de sous-vêtements
2. Il s'installait
3. dur comme du béton
4. se préparait
5. faiblard
6. allait en profiter
7. elle s'assoupissait
8. parfum délicat de l'airelle des marais
9. odeur désagréable, agressive, humide et froide
10. Ridicule !
11. folle
12. qu'elle traînait comme un boulet
13. surmontée
14. en était consciente

1. Maintenant que la saison [touristique] était terminée
2. de la belle brocante à saisir
3. banquette à l'ancienne
4. salon
5. à haut dossier
6. banc à dossier
7. au XVIIIe siècle
8. buanderie
9. donnant sur
10. tria
11. jeta
12. de l'eau de Javel
13. fit un détour
14. de plus en plus fort
15. brûleur
16. pressée de consulter
17. les petites annonces
18. feuilleta rapidement jusqu'à
19. manchette spectaculaire
20. façon confiante de se cramponner, de se blottir contre elle
21. Malgré un bourdonnement d'oreilles,
22. eut un souvenir très net du moment où
23. s'étaient lovés contre
24. prenait la photo
25. se cambra de douleur
26. Elle tendit un bras tremblant
27. et le renversa

ning to respond to her overprotection. She'd turn the wash on, then call them in. While they watched their ten-thirty television program, she'd have a second cup of coffee and look at the weekly *Cape Cod Community News*. With the season over[1], there might be some good antiques available[2] and not at tourist prices. She wanted an old-fashioned settee[3] for the parlor[4]—the high-backed[5] kind they used to call a "settle[6]" in the seventeen-hundreds[7].

In the laundry room[8] off[9] the kitchen she sorted[10] the wash, tossed[11] the sheets and towels into the machine, added detergent and bleach[12] and finally pushed the button to start the cycle.

Now it surely was time to call the children. But at the front door she detoured[13]. The paper had just arrived. The delivery boy was disappearing around the curve in the road. She picked it up, shivering against the increasing[14] wind, and hurried into the kitchen. She turned the burner jet[15] under the still-warm coffeepot. Then, anxious to get a look at[16] the classified page[17], she thumbed quickly to[18] the second section of the paper.

Her eyes focused on the blaring headline[19] and the pictures—all the pictures: of her and Carl and Rob Legler; the one of her with Peter and Lisa... that clinging, trusting way they'd always huddled up to her[20]. Through a roaring in her ears[21] she remembered vividly the time[22] they'd posed for that one. Carl had taken it.

"Don't pay attention to me," he'd said; "pretend I'm not here." But they'd known he was there and had shrunk against[23] her, and she had looked down at them as he snapped the picture[24]. Her hands were touching their silky, dark heads.

"No... no... no... no...!" Now her body arched in pain[25]. Unsteadily she reached out her hand[26], and it hit the coffeepot, knocking it over[27]. She drew it back, only dimly[1] feeling the searing[2] liquid that splattered on[3] her fingers.

She had to burn the paper. Michael and Missy mustn't see it. That was it. She'd burn the paper so that no one could see it. She ran to the fireplace in the dining room.

The fireplace... that wasn't cheery[4] and warm and protecting anymore. Because there was no haven[5]... there never could be a haven for her. She squeezed the paper together[6] and reached unsteadily for the box of matches[7] on the mantel[8]. A wisp[9] of smoke and a flame, and then the paper began to burn as she stuffed it between the logs[10].

Everyone on the Cape was reading that paper. They'd know... they'd all know. The one picture they'd surely recognize.[11] She didn't even remember that anyone had seen her after she'd cut her hair and dyed it. The paper was burning brightly now. She watched as the picture with Peter and Lisa flamed, and charred and curled[12]. Dead, both of them; and she'd be better off with them[13]. There was no place to hide for her... or to forget. Ray could take care of Michael and Missy. Tomorrow in Michael's class the children would be looking at him, whispering, pointing their fingers[14].

The children. She must save the children. No, *get*[15] the children. That was it. They'd catch cold.

She stumbled[16] to the back door and pulled it open. "Peter... Lisa... she called. No, no! It was Michael and Missy. *They* were her children.

"Michael. Missy. Come here. Come in now!" Her wail heightened to a shriek.[17] Where were they? She hurried out to the backyard[18], unmindful[19] of the cold that bit through her light sweater.

The swing. They must have gotten off[20] the swing. They were probably in the woods. "Michael. Missy. Michael! Missy! Don't hide! Come here now!"

The swing was still moving. The wind was making it sway[21]. Then she saw the mitten. Missy's mitten, caught in the metal loops[22] of the swing.

1. à peine
2. brûlant
3. éclaboussa
4. joyeux
5. refuge
6. roula le journal en boule
7. allumettes
8. manteau de la cheminée
9. volute
10. bûches
11. Et ils la reconnaîtraient sûrement sur la photo.
12. s'enflammer et se carboniser en s'enroulant
13. il aurait mieux valu qu'elle le soit aussi
14. chuchotant, le montrant du doigt
15. aller chercher
16. tituba
17. Son appel plaintif devint un cri perçant.
18. se précipita dans l'arrière-cour
19. insensible
20. descendre de
21. osciller
22. anneaux

From far off[1] she heard a sound. What sound? The children.

The lake! They must be at the lake. They weren't supposed[2] to go there, but maybe they had. They'd be found. Like the others. In the water. Their faces wet and swollen[3] and still.

She grabbed[4] Missy's mitten, the mitten with the smile face, and staggered[5] toward the lake. She called their names over and over again. She pushed her way through[6] the woods and out onto the sandy beach.

In the lake a little way out, something was glistening[7] below the surface. Was it something red... another mitten... Missy's hand? She plunged into the icy water as far as her[8] shoulders and reached down. But there wasn't anything there. Frantically[9] Nancy clutched her fingers together so that they formed a strainer[10], but there was nothing—only the terrible numbing[11] cold water. She looked down, trying to see to the bottom; leaned over[12] and fell. The water gushed into her nostrils[13] and mouth and burned her face and neck.

Somehow she staggered up and back[14] before her wet clothes pulled her down again. She fell onto the ice-crusted[15] sand. Through the roar in her ears and the mist that was closing in front of[16] her eyes, she looked into the woods and saw him—his face... *Whose* face?

The mist closed over her eyes completely. Sounds died away[17]: the mournful cackle[18] of the sea gull[19]... the lapping[20] of the water... Silence.

It was there that Ray and Dorothy found her. Shivering uncontrollably, lying on the sand, her hair and clothes plastered to[21] her head and body, her eyes blank and uncomprehending[22], angry blisters raised on[23] the hand that clutched[24] a small red mitten to her cheek.

1. Au loin,
2. n'avaient pas le droit
3. gonflés
4. empoigna
5. se dirigea en vacillant
6. se fraya un chemin dans
7. brillait
8. jusqu'aux
9. Prise de frénésie,
10. entrecroisa les doigts pour faire passoire
11. qui engourdit
12. se pencha encore
13. s'engouffra dans ses narines
14. Elle parvint à se relever en titubant et ressortit de l'eau
15. couvert de givre
16. le voile qui se formait devant
17. s'atténuèrent
18. gloussement lugubre
19. mouette
20. clapotis
21. plaqués contre
22. qui fixaient le vide sans comprendre
23. de belles ampoules sur
24. tenait serrée

6

JONATHAN CAREFULLY WASHED and rinsed his breakfast dishes, scoured[1] the omelet pan[2] and swept the kitchen floor. Emily had been naturally, effortlessly neat[3], and years of living with her had made him appreciate the intrinsic comfort of tidiness[4]. He always hung his clothes in the closets[5], put his laundry[6] in the bathroom hamper[7] and cleared up[8] immediately after his solitary meals. He even had an eye for[9] the kind of detail that his cleaning woman[10] missed and after she left on Wednesdays would do small jobs like washing canisters[11] and bric-a-brac and polishing surfaces that she'd left cloudy with wax[12].

In New York he and Emily had lived on Sutton Place, on the southeast corner of Fifty-fifth Street. Their apartment building[13] had extended over the FDR Drive[14] to the edge of the East River. Sometimes they had sat on their seventeenth-floor balcony[15] and watched the lights of the bridges that spanned[16] the river and talked about the time when they'd be retired[17] at the Cape and looking out over Maushop Lake.

"You won't have Bertha in every day to keep the wheels spinning[18]", he'd teased her[19].

1. récura
2. la poêle
3. soigneuse
4. confort garanti par le goût de l'ordre
5. penderies
6. linge sale
7. panier à linge
8. débarrassait
9. relevait
10. femme de ménage
11. boîtes de rangement
12. couverts d'encaustique
13. immeuble
14. avenue Franklin D. Roosevelt
15. balcon au 17e étage
16. enjambaient
17. après la retraite, ils habiteraient
18. s'occuper de tout
19. l'avait-il taquinée

1. en âge de prendre sa retraite
2. te formerai pour être
3. Ça te manquera
4. Je le ferais bien dès maintenant
5. si cela se savait
6. vélo à dix vitesses
7. t'essaieras à l'écriture
8. suggéré
9. Le combat d'une femme
10. fait des bénéfices
11. répliqué
12. je ne me plains pas
13. ne serait-ce que
14. torchon
15. dans l'encadrement de
16. le début du long hiver
17. nerveux
18. inquiet
19. le tracassait
20. sensation de malaise
21. travaillait sur un dossier [d'affaire à plaider]
22. que, rien à faire, des points ne concordaient pas
23. une retraite anticipée
24. De fait,
25. de toute façon
26. donné sa démission
27. versé une pension à
28. léchant ses plaies

"By the time we get up there, Bertha will be ready to retire[1] and I'll break you in as[2] my assistant. All we'll really need is a weekly cleaning woman. How about you? Will you miss[3] having a car pick you up at the door anytime you want it?"

Jonathan had answered that he'd decided to buy a bicycle. "I'd do it now[4]," he'd told Emily, "but I'm afraid some of our clients might get upset if the word was around[5] that I arrived at work on a ten-speeder[6]."

"And you'll try your hand at writing[7]," Emily had prodded[8]. "I sometimes wish you'd just taken a chance and done it years ago."

"Never could afford to, married to you," he'd said. "The one-woman war[9] against recession. All Fifth Avenue stays in the black[10] when Mrs. Knowles goes shopping."

"It's your fault," she'd retorted[11]. "You're always telling me to spend your money."

"I like spending it on you," he'd told her, "and I have no complaints[12]. I've been lucky."

If only they'd had even[13] a few years up here together... Jonathan sighed and hung up the dish towel[14]. Seeing Nancy Eldredge and her children framed in[15] the window this morning had vaguely depressed him. Maybe it was the weather or the long winter setting in[16], but he was restless[17], apprehensive[18]. Something was bothering him[19]. It was the kind of itch[20] he used to get when he was preparing a brief[21] and some facts just didn't jibe[22].

Well, he'd get to his desk. He was anxious to start working on the Harmon chapter.

He could have taken early retirement[23], he thought, as he walked slowly into his study. As it turned out,[24] that was just what he had done anyway[25]. The minute he lost Emily, he'd sold the New York apartment, put in his resignation[26], pensioned off[27] Bertha and, like a dog licking its wounds[28], had come here to this house that they'd picked out[1] together. After the first bleak grief[2], he'd found a measure of contentment[3].

Now writing the book was a fascinating and absorbing experience. When he'd gotten the idea for doing it, he had asked Kevin Parks, a meticulous free-lance researcher[4] and old friend, to come up for a weekend. Then he had outlined his plan to him[5]. Jonathan had selected ten controversial[6] criminal trials. He'd proposed that Kev take on the job of putting together a file of[7] all available material[8] on those trials: court transcripts[9]; depositions; newspaper accounts[10]; pictures; gossip[11]—anything he could find. Jonathan planned to study each file thoroughly[12] and then decide how to write the chapter—either agreeing[13] with the verdict or rejecting it, and giving his reasons. He was calling the book "Verdict in Doubt[14]."

He'd already finished three chapters. The first was called "The Sam Sheppard Trial." His opinion: not guilty[15]. Too many loopholes[16]; too much suppressed evidence[17]. Jonathan agreed with the Dorothy Kilgallen opinion that the jury had found Sam Sheppard guilty of adultery, not murder.

The second chapter was "The Cappolino Trial." Marge Farger, in his opinion, belonged[18] in a prison cell with her former[19] boyfriend.

The just-completed chapter[20] was "The Edgar Smith Trial." Jonathan's view[21] was that Edgar Smith was guilty but deserved[22] his freedom. Fourteen years constituted a life sentence[23] today, and he had rehabilitated and educated himself in a grisly cell on Death Row[24].

Now he sat down at his massive desk and reached into the file drawer for the thick cardboard folders[25] that had arrived the previous day[26]. They were labeled[27] THE HARMON CASE.

1. choisie
2. la peine infinie des premiers temps
3. forme de tranquillité
4. documentaliste
5. avait donné les grandes lignes de l'ouvrage
6. controversés
7. s'occupe de compiler
8. les documents disponibles
9. les minutes du procès
10. les comptes rendus
11. les potins
12. minutieusement
13. en accord
14. Coupable ou non coupable ?
15. non coupable
16. de failles
17. d'éléments cachés à la défense
18. avait sa place
19. ancien
20. chapitre qu'il venait d'achever
21. L'opinion
22. méritait
23. ça représentait la perpétuité
24. sinistre cellule du couloir de la mort
25. classeurs en carton
26. la veille
27. Sur l'étiquette était inscrit

A note from Kevin was stapled[1] to the first envelope. It read:

> Jon, I have a hunch[2] you'll enjoy getting your teeth[3] into this one. The defendant[4] was a sitting duck[5] for the prosecutor[6]; even her husband broke down on the stand[7] and practically[8] accused her in front of the jury. If they ever locate the missing[9] prosecution witness and try her again, she'd better[10] have a stronger story than last time. The District Attorney's office out there[11] knows where she is, but I couldn't get it from them; somewhere in the East is the best I can do.

Jonathan opened the file with the accelerating pulse[12] that he always associated with the beginning of an interesting new case. He never allowed himself to do much speculating until he got the research all together[13], but his memory[14] of this case when it was being tried six or seven years ago made him curious. He remembered how at that time just reading the trial testimony[15] had left so many questions in his mind... questions he wanted to concentrate on now. He recalled that his overall[16] impression of the Harmon case was that Nancy Harmon never had told all she knew about the disappearance of her children.

He reached into the folder and began to lay out[17] the meticulously labeled items[18] on the desk. There were pictures of Nancy Harmon taken during her trial. She certainly was a pretty little thing with that waist-length hair[19]. According to the papers she was twenty-five at the time the murders were committed. She looked even younger—not much more than a teenager. The dresses she wore were so youthful[20]... almost childish[21]... they added to the overall effect. Probably her attorney[22] had suggested[23] that she look as young as possible.

1. agrafée
2. j'ai dans l'idée
3. t'attaquer
4. L'accusée
5. cible facile
6. procureur
7. s'est effondré à la barre
8. pour ainsi dire
9. disparu
10. elle aura intérêt à
11. de là-bas
12. excitation
13. Il s'interdisait toute présomption avant d'avoir bouclé la phase de recherche
14. le souvenir qu'il avait
15. la simple lecture des dépositions
16. d'ensemble
17. étaler
18. éléments
19. chevelure jusqu'à la taille
20. faisaient si jeune
21. enfantin
22. avocat
23. conseillé

Funny, but ever since he'd started planning this book he'd felt that he'd seen that girl somewhere. He stared at[1] the pictures in front of him. Of course. She looked like a younger version of Ray Eldredge's wife! That explained the nagging[2] resemblance. The expression was totally different, but wouldn't it be a small world[3] if there was some family relationship?

His eye fell on the first typewritten[4] page, which gave a rundown on[5] Nancy Harmon. She had been born in California and raised in Ohio. Well, that let out[6] any possibility of her being a close relative to[7] Nancy Eldredge. Ray's wife's family had been neighbors[8] of Dorothy Prentiss in Virginia.

Dorothy Prentiss. He felt a quick dart[9] of pleasure at the thought of the handsome[10] woman who worked with Ray. Jonathan often stopped by[11] their office around five o'clock, when he picked up the evening paper, the *Boston Globe*. Ray had suggested some interesting land investments[12] to him, and they had all proved sound[13]. He'd also persuaded Jonathan to become active in the town, and as a result they'd become good friends.

Still, Jonathan realized that he went into Ray's office more often than necessary. Ray would say, "You're just in time for an end-of-the-day drink[14]" and call out to Dorothy to join them.

Emily had liked daiquiris. Dorothy always had Jonathan's favorite drink—a Rob Roy[15] with a twist[16]. The three of them would sit for a half hour or so[17] in Ray's private office.

Dorothy had a penetrating humor that he enjoyed.[18] Her family had been show-business people[19], and she had countless[20] great stories about traveling with them. She'd planned a career too[21], but after three small parts[22] Off Broadway[23] she had gotten married and settled down in Virginia. After her husband died she'd come up to the Cape planning to open an interior-decorating shop, then had gotten started working

1. scruta
2. l'impression tenace de
3. ne dirait-on pas que le monde est tout petit
4. imprimée
5. un récapitulatif de la vie de
6. annulait
7. proche parenté avec
8. des voisins
9. bouffée
10. séduisante
11. passait à
12. placements fonciers
13. judicieux
14. Tu arrives à point pour un petit apéritif
15. [cocktail, scotch + vermouth]
16. zeste de citron
17. environ
18. Il appréciait l'humour corrosif de Dorothy.
19. faisait partie du monde du spectacle
20. d'innombrables
21. Elle aussi avait prévu une carrière d'actrice
22. rôles
23. dans des spectacles à petit budget

1. un excellent agent immobilier
2. aussi miteux soit-il au premier abord
3. ces derniers temps,
4. hésité à
5. composer
6. s'engager trop rapidement dans une relation avec quelqu'un qu'il croisait très souvent
7. l'impressionnait-elle un peu trop
8. [= feminity]
9. être troublé par
10. à partir dans des rêvasseries
11. Fermement
12. une première liasse
13. le tic-tac
14. croissante
15. les ronchonnements qui marquaient de temps en temps son incrédulité
16. les sourcils froncés par
17. n'allait pas
18. En se basant sur ce qu'il avait déjà lu,
19. de louche
20. un élément sous-jacent
21. se combiner
22. cohérente
23. l'esprit ailleurs, emplit à demi la bouilloire
24. Le coinçant

with Ray. Ray said that Dorothy was a hell of a real estate saleswoman[1]. She could help people visualize the possibilities in a place, no matter how seedy it looked at first glance[2].

More and more often lately[3] Jonathan had toyed with the idea of[4] suggesting that Dorothy join him for dinner. Sundays were long, and a couple of Sunday afternoons recently he'd actually started to dial[5] her number, then stopped. He didn't want to rush into getting involved with someone he'd run into constantly[6]. And he just wasn't sure. Maybe she came on a little too strong for him[7]. All those years of living with Emily's total femininity[8] had made him somewhat unprepared for reacting on a personal level to[9] a terribly independent woman.

God, what was the matter with him? He was so easily diverted into woolgathering[10] this morning. Why was he letting himself get distracted from this Harmon case?

Resolutely he lit his pipe, picked up the file and leaned back in his chair. Deliberately[11] he picked up the first batch[12] of papers.

An hour and fifteen minutes passed. The silence was unbroken except for the ticking[13] of the clock, the increasing[14] insistence of the wind through the pines outside his window and Jonathan's occasional snort of disbelief[15]. Finally, frowning in[16] concentration, he laid the papers down and walked slowly to the kitchen to make coffee. Something smelled[17] about that whole Harmon trial. From as much of the transcript as he'd read through so far[18] it was evident that there was something fishy[19] there... an undercurrent[20] that made it impossible for the facts to hang together[21] in any kind of reasonably cohesive[22] way.

He went into the immaculate kitchen and absently half-filled the kettle[23]. While he waited for it to heat, he walked to the front door. The *Cape Cod Community News* was already on the porch. Tucking it[24] under his arm, he went back into the kitchen, poured a rounded teaspoon of Taster's Choice[1] into a cup, added the boiling water, stirred[2] and began to sip[3] as with the other hand he turned the pages of the paper, scanning the contents[4].

He had almost finished the coffee when he got to the second section. His hand with the cup stopped in mid-air as his gaze froze on the picture of Ray Eldredge's wife.

In that first instant of realization, Jonathan sadly accepted two irrefutable facts: Dorothy Prentiss had deliberately lied to him about having known Nancy as a child in Virginia; and retired or not, he should have been enough of a lawyer to trust his own instincts[5]. Subconsciously, he had always suspected that Nancy Harmon and Nancy Eldredge were one and the same[6] person.

1. versa une bonne cuillerée de café instantané
2. touilla
3. boire le café
4. parcourant les articles en diagonale
5. en tant qu'ancien avocat, il aurait dû se fier à son instinct
6. la même

7

It was so cold. There was a gritty taste[1] in her mouth. Sand—why? Where was she?

She could hear Ray calling her, feel him bending over her, cradling her against him[2]. "Nancy, what's the matter? Nancy, where are the children?"

She could hear the fear in his voice. She tried to raise her hand, then felt it fall loosely by her side[3]. She tried to speak, but no words formed on her lips[4]. Ray was there, but she couldn't reach him.

She heard Dorothy say, "Pick her up, Ray. Take her to the house. We have to get help looking for the[5] children."

The children. They must find them. Nancy wanted to tell Ray to look for them. She felt her lips trying to form words, but the words wouldn't come.

"Oh, my God!" She heard the break in Ray's voice[6]. She wanted to say, "Don't bother with me[7]; don't bother with me. Look for the children." But she couldn't speak. She felt him pick her up and hold her against him. "What's happened to her, Dorothy?" he asked. "What's the matter with her?"

"Ray, we've got to call the police."

1. Elle avait comme des gravillons
2. se pencher sur elle, la bercer contre lui
3. la sentit retomber mollement à son côté
4. aucun mot ne sortit
5. trouver de l'aide pour partir à la recherche des
6. la voix de Ray se briser
7. Ne t'inquiète pas pour moi

"The police!" Vaguely[1] Nancy could hear the resistance[2] in his voice.

"Of course. We need help finding the children. Ray, hurry! Every moment is precious. Don't you see—you can't protect Nancy now. Everyone will know her from[3] that picture."

The picture. Nancy felt herself being carried[4]. Remotely[5] she knew she was shivering. But that wasn't what she had to think about. It was the picture of her in the tweed suit she'd bought after the conviction was overturned. They'd taken her out of prison and brought her to court. The state hadn't tried her again.[6] Carl was dead, and the student who'd testified against her had disappeared, and so she'd been released.

The prosecuting attorney[7] had said to her, "Don't think this is over[8]. If I spend[9] the rest of my life, I'll find a way to get a conviction that sticks[10]." And with his words beating against her, she'd left the courtroom.

Afterward, when she'd received permission to leave the state, she'd had her hair cut and dyed[11] and gone shopping. She had always hated[12] the kind of clothes Carl liked her to wear and had bought the three-piece suit[13] and brown turtleneck sweater. She still wore the jacket[14] and slacks[15]; she'd worn them shopping only last week. That was another reason the picture was so recognizable. The picture... it had been taken in the bus terminal[16]; that was where she'd been.

She hadn't known[17] that anyone[18] was taking a picture of her. She'd left on the last evening bus for Boston. The terminal hadn't been crowded[19], and no one had paid any attention to her[20]. She'd really thought that she could just slip away[21] and try to begin again. But someone had just been waiting to start it all over again.

I want to die, she thought. *I want to die.*

Ray was walking swiftly[22], but trying to[23] shield her[24] with his jacket. The wind was biting through[25]

1. Confusément
2. réticence
3. va la reconnaître, avec
4. qu'on la portait
5. Confusément,
6. Elle n'était pas de nouveau inculpée.
7. procureur
8. que ce soit fini
9. Même si je dois y consacrer
10. vous faire condamner
11. s'était fait couper et teindre les cheveux
12. détesté
13. ensemble trois pièces
14. veste
15. le pantalon
16. gare routière
17. ne s'était pas rendu compte
18. quelqu'un
19. Il y avait peu de monde à la gare
20. personne n'avait fait attention à elle
21. partir discrètement
22. d'un pas rapide
23. tout en s'efforçant de
24. la protéger
25. vent mordant transperçait

the wet clothes. He couldn't shield her; not even he could[1] shield her. It was too late.... Maybe it had always been too late. Peter and Lisa and Michael and Missy. They were all gone.... It was too late for all of them.

No. No. No. Michael and Missy. They were here a little while ago. They were playing. They were out on the swing and then the mitten was there. Michael wouldn't leave[2] Missy. He was so careful of[3] her. It was like last time. Last time, and they'd find them the way[4] they found Peter and Lisa, with the wet seaweed[5] and bits of plastic on their faces and in their hair and their bodies swollen.

They must be at the house. Dorothy was opening the door and saying, "I'll call the police, Ray."

Nancy felt the darkness coming at her[6]. She began sliding back and away[7].... No... no... no....

1. même lui ne pouvait

2. n'aurait jamais abandonné

3. faisait si attention à

4. dans le même état où

5. algues

6. un voile noir se profiler

7. à se sentir glisser en arrière, à partir

8

Oh, the activity[1]. Oh, the way they were all scurrying around[2] like ants[3]—all milling around[4] her house and yard. He licked his lips anxiously[5]. They were so dry when all the rest of him was wet—his hands and feet and groin and underarms[6]. Perspiration was streaming down[7] his neck and back.

As soon as he got back to the big house, he carried the children in and brought them right up to[8] the room with the telescope. He could keep an eye on[9] them here and talk to them when they woke up and touch them.

Maybe he'd give the little girl a bath and dry her off in a nice soft towel and rub baby powder[10] on her and kiss her. He had all day to spend with the children. All day; the tide wouldn't come in[11] until seven tonight. By then[12] it would be dark[13], and no one would be nearby[14] to see or hear. It would be days[15] before they'd be washed in[16]. It would be like last time.

It was so much more enjoyable[17] touching them when he knew[18] their mother was being questioned[19] by now. "What did you do with your children?" they'd ask her.

1. remue-ménage
2. s'agitaient dans tous les sens
3. des fourmis
4. grouillant
5. avec inquiétude
6. ses aisselles
7. coulait dans
8. les transporta directement jusqu'à
9. surveiller
10. du talc
11. ce ne serait pas marée haute
12. À ce moment-là,
13. il ferait nuit
14. là
15. Des jours et des jours s'écouleraient
16. ramenés sur le rivage
17. plaisant
18. en sachant que
19. interrogée

1. arriver les uns après les autres
2. par
3. dépassaient
4. Un merveilleux sentiment de satisfaction l'envahit.
5. la toute fin
6. quand le juge l'eut condamnée
7. à l'exécution par asphyxie
8. à sangloter
9. avait enfoui
10. policiers de service l'avaient menottée
11. s'étaient défaits
12. baigné de larmes
13. guettait désespérément
14. ses cheveux blond vénitien
15. régulières
16. ravissants
17. sourcils et cils très noirs
18. avec irritation
19. boucles humides
20. peau claire
21. pleurnichait
22. le produit ne devait plus faire effet
23. à chaque bout
24. à l'odeur de moisi
25. canapé en velours
26. pleurait vraiment
27. Elle serrait les yeux très fort.

He watched more police cars swarm[1] up[2] the dirt road into her backyard. But some of them were passing[3] the house. Why were so many of them going to Maushop Lake? Of course. They thought she had taken the children there.

He felt wonderfully gratified.[4] Here he could see everything that was happening without risk, perfectly safe and comfortable. He wondered if Nancy was crying. She had never cried once at her trial until the very end[5]—after the judge sentenced her[6] to the gas chamber[7]. She'd begun sobbing[8] and buried[9] her face in her hands to cover the sound. The court attendants had snapped handcuffs on her[10], and her long hair had spilled forward[11], covering the tearstained[12] face that looked hopelessly out at[13] the hostile faces.

He remembered the first time he'd seen her walking across the campus. He'd been immediately attracted to her—the way the wind blew her strawberry-gold hair[14] around her shoulders; the delicately formed face; the small, even[15] white teeth; the enchanting[16] round blue eyes that looked gravely out from thick, sooty brows and lashes[17].

He heard a sob. Nancy? But of course not. It was coming from the girl. Nancy's child. He turned from the telescope and stared resentfully[18]. But his expression changed to a smile as he studied her. Those damp ringlets[19] on her forehead; the tiny straight nose; the fair skin[20]... she looked a lot like Nancy. Now she wailed[21] as she started to wake up. Well, it was just about time for the drug to wear off[22]; they'd been unconscious nearly an hour.

Regretfully, he left the telescope. He'd laid the children on opposite ends[23] of the musty-smelling[24] velour couch[25]. The little girl was crying in earnest[26] now. "Mommy... Mommy." Her eyes were squeezed shut.[27] Her mouth was open.... Her little tongue was so pink! Tears were running down her cheeks.

He sat her up and unzipped her jacket. She shrank away from him[1]. "There, there," he said soothingly[2]. "It's all right."

The boy stirred[3] and woke up too. His eyes were startled, just as they had been when he had seen him in the yard. Now he sat up slowly. "Who are you?" he demanded. He rubbed his eyes, shook his head and looked around. "Where are we?"

An articulate child... well spoken[4]... his voice clear and well modulated. That was good. Well-trained[5] children were easier to handle[6]. Didn't make a fuss.[7] Taught respect for older people, they tended[8] to be pliable[9]. Like the others. They'd come with him so quietly that day. They had knelt in the trunk[10] of the car unquestioningly[11] when he had said they were going to play a game on[12] Mommy.

"It's a game," he told this little boy. "I'm an old friend of your mommy's and she wants to play a birthday game. Did you know it was her birthday today?" He kept patting the little girl while he spoke. She felt so soft and good.

The boy—Michael—looked uncertain[13]. "I don't like this game," he said firmly. Unsteadily[14] he got to his feet. He pushed aside[15] the hands that were touching Missy and reached for her. She clung to him. "Don't cry. Missy," he said soothingly[16]. "It's just a silly game. We'll go home now."

It was obvious that he wasn't going to be fooled[17] easily. The boy had Ray Eldredge's candid expression. "We're not going to play any of your games," he said. "We want to go home."

There was a wonderful way he could make the little boy cooperate. "Let go of[18] your sister," he ordered. "Here, give her to me." He yanked her from[19] the boy. With the other hand he took Michael's wrist[20] and pulled him over to the window. "Do you know what a telescope is?"

1. eut un mouvement de recul
2. d'un ton rassurant
3. bougea
4. enfant sachant s'exprimer
5. bien élevés
6. manier
7. Ils ne faisaient pas d'histoires.
8. avaient tendance
9. dociles
10. coffre
11. sans poser de questions
12. faire une blague à
13. hésitant
14. En chancelant,
15. écarta
16. sur un ton apaisant
17. trompé
18. Lâche
19. l'arracha au
20. poignet

Michael nodded uncertainly[1]. "Yes. It's like the glasses[2] my daddy has. It makes things bigger."

"That's right. You're very smart[3]. Now, look in here." The boy put his eye to the viewer[4]. "Now tell me what you see... No, squeeze your other eye shut[5]."

"It's looking at my house."

"What do you see there?"

"There are lots of cars... police cars. What's the matter?" Alarm[6] made his voice quiver[7].

He looked down happily at the worried[8] face. A faint[9] pinging sound[10] came from the window. It was starting to sleet.[11] The wind was driving[12] hard little pellets[13] against the glass panes. The visibility would be very poor[14] soon. Even with the telescope it would be hard to see much. But he could have a wonderful time with the children—the whole, long afternoon. And he knew how to make the boy obey. "Do you know what it's like to be dead?" he asked.

"It means to go to God," Michael answered.

He nodded approvingly. "That's right. And this morning your mother went to God. That's why all the police cars are there. Your daddy asked me to mind you[15] for a while and said for you[16] to be good and help me take care of your sister."

Michael looked as though he'd cry too. His lip quivered as he said, "If my mommy went to God, I want to go too."

Running his fingers through Michael's hair, he rocked[17] the still-wailing[18] Missy. "You will," he told him. "Tonight. I promise."

1. fit un oui hésitant de la tête
2. jumelles
3. intelligent
4. oculaire
5. ferme l'autre œil
6. L'inquiétude
7. trembler
8. inquiet
9. léger
10. crépitement
11. Du grésil commençait à tomber.
12. envoyait
13. granules
14. mauvaise
15. te garder
16. te fait dire
17. berça
18. qui continuait de pleurnicher

9

The first reports[1] went over the wire-service tickers[2] at noon, in time to make bulletins on the news broadcasts[3] throughout the country. Newscasters[4], hungering for[5] a story, seized upon it[6] and sent researchers scurrying to[7] the files for records[8] of the Nancy Harmon murder trial.

Publishers[9] chartered[10] planes to send their top crime reporters to Cape Cod.

In San Francisco, two assistant district attorneys listened to the bulletin. One said to the other, "Have I always said[11] that bitch[12] was as guilty as if I'd seen her kill those kids myself? Have I said it? So help me, if they don't hang this one on her[13], I'll take a leave of absence[14] and personally comb[15] the globe to find that Legler slob[16] and get him back here to testify against her."

In Boston, Dr. Lendon Miles was enjoying the beginning of his lunch break. Mrs. Markley had just left. After a year of intense therapy she was finally beginning to get pretty good insight[17]. She'd made a funny remark a few minutes ago. She'd been discussing an episode from her fourteenth year and said, "Do you realize that thanks to you I'm going through ado-

1. dépêches
2. téléscripteurs
3. être aux informations
4. Les présentateurs
5. toujours à l'affût d'
6. s'en emparèrent
7. filer chercher
8. leurs archives
9. Les journaux
10. affrétèrent
11. N'ai-je pas toujours dit
12. garce
13. elle ne se fait pas coincer cette fois-ci
14. congé
15. je ratisserai
16. plouc
17. les choses commençaient à se clarifier pour elle

lescence and change of life all at once? It's a hell of a deal[1]." Only a few months ago she hadn't been doing much joking.

Lendon Miles enjoyed his profession. To him the mind was a delicate, complicated phenomenon—a mystery that could be unraveled[2] only by a series of infinitely small revelations... one leading slowly, patiently into the next. He sighed. His ten-o'clock patient was in early analysis and had been extremely hostile.

He switched on the radio next to his desk to catch the balance[3] of the noon news and was just in time to hear the bulletin.

A shadow of an old pain crossed his face.[4] Nancy Harmon... Priscilla's daughter. After fourteen years he could still see Priscilla so clearly: the slender[5], elegant body; the way she held her head; the smile that came like quicksilver[6].

She had started working for him a year after her husband's death. She'd been thirty-eight then, two years his junior. Almost immediately he began taking her out to dinner when they worked late, and soon he realized that for the first time in his life the idea of marriage seemed logical and even essential. Until he met Priscilla, work, study, friends and freedom had been enough; he'd simply never met anyone who made him want to alter his status quo.

Gradually she'd told him about herself. Married after her first year in college[7] to an airline pilot, she had one child, a daughter. The marriage had obviously been a happy one. Then on a trip to India her husband had come down with[8] viral pneumonia and had died within twenty-four hours.

"It was so hard to take[9]," Priscilla told him. "Dave flew over a million miles. He brought 707's down in blizzards[10]. And then something so totally unexpected[11]... I didn't realize people still died of pneumonia...."

1. Ça fait beaucoup à la fois
2. dissiper
3. fin
4. Le souvenir d'une ancienne blessure l'assombrit.
5. svelte
6. du vif-argent
7. d'université
8. contracté
9. encaisser
10. faisait atterrir des Boeing 707 en pleine tempête
11. inattendu

Lendon never did meet Priscilla's daughter. She had left for school in San Francisco soon after Priscilla had come to work for him. Priscilla had talked out[1] her reasons for sending her so far away. "She was growing too close to me," Priscilla had worried. "She's taken Dave's death so hard.[2] I want her to be happy and young and to get away from the whole climate of grief that I think is closing in on us[3]. I went to Auberley and met Dave while I was there. Nancy had been with me to reunions[4] so it isn't as if it's too strange to her."

In November Priscilla had taken a couple of days off[5] to visit Nancy at college. Lendon had driven her to the airport. For a few minutes they had stood in the terminal waiting for her flight to be called. "Of course you know I'll miss you[6] terribly" he'd said.

She was wearing a dark brown suede[7] coat that showed off[8] her patrician[9] blond beauty. "I hope so," she said, and her eyes were clouded[10]. "I'm so worried," she told him. "Nancy's letters are so down[11] lately. I'm just terribly afraid. Did you ever have a feeling of something awful hanging over you[12]?"

Then when he stared at her, they both began to laugh. "You see why I didn't dare mention this before," she said. "I knew you'd think I was crazy."

"On the contrary, my training[13] has taught me to appreciate the value of hunches[14], only I call it intuition. But why didn't you tell me you were so worried? Maybe I should be going with you. I only wish I'd met Nancy before she left."

"Oh, no. It's probably me being a mother hen[15]. Anyhow, I'll pick your brains[16] when I get back." Somehow their fingers had become entwined[17].

"Don't worry. Kids all straighten out[18], and if there are any real problems, I'll fly out[19] over the weekend if you want me[20]."

"I shouldn't bother you[21]...."

1. expliqué
2. La mort de Dave l'a tellement affectée.
3. tout ce chagrin qui nous oppresse, à mon avis
4. des réunions de famille
5. deux jours de congé
6. vous allez me manquer
7. en daim
8. mettait en valeur
9. distinguée
10. voilés
11. sont de quelqu'un qui n'a pas le moral
12. et imminent
13. formation
14. pressentiments
15. mon côté mère poule
16. je ferai appel à vos lumières
17. s'étaient entrelacés
18. Les enfants s'en sortent toujours
19. ferai un saut en avion
20. avez besoin de moi
21. vous embêter

An impersonal voice came over the loudspeaker[1]. "Flight Five-six-nine now boarding[2] for San Francisco..."

"Priscilla, for God's sake[3], don't you realize that I love you?"

"I'm glad.... I think... I know... I love you too."

Their last moment together. A beginning... a promise of love.

She had called him the next night. To say that she was worried and had to talk to him. She was at dinner with Nancy, but would call as soon as she got back to her hotel. Would he be home?

He waited all night for the call. But it never came. She never got back to the hotel. The next day he learned about the accident. The steering apparatus[4] of the car she'd rented had failed[5]. The car had careened off the road into a ditch[6].

He probably should have gone to Nancy. But when he finally got through to where she was staying[7], he spoke to Carl Harmon, the professor who said he and Nancy were planning to marry. He sounded[8] perfectly competent and very much in charge[9]. Nancy wouldn't be returning to Ohio. They had told her mother of their plans at dinner. Mrs. Kiernan had been concerned[10] about Nancy's youth[11], but that was natural. She would be buried[12] out there, where her husband was interred[13]; the family had, after all, been residents of California for three generations until Nancy was a baby. Nancy was bearing up well[14]. He thought that it was best for them to have a quiet wedding immediately. Nancy should not be alone now.

There had been nothing for Lendon to do. What could he do? Tell Nancy that he and her mother had been falling in love? The odds were[15] that she would simply have resented him[16]. This Professor Harmon sounded fine[17], and undoubtedly[18] Priscilla had simply been worried about Nancy's taking such a decisive step as[19] marriage at barely[20] eighteen. But surely

1. haut-parleur
2. embarquement immédiat
3. pour l'amour du ciel
4. direction
5. s'était bloquée
6. était sortie de la route pour finir dans le fossé
7. eut enfin réussi à la joindre au téléphone
8. paraissait
9. prêt à se charger de tout
10. un peu inquiète,
11. vu le jeune âge de Nancy
12. enterrée
13. inhumé
14. tenait le coup
15. Il y avait de fortes chances
16. qu'elle lui soit hostile
17. avait l'air très bien
18. sans doute
19. un engagement aussi important que
20. à peine

there was nothing that he, Lendon, could do about that decision.

He'd been glad to accept the offer to teach at the University of London. That was why he'd been out of the country and had never learned of[1] the Harmon murder trial until after it was over[2].

It was at the University of London that he had met Allison. She was a teacher there, and the sense of sharing[3] that Priscilla had begun to show him had made it impossible to go back to his well-ordered, solitary—selfish[4]—life. From time to time he had wondered where Nancy Harmon had vanished[5]. He'd been living in the Boston area for the last two years, and she was only an hour and a half away. Maybe now he could somehow[6] make up[7] for the way he had failed[8] Priscilla before.

The phone rang. An instant later, the intercom light[9] blinked[10] on his phone. He picked up the receiver[11]. "Mrs. Miles is on the phone, Doctor," his secretary said.

Allison's voice was filled with concern[12]. "Darling, did you by chance[13] hear the news about the Harmon girl?"

"Yes, I did." He had told Allison about Priscilla.

"What are you going to do?"

Her question crystallized the decision he had already made subconsciously. "What I should have done years ago. I'm going to try to help that girl. I'll call you as soon as I can."

"God bless[14], darling."

Lendon picked up the intercom and spoke crisply[15] to his secretary. "Ask Dr. Marcus to take over[16] my afternoon appointments[17], please. Tell him it's an emergency[18]. And cancel[19] my four-o'clock class. I'm driving to Cape Cod immediately."

1. entendu parler
2. avant que l'affaire soit terminée
3. partage
4. égoïste
5. disparu
6. trouver une façon
7. de se racheter
8. fait défaut à
9. voyant de l'Interphone
10. clignota
11. combiné
12. très inquiète
13. par hasard
14. à plus
15. donna des ordres brefs
16. me remplacer pour
17. rendez-vous
18. urgence
19. annulez

10

"WE'VE STARTED DRAGGING[1] the lake, Ray. We've got bulletins going out on the radio and TV stations, and we're getting manpower[2] from all over[3] to help in the search[4]." Chief Jed Coffin of the Adams Port police tried to adopt the hearty tone[5] that he would normally use if two children were missing.

But even looking at the agony[6] in Ray's eyes and the ashen pallor of his face[7], it was difficult to sound reassuring and solicitous[8]. Ray had deceived him[9]—introduced him to[10] his wife, talked about her coming from Virginia and having known Dorothy there. He'd filled him with[11] talk and never once told the truth. And the Chief hadn't guessed[12]—or even suspected. That was the real irritation. Not once had he suspected.

To Chief Coffin, what had happened was very clear. That woman had seen the article about herself in the paper, realized that everyone would know who she was and gone berserk[13]. Did to these poor kids the same thing she'd done to her others. Studying Ray shrewdly[14], he guessed that Ray was thinking pretty much the same thing.

1. à draguer
2. des renforts
3. de partout
4. aux recherches
5. ton enjoué
6. angoisse
7. son teint terreux
8. plein de sollicitude
9. l'avait trompé
10. lui avait présenté
11. l'avait saoulé de
12. deviné
13. avait complètement déraillé
14. attentivement

Charred[1] bits of the morning paper were still in the fireplace. The Chief realized Ray was looking at them. From the jagged[2] way the unburned parts were torn[3], it was obvious they'd been pulled apart by someone in a frenzy[4].

"Doc Smathers still upstairs with her?" There was unconscious discourtesy in the question.[5] He'd always called Nancy "Mrs. Eldredge" till now.

"Yes. He's going to give her a needle[6] to relax her but not to put her out[7]. We've got to talk to her. Oh, God!"

Ray sat down at the dining-room table and buried his face in his hands. Only a few hours ago Nancy had been sitting in this chair with Missy in her arms and Mike asking, "Is it really your birthday, Mommy?" Had he triggered[8] something in Nancy by demanding she celebrate[9]?... And then that article. Had...?

"No!" Ray looked up and blinked[10], turning his head away from the sight of the policeman standing by the back door.

"What is it?" Chief Coffin asked.

"Nancy is incapable of harming the[11] children. Whatever happened, it wasn't that."

"Your wife when she's herself[12] wouldn't harm them, but I've seen women go off the deep end[13], and there is the history..."

Ray stood up. His hands clenched[14] the edge[15] of the table. His glance went past the Chief, dismissing him[16]. "I need help," he said. "Real help."

The room was in chaos. The police had made a quick search of[17] the house before concentrating on the outside. A police photographer was still taking pictures of the kitchen, where the coffeepot had fallen, spewing streams[18] of black coffee onto the stove[19] and floor. The telephone rang incessantly. To every call the policeman answering said, "The Chief will have a statement[20] later."

1. carbonisés
2. très irrégulier
3. déchirées
4. en pleine agitation
5. Sa question manquait involontairement de courtoisie.
6. lui faire une piqûre
7. l'endormir
8. déclenché
9. en insistant pour qu'elle le fête
10. cligna des yeux
11. faire du mal à nos
12. dans son état normal
13. perdre complètement la tête
14. agrippaient
15. bord
16. sans le voir
17. rapidement fouillé
18. projetant des traînées
19. la gazinière
20. fera une déclaration

The policeman at the phone came over to the table. "That was the A.P.[1]," he said. "The wire services have gotten hold of this[2]. We'll be mobbed[3] in an hour."

The wire services. Ray remembered the haunted look[4] that had only gradually left Nancy's face. He thought of the picture in this morning's paper, with her hand up as though trying to fend off blows[5]. He pushed past[6] Chief Coffin and hurried upstairs, opening the door of the master bedroom. The doctor was sitting next to Nancy, holding her hands. "You can hear me, Nancy," he was saying. "You know you can hear me. Ray is here. He's very worried about you. Talk to him, Nancy."

Her eyes were closed. Dorothy had helped Ray strip off[7] the wet clothes. They'd put a fluffy[8] yellow robe[9] on her, but she seemed curiously small and inert inside it—not unlike a child herself.

Ray bent over[10] her. "Honey, please, you've got to help the children. We've got to find them. They need you. Try, Nancy—please try."

"Ray, I wouldn't[11]," Dr. Smathers warned[12]. His lined[13], sensitive[14] face was deeply creased[15]. "She's had some kind of terrible shock—whether it was[16] reading the article or something else. Her mind is fighting confronting it.[17]"

"But we've got to know what it was," Ray said intently[18]. "Maybe she even saw someone take the children away. Nancy, I know. I understand. It's all right[19] about the newspaper. We'll face[20] that together. But, darling, where are the children? You must help us find them. Do you think they went near the lake?"

Nancy shuddered[21]. A strangled cry came from somewhere in her throat. Her lips formed words: "Find them... find them."

"We will find them. But you must help, please. Honey, I'm going to help you sit up. You can. Now, come on."

1. Associated Press
2. sont sur le coup
3. Ce sera la ruée
4. l'air hagard
5. parer des coups
6. bouscula
7. à lui enlever
8. très doux
9. peignoir
10. se pencha sur
11. non, ce n'est pas une bonne idée
12. protesta
13. ridé
14. sensible
15. creusé
16. que ce soit en
17. Elle est encore ébranlée.
18. avec force
19. Ne t'en fais pas
20. affronterons
21. frissonna

Ray leaned down and supported her in[1] his arms. He saw the raw[2] skin on her face where the sand had burned it. There was wet sand still clinging to her hair. Why? Unless....

"I gave her a shot[3]," the doctor said. "It should relieve[4] the anxiety, but it won't be enough to knock her out[5]."

She felt so heavy and vague[6]. This was the way she'd felt for such a long time—from the night Mother died... or maybe even before that—so defenseless[7], so pliable[8]... so without ability to choose or move or even speak. She could remember how so many nights her eyes would be glued together[9]—so heavy, so weary[10]. Carl had been so patient with her. He had done everything for her. She had always told herself that she had to get stronger, had to overcome[11] that terrible lethargy, but she never could.

But that was so long ago. She didn't think about that anymore—not about Carl; not about the children; not about Rob Legler, the handsome student who'd seemed to like her, who made her laugh. The children had been so gay when he was there, so happy. She had thought he was a real friend—but then he sat on the witness stand[12] and said, "She told me that her children would be smothered[13]. That was exactly what she said, four days before they disappeared."

"Nancy. Please. Nancy. Why did you go to the lake?"

She heard the stifled[14] sound she made. The lake. Did the children go there? She must search for them.

She felt Ray lifting her and slumped against him, but then forced her body to begin to sit up. It would be so much easier to slip away, to slide[15] into sleep just as she used to do.

"That's it. That's right, Nancy." Ray looked at the doctor. "Do you think a cup of coffee... ?"

The doctor nodded. "I'll ask Dorothy to make it." Coffee. She'd been making coffee when she saw that picture in the paper. Nancy opened her eyes. "Ray,"

1. la soutint de
2. à vif
3. lui ai fait une injection
4. soulager
5. sans pour autant l'assommer
6. confuse
7. vulnérable
8. docile
9. étaient comme collés
10. las
11. surmonter
12. était assis dans le box des témoins
13. étouffés
14. sourd
15. se laisser glisser

she whispered[1], "they'll know. Everyone will know. You can't hide... you can't hide." But there was something else. "The children." She clutched his arm. "Ray, find them—find my babies."

"Steady[2], honey. That's where we need you. You've got to tell us. Every single thing.[3] Just get your bearing[4] for a few minutes."

Dorothy came in with a cup of steaming coffee in her hand. "I made the instant[5]. How is she?"

"She's coming round[6]."

"Captain Coffin is anxious to[7] begin questioning her."

"Ray!" Panic made Nancy clutch Ray's arm.

"Darling, it's just that we have to have help[8] finding the children. It's all right."

She gulped the[9] coffee, welcoming the searing, hot taste[10] as she swallowed it. If she could just think... just wake up... just lose[11] this terrible sleepiness[12].

Her voice. She could talk now. Her lips felt rubbery[13], thick, spongelike[14]. But she had to talk... make them find[15] the children. She wanted to go downstairs. She mustn't stay here... like last time... waiting in her room... unable to go downstairs... to see all the people downstairs... the policemen... the faculty wives[16].... Are there any relatives[17]?... Do you want us to call anyone?... No one... no one... no one...

Leaning heavily[18] on Ray's arm, she stood up unsteadily. Ray. She had his arm to lean on now. His children. His children.

"Ray... I didn't hurt them...."

"Of course not, darling."

The voice too soothing[19]... the shocked sound[20]. Of course he was shocked. He was wondering why she would deny it[21]. No good mother spoke of hurting her children. Why then did she... ?

With a supreme effort she groped toward[22] the door. His arm around her waist[23] steadied her steps[24]. She couldn't feel her feet. They weren't there. She wasn't

1. chuchota
2. Doucement
3. Tout dans le détail.
4. Mais prends le temps de te remettre
5. du café instantané
6. reprend ses esprits
7. a hâte de
8. il nous faut de l'aide
9. prit une gorgée de
10. appréciant le liquide très chaud
11. se débarrasser de
12. somnolence
13. caoutchouteuses
14. comme des éponges
15. faire en sorte qu'on retrouve
16. femmes des professeurs
17. membres de la famille
18. S'appuyant lourdement
19. trop apaisante
20. ton bouleversé
21. avait besoin de se défendre
22. se traîna jusqu'à
23. taille
24. l'aidait à assurer ses pas

1. cauchemars
2. la serreraient contre lui
3. sa douce tiédeur
4. se mirent à descendre
5. de pure forme
6. indifférente
7. pris la peine
8. recherchons
9. Je suis convaincu
10. faire tourner une machine
11. tournait le coin de la rue
12. j'ai rallumé
13. à feuilleter le journal
14. regarda droit devant elle

there. It was one of the nightmares[1]. In a few minutes she'd wake up, as she had so many nights, and slip out of bed and go in to see Missy and Michael and cover them and then get back into bed—softly, quietly, not waking Ray. But in sleep he'd reach out and his arms would pull her close[2], and against the warm scent of him[3] she'd be calmed and sleep.

They started down[4] the stairs. So many policemen. Everybody looking up... curiously still... suspended in time.

Chief Coffin was at the dining-room table. She could feel his hostility.... It was like last time.

"Mrs. Eldredge, how do you feel?"

A perfunctory[5] question, noncaring[6]. Probably he wouldn't have bothered[7] to ask except that Ray was there.

"I'm all right." She had never liked this man.

"We're searching for[8] the children. I have every confidence[9] that we'll find them quickly. But you must help us. When did you last see the children?"

"A few minutes before ten. I put them outside to play and went upstairs to make the beds."

"How long were you upstairs?"

"Ten minutes... not more than fifteen."

"Then what did you do?"

"I came downstairs. I was going to turn on a wash[10] and call the children. But after I started the wash, I decided to heat the coffee. Then I saw the boy deliver the community paper."

"Did you speak to him?"

"No. I don't mean I saw him. I went to get the paper and he was just going around the corner[11]."

"I see. What happened then?"

"I went back into the kitchen. I turned on[12] the coffeepot—it was still quite warm. I started turning the pages of the paper[13]."

"And you saw the article about yourself."

Nancy stared straight ahead[14] and nodded her head.

"How did you react to seeing[1] that article?"

"I think I started to scream[2]... I don't know...

"What happened to the coffeepot?"

"I knocked it over[3].... The coffee went all over[4]. It burned my hand."

"Why did you do that?"

"I don't know. I didn't mean to.[5] It was just that[6] I was going to burst[7]. I knew that everyone would start looking at me again. They'd stare and whisper. They'd say I killed the children. And Michael mustn't ever see that.[8] I ran with the paper. I pushed it into the fireplace. I lit a match and it burned... it started to burn... and I knew I had to get Michael and Missy—I had to hide them. But it was the way it was last time[9]. When the children were gone[10]. I ran out to get Michael and Missy. I was afraid."

"Now, this is important. Did you see the children?"

"No. They were gone. I started calling. I ran to the lake."

"Mrs. Eldredge, this is very important: Why did you go to the lake? Your husband tells me the children have never once been disobedient about going there[11]. Why didn't you look on the road for them, or in the woods, or see if they'd decided to walk into town to buy you a birthday present? Why the lake?"

"Because I was afraid. Because Peter and Lisa were drowned[12]. Because I had to find Michael and Missy. Missy's mitten was caught on the swing. She's always losing a mitten. I ran to the lake. I had to get the children. It's going to be just like last time[13]... their faces all wet and quiet... and they won't talk to me...."

Chief Coffin straightened up[14]. His tone became formal.[15] "Mrs. Eldredge," he said, "it is my duty[16] to inform you that you have a right to legal advice[17] before you answer any further[18] questions and that anything you say[19] can be used against you[20]."

Without waiting for her response, he got up and stalked out of the room[21] and to the back door. A

1. en voyant
2. hurler
3. l'ai renversée
4. a tout éclaboussé
5. Je ne l'ai pas fait exprès.
6. J'avais tout simplement l'impression que
7. éclater
8. Et Michael ne doit jamais assister à ça.
9. c'était comme la dernière fois
10. avaient disparu
11. n'ont jamais enfreint l'interdiction d'y aller
12. sont morts noyés
13. Ça va être comme la dernière fois
14. se redressa
15. Il prit un ton officiel.
16. il est de mon devoir
17. avez le droit de vous faire assister d'un avocat
18. à de nouvelles
19. tout ce que vous direz
20. retenu contre vous
21. sortit de la pièce d'un pas raide

car with a policeman at the wheel[1] was waiting for him in the rear driveway[2]. As he stepped from[3] the house, thin, driving pellets of sleet stung his face[4] and head. He got into the car and the wind blew the door closed behind him[5], scraping it against[6] his shoe. He winced[7] at the short stab of pain[8] in his ankle[9] and growled[10], "The lake."

Fat chance they had of doing any searching[11] if this weather got any worse[12]. At noon it was already so dark you'd think it was nighttime. The diving operation[13] was a mess[14] under optimal conditions. Maushop was among the biggest lakes on the Cape and one of the deepest and most treacherous. That was why over the years there'd been so many drownings[15] there. You could be wading up to your waist[16] and at the next step[17] be in forty feet of water[18]. If those kids had been drowned, it might be spring before their bodies surfaced. The way[19] the temperature was dropping, the lake would be fit for ice skating[20] in a few days.

The lakeside, normally deserted at this time of the year and certainly in this kind of weather, was crowded[21] with bystanders[22], who huddled together[23] in small clusters[24], silently watching the roped-off area[25] where the divers and their apparatus[26] were flanked[27] by police.

Chief Coffin jumped out of the squad car[28] and hurried to the beach. He went directly to Pete Regan, the lieutenant who was supervising the operation. Pete's eloquent shrug answered his unasked[29] question.

Hunching his shoulders[30] inside his coat, the Chief stamped his[31] feet as the sleet melted[32] into his shoes. He wondered if this was the spot from which Nancy Eldredge had dragged her kids into the water. Now men were risking their own lives because of her. God only knew where or when those poor little kids would be found. Shows what happens... A technicality[33]... a convicted murderess gets off[34] because

1. au volant
2. l'allée à l'arrière de la maison
3. franchissait le seuil de
4. un fin grésil lui fouetta le visage
5. rabattit la portière sur lui
6. raclant
7. grimaça
8. élancement
9. cheville
10. grogna
11. Des recherches par là-bas, ça m'étonnerait
12. empirait
13. Envoyer des plongeurs
14. était déjà compliqué
15. noyades
16. avoir de l'eau jusqu'à la taille
17. en une enjambée
18. 12 m de profondeur
19. À l'allure
20. bon pour servir de patinoire
21. envahi
22. de badauds
23. se serraient les uns contre les autres
24. par petits groupes
25. zone délimitée
26. équipement
27. encadrés
28. voiture de police
29. muette
30. Se voûtant
31. tapa des
32. fondait
33. vice de forme
34. s'en sort

a smart-ass lawyer[1] gets a couple of bleeding-heart[2] judges to declare a mistrial[3].

Angrily, he spat out Pete's name[4].

Pete turned to him quickly. "Sir?"

"How long are those guys planning to keep diving?"

"They've been down twice, and after this session, they'll try once more, then take a break[5] and set up in a different location[6]." He pointed to the television equipment. "Looks like[7] we'll make the headlines tonight. You'd better have a statement ready."

With numbed[8] fingers, the Chief dug into his coat pocket. "I've scribbled one down[9]." He read it quickly. "We are conducting[10] a massive effort[11] to find the Eldredge children. Volunteers are making a block-by-block search of[12] the immediate vicinity[13] of her home as well as the neighboring wooded areas[14]. Helicopters are conducting an air reconnaissance. The search of Maushop Lake, because of its proximity to the Eldredge home must be considered a normal extension of the investigation."

But a few minutes later, when he delivered that statement to the growing assemblage of reporters, one of them asked, "Is it true that Nancy Eldredge was found hysterical and drenched[15] in this area of Maushop Lake this morning after her children disappeared?"

"That is true."

A thin, sharp-eyed[16] reporter who he knew was connected with Boston Channel 5's news team asked, "In view[17] of that fact and her past history[18], doesn't the search of the lake take on a new aspect?"

"We are exploring all possibilities."

Now the questions came thick and fast[19], the reporters interrupting one another to ask them. "In view of the past tragedy, wouldn't the disappearance of the Eldredge children be considered of suspicious[20] origin?"

"To answer that question could prejudice[21] Mrs. Eldredge's rights[22]."

1. petit malin d'avocat
2. au cœur tendre
3. qu'il y a eu vice de procédure
4. interpella Pete brusquement
5. faire une pause
6. essayer ailleurs
7. On dirait
8. engourdis
9. griffonné un truc
10. menons
11. opération d'envergure
12. quadrillent
13. voisinage
14. bois
15. trempée
16. à l'œil vif
17. Compte tenu
18. son passé
19. s'enchaînèrent vivement
20. suspecte
21. porter atteinte aux
22. droits

1. avait pris connaissance de
2. la plupart, sinon tous
3. ne savaient rien
4. l'air pincé
5. lui barra le chemin
6. correspondants de presse
7. d'une voix forte
8. inexpliquées
9. côte

"When will you question her again?"

"As soon as possible."

"Is it known whether Mrs. Eldredge was aware of[1] the article about her that came out this morning?"

"I believe she was."

"What was her reaction to that article?"

"I can't say."

"Isn't it a fact that most if not all of[2] the people in this town were unaware[3] of Mrs. Eldredge's past?"

"That is true."

"Were you aware of her identity?"

"No. I was not." The Chief spoke through clenched teeth[4]. "No more questions."

Then, before he could get away, another question came. A reporter from the *Boston Herald* blocked his path[5]. All the other news personnel[6] stopped trying to get the Chiefs attention when they heard him ask loudly[7], "Sir, in the past six years haven't there been several unsolved[8] deaths of young children both on the Cape and on the nearby mainland[9]?"

"That is true."

"Chief Coffin, how long has Nancy Harmon Eldredge been living on the Cape?"

"Six years, I believe."

"Thank you, Chief."

11

Jonathan Knowles did not realize how much time was slipping by[1]. Neither was he aware of the activity in the area near Maushop Lake. His subconscious had registered the fact that heavier-than-usual[2] traffic[3] was passing on the road in front of his house. But his study[4] was to the back of the house, and much of the sound was filtered out[5] before it came to his ears.

After the first shock of realizing that Ray Eldredge's wife was the notorious[6] Nancy Harmon, he'd gotten another cup of coffee and settled down at his desk. He resolved to stick to[7] his schedule[8]—to begin to study the Harmon murder case just as he'd planned. If he found that knowing Nancy Harmon personally in some way clouded[9] his ability[10] to write about her, he'd simply eliminate this chapter from his book.

He began his research by carefully studying the sensational article in the Cape paper. With grim detail[11] that insidiously evoked horror in[12] the reader, it reviewed[13] Nancy Harmon's background as the young wife of a college professor... two children... a home on the college campus. An ideal situation until the day Professor Harmon sent a student to his house to repair the oil burner[14]. The student was good-looking[15],

1. s'écoulait
2. plus dense que d'habitude
3. une circulation
4. bureau
5. assourdi
6. tristement célèbre
7. s'en tenir à
8. programme
9. entravait d'une façon ou d'une autre
10. capacité
11. un souci du détail
12. suscitait l'horreur chez
13. brossait
14. chaudière à mazout
15. beau garçon

glib[1] and experienced with women. And Nancy—barely twenty-five herself—had flipped over[2] him.

Jonathan read excerpts from the[3] trial testimony in the article. The student, Rob Legler, explained how he had met Nancy. "When Professor Harmon got that call from his wife about the oil burner not working, I was in his office. There's just nothing mechanical I can't fix[4], so I volunteered[5] to go over[6]. He didn't want me to do it, but he couldn't get the regular maintenance[7] service and had to get the heat back on[8] in his house."

"Did he give you any specific instructions concerning his family?" a district attorney asked.

"Yes. He said that his wife wasn't well and I shouldn't bother her; that if I needed anything, or wanted to discuss whatever problem I found[9], I should call him."

"Did you follow Professor Harmon's instructions?"

"I would have, sir, but I couldn't help the fact that[10] his wife followed me around like a little dog."

"Objection! Objection!" But the defense attorney[11] had been too late[12]. The point had been made.[13] And further evidence[14] from the student had been totally damaging[15]. He was asked if he had had any physical contact with Mrs. Harmon.

His answer was direct. "Yes, sir."

"How did it happen?"

"I was showing her where the emergency switch[16] was on the oil burner. It was one of those old-fashioned hot-air-blower types[17], and the switch had caused the problem."

"Didn't Professor Harmon tell you not to trouble Mrs. Harmon with any questions or explanations[18]?"

"She insisted on knowing about it[19]. Said she had to learn how to manage things[20] in her house. So I showed her. Then she was sort of leaning[21] over me to try the switch, and... well, I figured[22], why not?... so I made a pass[23]."

"What did Mrs. Harmon do?"

"She liked it. I could tell.[24]"

1. beau parleur
2. flashé sur
3. des extraits du
4. Je répare tout ce qui est mécanique
5. ai proposé
6. passer voir
7. d'entretien
8. rétablir le chauffage
9. un problème éventuel sur place
10. que vouliez-vous que je fasse :
11. avocat de la défense
12. réagissait trop tard
13. L'argument avait été présenté.
14. la suite du témoignage
15. causé un tort énorme
16. dispositif d'arrêt d'urgence
17. vieux modèles à air pulsé
18. explications
19. pour que je lui explique
20. se débrouiller
21. se penchait
22. me suis dit
23. tenté ma chance
24. Ça se voyait.

"Will you please explain exactly what happened?"

"It wasn't really what happened. 'Cause nothing much actually happened.[1] It was just that she liked it. I sort of spun her around[2] and grabbed her[3] and kissed her—and after a minute she pulled away[4], but she didn't want to."

"What happened then?"

"I said something about that being[5] pretty good."

"What did Mrs. Harmon say?"

"She just looked at me and said... almost like she wasn't talking to me... she said, 'I've got to get away.' "

"I figured I didn't want to get in any trouble[6]. I mean, I didn't want to do anything to get kicked out[7] of school and end up being drafted[8]. That was the whole reason for the college scene.[9] So I said, 'Look[10], Mrs. Harmon'... only then I decided it was about time[11] to call her Nancy... so I said, 'Look, Nancy, this doesn't have to be a problem. We can work something out[12] so we can get together without anyone ever guessing[13]. You can't leave here—you've got the kids.' "

"How did Mrs. Harmon respond to that statement[14]?"

"Well, it's funny. Just then the boy... Peter... came down the stairs looking for her. He was a real quiet kid—didn't say 'Boo[15].' She looked mad and said, 'The children'; then she sort of laughed[16] and said, 'But they're going to be smothered.' "

"Mr. Legler, this is a crucial sentence[17] you're quoting[18]. Are you sure you are repeating Mrs. Harmon's exact phrasing[19]?"

"Yes, sir, I am. It really made me feel spooky[20] right then[21]. That's why I'm so sure of it. But of course you don't really believe that anyone means it[22] when they say something like that."

"On what date did Nancy Harmon make that statement?"

1. Passque y a pas eu grand-chose, en fait
2. Je l'ai retournée vers moi
3. l'ai prise par les épaules
4. s'est écartée
5. comme quoi c'était
6. m'attirer des ennuis
7. viré
8. me retrouver à faire mon service militaire
9. Parce que, la fac, c'était pour éviter l'armée.
10. Écoutez
11. qu'il était temps
12. s'arranger
13. sans que personne s'en doute
14. déclaration
15. très timide
16. a eu une espèce de rire
17. phrase capitale
18. que vous rapportez là
19. les termes exacts
20. Ca m'a vraiment donné la chair de poule
21. sur le moment
22. le pense vraiment

1. la réparation de la chaudière

2. pour être finalement retrouvés échoués sur la plage

3. effectivement

4. atténuer

5. que vous lui avez imposé

6. sais reconnaître

7. nana qui aime ça

8. sous serment

9. l'ai laissé faire

10. fixa sans les voir

11. rêveuse

12. jura

13. autorisée

14. à témoigner

15. n'avait fait que nuire à sa défense

16. découverte

17. infortunés

18. à 80 km l'un de l'autre

19. horriblement

20. des morsures de requin

"It was on November thirteenth. I know because when I went back to school, Professor Harmon insisted on giving me a check for fixing the burner[1]."

"November thirteenth... and four days later the Harmon children disappeared from their mother's automobile and eventually were washed in on the shores[2] of San Francisco Bay with plastic bags over their heads—in effect[3], smothered."

"That's right."

The defense attorney had tried to reduce[4] the impact of the story. "Did you continue to embrace Mrs. Harmon?"

"No. She went upstairs with the kids."

"Then we have only your statement that she enjoyed the kiss you forced on her[5]."

"Believe me, I can tell[6] a receptive babe[7] when I'm with one."

And Nancy's sworn[8] testimony when asked about that incident: "Yes, he did kiss me. Yes, I believe that I knew he was going to and I let him[9]."

"Do you also remember making the statement that your children were going to be smothered?"

"Yes, I do."

"What did you mean by that statement?"

According to the article, Nancy simply looked past her attorney and stared unseeingly over[10] the faces in the courtroom. "I don't know," she said in a dreamy[11] voice.

Jonathan shook his head and swore[12] silently. That girl should never have been permitted[13] to take the witness stand[14]. She did nothing except damage her own case[15]. He continued reading and winced as he came to the description of the finding[16] of those pathetic[17] children. Washed in, both of them, two weeks and fifty miles apart[18]. Bodies badly[19] swollen, seaweed clinging to them, the little girl's body savagely mutilated—probably by shark bites[20]; the handmade bright red sweaters[1] with the white design still miraculously colorful against the small bodies.

After he'd finished reading the article, Jonathan turned his attention to the voluminous file Kevin had sent him. Leaning back in his chair, he began to read through it, starting with the first newspaper clipping[2] headlining[3] the disappearance of the Harmon children from their mother's automobile while she was shopping. Blowups[4] of fuzzy[5] snapshots of both of the children; a minutely detailed[6] description of their weight and size and what they were wearing; anyone with any information please call this special number. With his carefully trained[7] mind and eyes, Jonathan read rapidly, assorting[8] and assimilating information, lightly underlining[9] cogent[10] facts he wanted to refer to[11] later. When he began reading the transcript of the trial, he understood why Kevin had referred to Nancy Harmon as a sitting duck for the prosecutor. The girl didn't even make sense.[12] She had played so completely into the prosecutor's hands the way she testified[13]—without fight; her protestations of innocence sounding perfunctory and emotionless[14].

What had been the matter with her? Jonathan wondered. It was almost as though she didn't want to get off[15]. At one point[16] she'd even said to the husband right from[17] the witness stand, "Oh, Carl, can you forgive me?"

The creases[18] along Jonathan's forehead deepened[19] as he recalled that just a few hours before he'd passed the Eldredges' house and glanced in at that young family around the breakfast table. He'd compared them with his own solitary state and had been envious[20]. Now their life was ripped apart[21]. They'd never be able to stay in as insular a community as the Cape[22], knowing that everywhere they went people were pointing[23] and talking. Anyone would instantly recognize Nancy from that one picture[24]. Even he

1. pulls
2. coupure
3. avec, à la une,
4. Des agrandissements
5. flous
6. très précise
7. exercés
8. classant
9. soulignant
10. décisifs
11. sur lesquels il voulait revenir
12. L'attitude de cette fille était absurde.
13. Sa déposition faisait entièrement le jeu du procureur
14. indifférentes
15. être acquittée
16. À un moment,
17. sans quitter
18. rides
19. se creusèrent
20. jaloux
21. volé en éclats
22. dans un microcosme tel que Cape Cod
23. les montreraient du doigt
24. rien qu'avec cette photo

remembered her wearing that tweed suit—and recently, too.

Suddenly Jonathan recalled the occasion. It had been at Lowery's Market. He'd run into[1] Nancy when they were both shopping and they'd stopped for a few minutes to talk. He'd admired the suit, telling her that there was nothing better-looking[2] than a good tweed—and pure wool, of course; none of that synthetic junk[3] that had no depth[4] or sheen[5].

Nancy had looked very pretty. A yellow scarf[6] knotted[7] casually[8] at her neck had picked up[9] the glint[10] of yellow in the predominantly brown and rust-colored[11] material[12]. She'd smiled—a warm, lovely smile that wrapped you in it[13]. The children were with her—nice, polite children, both of them. Then the boy had said, "Oh, Mommy, I'll get the cereal," and as he reached for it, he knocked over[14] a pyramid of soup cans[15].

The clatter[16] had brought everyone in the store running, including Lowery himself, who was a sour[17], disagreeable man. Many young mothers might have been embarrassed and started berating[18] the child. Jonathan had admired the way Nancy said very quietly, "We're sorry, Mr. Lowery. It was an accident. We'll take care of it[19]."

Then she said to the little boy, who looked stricken[20] and worried[21], "Don't be upset[22], Mike. You didn't mean it[23]. Come on. Let's pile them back up."

Jonathan had helped with the restacking[24], after first shooting a menacing glare[25] at Lowery, who'd obviously been about to[26] make some kind of remark. It seemed so hard to believe that seven years ago today that same considerate[27] young woman could have deliberately taken the life of two other children—children she had brought into life[28].

But passion was a powerful motive[29], and she had been young. Maybe her very indifference[30] at her trial had been acceptance of[31] guilt, even though she

1. tombé sur
2. de plus seyant
3. camelote
4. consistance
5. éclat
6. foulard
7. noué
8. négligemment
9. relevait
10. soupçon
11. couleur rouille
12. tissu
13. qui vous enveloppait
14. avait renversé
15. conserves
16. vacarme
17. revêche
18. à réprimander
19. tout remettre en ordre
20. penaud
21. inquiet
22. Ne t'en fais pas
23. Tu ne l'as pas fait exprès
24. à remettre les boîtes en place
25. avoir lancé un regard menaçant
26. qui, de toute évidence, s'apprêtait à
27. prévenante
28. à qui elle avait donné la vie
29. moteur
30. indifférence même
31. admettre

couldn't publicly bring herself[1] to admit such a heinous[2] crime. He'd seen that kind of thing happen too.

The doorbell rang. Jonathan got up from his chair, surprised. Few people visited unannounced[3] at the Cape, and any door-to-door selling[4] was absolutely forbidden.

As he walked to the door Jonathan realized how stiff[5] he'd become from sitting. To his amazement[6], his visitor was a policeman, a young man whose face he only vaguely recognized from seeing him in a squad car. *Selling some kind of tickets* was Jonathan's immediate thought, but he discarded[7] that idea at once. The young officer accepted his invitation to step inside. There was something crisply efficient and serious about his demeanor.[8] "Sir, I'm sorry to bother you but we're investigating[9] the disappearance of the Eldredge children."

Then, while Jonathan stared at him, he pulled out a notebook. His eyes darting around[10] the orderly[11] house, he began his questions. "You live alone here, sir, do you not?"

Without answering, Jonathan reached past him[12] and opened the massive front door. At last he became aware of[13] the presence of cars driving down the road toward the lake and the sight of grim-faced[14] men in heavy rain gear[15] swarming[16] through the neighborhood[17].

1. se résoudre
2. odieux
3. venaient à l'improviste
4. démarchage à domicile
5. raide
6. grand étonnement
7. écarta
8. Son attitude se voulait sèche et grave.
9. enquêtons sur
10. Tout en inspectant du regard
11. bien tenue
12. le contourna du bras
13. perçut
14. à la mine sévère
15. gros imperméables
16. présents en masse
17. dans le quartier

12

"**JUST SIP THIS,**[1] **NANCY.** Your hands are so cold. It will help you. You need your strength." Dorothy's voice was cajoling. Nancy shook her head. Dorothy set the cup on the table, hoping the aroma of the fresh vegetables, bubbling[2] in a spicy[3] base of tomato soup, might tempt her.

"I made that yesterday," Nancy said tonelessly[4], "for the children's lunch. The children must be hungry."

Ray was sitting next to her, his arm slung protectively across the back of her chair, an ashtray[5] filled high[6] with ground-out[7] cigarettes in front of him.

"Don't torture yourself, dear," he said quietly.

Outside, over the rattling[8] of the shutters[9] and windowpanes, they could hear the staccato sound[10] of helicopters flying low.

Ray answered the question he saw on Nancy's face. "They've got three helicopters scanning[11] the area. They'll spot[12] the kids if they just wandered away[13]. They've got volunteers from every town on the Cape. There are two planes over the bay and sound[14]. Everyone's helping."

1. Buvez quelques gorgées
2. bouillottant
3. épicé
4. d'une voix terne
5. cendrier
6. rempli à ras bord
7. écrasées
8. claquement
9. volets
10. tac tac
11. qui balayent
12. repéreront
13. se sont juste égarés
14. détroit

"And there are divers in the lake," Nancy said, "looking for my children's bodies." Her voice was a remote monotone.[1]

After giving the statement to the news media, Chief Coffin had gone back to the police station to make a series of phone calls. When they were completed, he returned to the Eldredge house, coming in[2] just in time to hear Nancy's words. His practiced glance[3] took in[4] the staring quality of her eyes[5], the ominous stillness[6] of her hands and body, the facile[7] expression and voice. Approaching a state of shock again[8], and they'd be lucky if she was able to answer to her own name before long.

He looked past her, his eyes seeking[9] Bernie Mills, the policeman he'd left on duty[10] in the house. Bernie was standing at the doorway of the kitchen, poised[11] to pick up the telephone if it rang. Bernie's sandy[12] hair was plastered neatly over his bony[13] skull[14]. His prominent[15] eyes, softened[16] by short, blond lashes[17], moved horizontally. Accepting the signaled message[18], Chief Coffin looked again at the three people around the table. Ray got up, walked behind his wife's chair and put his hands on her shoulders.

Twenty years disappeared for Jed Coffin. He remembered the night he'd gotten a call at the precinct house[19] when he was a rookie cop[20] in Boston that Delia's folks[21] had been in an accident and it wasn't likely they'd make it[22].

He'd gone home. She'd been sitting in the kitchen in her nightgown[23] and robe[24], sipping a cup of her favorite instant hot chocolate, reading the paper. She'd turned, surprised to see him early but smiling, and before he said one word, he'd done just what Ray Eldredge was doing now—pressed his hands on her shoulders, holding her.

Hell, wasn't that the guts of the departure speech[25] stewardesses[26] used to rattle off[27] on airplanes? "In the event of an emergency landing[28], sit straight, grip

1. Elle parlait d'un ton monocorde, lointain
2. arrivant
3. œil averti
4. nota
5. fixité de son regard
6. immobilité inquiétante
7. absents
8. L'état de choc menaçait de nouveau
9. cherchant
10. de garde
11. prêt à
12. blond roux
13. osseux
14. crâne
15. globuleux
16. adoucis
17. cils
18. leur message muet
19. commissariat
20. flic débutant
21. les parents
22. il y avait peu de chances qu'ils s'en sortent
23. chemise de nuit
24. robe de chambre
25. n'était-ce pas précisément le discours
26. que les hôtesses de l'air
27. débitaient
28. En cas d'atterrissage d'urgence

the arms of your seats, plant your feet solidly on the floor." What they were saying was[1] "Let the shock pass through you[2]."

"Ray, can I see you privately[3]?" he asked brusquely.

Ray's hands continued to steady[4] Nancy's shoulders as her body began to shake. "Did you find my children?" she asked. Now her voice was almost a whisper.

"Honey, he'd tell us if he found the kids. Just sit tight here.[5] I'll be right back.[6]" Ray bent down and for an instant laid his cheek on hers. Without seeming to expect a response, he straightened up and led the Chief through the connecting foyer[7] into the large living room.

Jed Coffin felt an unwilling[8] admiration for the tall young man who positioned himself by the fireplace before turning to face him. There was something so gut-level self-possessed about Ray[9] even in these circumstances. Fleetingly he remembered[10] that Ray had been decorated for outstanding leadership[11] under fire[12] in Vietnam and given a field promotion to[13] captain.

He had class, no doubt about that. There was class inherent in the way Ray stood and talked and dressed and moved; in the firm contours of his chin and mouth; in the strong, well-shaped hand that rested lightly on the mantel.

Stalling to[14] regain[15] his sense of rightness[16] and authority, Jed looked slowly around the room. The wide oak floorboards shone softly under oval hooked rugs[17]; a dry sink[18] stood between the leaded paned windows[19]. The mellow[20], creamy walls were covered with paintings. Jed realized that the scenes in them were familiar. The large painting over the fireplace was Nancy Eldredge's rock garden. The country-graveyard scene[21] over the piano was that old private cemetery down the road from Our Lady of the Cape Church. The pine-framed[22] painting over the

1. Ce qui revenait à dire
2. Laissez votre corps encaisser le choc
3. seul à seul
4. contenir
5. Ne bouge pas.
6. Je reviens tout de suite.
7. vestibule
8. involontaire
9. Ray faisait preuve d'une telle maîtrise de soi
10. Il se rappela l'espace d'un instant
11. son commandement remarquable
12. au combat
13. promu sur le champ de bataille au grade de
14. Gardant le silence le temps de
15. recouvrer
16. légitimité
17. tapis au crochet
18. buffet de toilette
19. fenêtres à vitraux
20. veloutés
21. cimetière rural peint
22. dans un cadre en pin

1. impression de retour au foyer
2. la tombée du jour
3. aquarelle
4. balayé par le vent
5. marais aux canneberges
6. esquissée
7. faisant des croquis
8. eût quelque talent
9. s'amusaient à
10. des trucs pareils à des dessins d'enfants
11. encastrées
12. encadraient
13. vieilli
14. en étain
15. rembourrées
16. fauteuil à bascule
17. brodé
18. Avec un léger malaise
19. de la moquette
20. une moquette à poils longs
21. s'accrochait
22. fidèlement
23. de pipi
24. que leur teckel encore mal dressé y déposait
25. ne s'était pas fait avoir par
26. rappel d'usage
27. acquise
28. innombrables
29. rechercha
30. faille
31. avec brusquerie
32. lueur
33. raidissement
34. lui donnèrent
35. franchi le pas décisif

couch had caught the homecoming flavor[1] of Sesuit Harbor at sundown[2] as all the boats came sailing in. The watercolor[3] of the windswept[4] cranberry bog[5] had the old Hunt house—The Lookout—barely outlined[6] in the background.

Jed had occasionally noticed Nancy Eldredge sketching[7] around town, but never dreamed that she was any good[8]. Most women he knew who fooled around with[9] that sort of thing usually ended up framing stuff that looked like exhibits from Show and Tell[10].

Built-in[11] bookcases lined[12] the fireplace. The tables made of heavy old distressed[13] pine weren't unlike the ones he remembered they'd donated to the church bazaar after his grandmother died. Pewter[14] lamps like hers were on the low tables next to comfortable overstuffed[15] chairs. The rocker[16] by the fireplace had a hand-embroidered[17] cushion and back.

Somewhat uncomfortably[18], Jed compared this room with his own newly decorated living room. Delia had picked out black vinyl for the couch and chairs; a glass-topped table with steel legs; wall-to-wall carpeting[19]—thick yellow shag[20] that clawed[21] at the shoes and faithfully[22] preserved and displayed every drop of saliva or pee[23] their still-untrained dachshund bestowed on it[24].

"What do you want, Chief?" Ray's voice was cold and unfriendly. The Chief knew that to Ray he was an enemy. Ray had seen through[25] his routine admonition[26] to Nancy about her rights. Ray knew exactly how he felt and was fighting him. Well if a fight was what he wanted...

With the ease born of experience garnered[27] from countless[28] similar sessions, Jed Coffin sought out[29] the weakness[30] and directed his attention to it. "Who is your wife's lawyer, Ray?" he asked curtly[31].

A flicker[32] of uncertainty, a stiffening[33] of the body betrayed[34] the answer. Just as Jed had figured, Ray hadn't taken the decisive step[35]. Still trying to pretend his wife was the average distraught mother[1] of missing children. Christ, he'd probably want to put her on a television news show tonight, handkerchief twisting in her hands, eyes swollen, voice pleading, "Give me back my children."

Well, Jed had news for Ray. His precious[2] wife had done that scene before. Jed could get copies of the seven-year-old film the newspapers had called "a moving plea[3]." In fact, the assistant district attorney in San Francisco had offered to provide it during their telephone conversation only half an hour ago. "It'll save that bitch the trouble of going through her act again[4]," he'd said.

Ray was speaking quietly, his tone a hell of a lot more subdued[5]. "We haven't contacted a lawyer," he said. "I hoped that maybe... with everyone searching..."

"Most of that search is going to be suspended[6] pretty soon," Jed said flatly. "With this weather, there isn't going to be anyone able to see anything. But I've got to take your wife down to the station[7] for questioning. And if you haven't arranged for a lawyer yet, I'll have the court appoint[8] one for her."

"You can't do that!" Ray snapped the words[9] furiously, then made an obvious effort[10] to control himself. "What I mean is that you would destroy Nancy if you took her to a police-station setting[11]. For years she used to have nightmares, and they were always the same: that she was in a police station being questioned and then that she was taken down a long corridor to the mortuary[12] and made to identify her children. My God, man, she's in shock right now. Are you trying to make sure that she won't be able to tell us anything she may have seen?"

"Ray, my job is to get your children back."

"Yes, but you see what just[13] reading that cursed[14] article has done to her. And what about the bastard who wrote that article? Anyone vile[15] enough to dig up[16]

1. incarnait la mère éplorée
2. fichue
3. émouvante supplique
4. refaire son petit numéro
5. infiniment plus contenu
6. interrompues
7. commissariat
8. je demanderai au tribunal d'en désigner
9. rétorqua
10. avant de faire un effort manifeste
11. cadre
12. morgue
13. l'effet que le simple fait
14. maudit
15. ignoble
16. déterrer

that story and send it out[1] might be capable of taking the children."

"Naturally we're working on that. That feature[2] is always signed with a fictitious staff name[3], but the articles are actually free-lance submissions[4] that if accepted involve a twenty-five-dollar payment[5]."

"Well, who is the writer, then?"

"That was what we tried to find out," Jed replied. He sounded angry. "The covering[6] letter instructed[7] that the story was offered only on condition that if accepted, it would not be changed at all, that all the accompanying pictures would be used and that it would be published on November seventeenth—today. The editor told me that he found the story both well written and fascinating. In fact, he felt it was so good that he thought the writer was a fool[8] to have submitted it to him for a lousy[9] twenty-five dollars. But of course, he didn't say so. He dictated a letter accepting the conditions and enclosing[10] the check."

Jed reached into his hip pocket[11] for his notebook and flipped it open[12]. "The letter of acceptance was dated October twenty-eighth. On the twenty-ninth the editor's secretary remembers receiving a phone call asking if a decision had been reached[13] about the Harmon article. It was a bad connection[14] and the voice was so muffled[15] she could hardly[16] hear the caller, but she told him—or her—that a check was in the mail[17], care of General Delivery[18], Hyannis Port. The check was made out to one[19] J. R. Penrose. The next day it was picked up[20]."

"Man or woman?" Ray asked quickly.

"We don't know. As you have to realize, a town like Hyannis Port has a fair[21] number of tourists going through it even at this time of the year. Anyone requesting[22] something from General Delivery would only have to ask for it. No clerk[23] seems to remember the letter, and so far the twenty-five-dollar check hasn't been cashed[24]. We can work our way back[25] to

1. l'envoyer à la presse
2. type d'article
3. attribué fictivement à un membre de la rédaction
4. des envois
5. rétribués 25 dollars
6. d'accompagnement
7. stipulait
8. imbécile
9. la somme ridicule de
10. qui serait jointe à
11. poche revolver
12. qu'il ouvrit d'un geste
13. prise
14. La communication n'était pas bonne
15. étouffée
16. à peine
17. avait été envoyé
18. poste restante
19. à l'ordre d'un(e) certain(e)
20. quelqu'un est venu le prendre
21. important
22. réclamant
23. employé
24. encaissé
25. pourrons remonter

J. R. Penrose when it is[1]. Frankly, it wouldn't surprise me if the writer turns out to be[2] one of our own little old ladies in town. They can be just wonderful at digging into gossip[3]."

Ray stared into[4] the fireplace. "It's cool[5] in here," he said. "A fire will feel good." His eye fell on the cameos[6] on the mantelpiece that Nancy had painted of Michael and Missy when they were babies. He swallowed over[7] the stinging lump[8] that suddenly closed his throat[9].

"I don't think you really need a fire in here now, Ray," Jed said quietly. "I asked you to step in here because I want you to tell Nancy to get dressed and come with us to the station house."

"No... no... please..." Chief Coffin and Ray whirled[10] to face the archway[11] leading into[12] the room. Nancy was standing there, one hand leaning against the carved[13] oak archway for support. Her hair had dried, and she had pulled it into[14] a bun[15] caught loosely against the nape of her neck[16]. The strain[17] of the past hours had turned her skin a chalky white[18] that was accentuated by the dark hair. An almost detached expression was settling into[19] her eyes.

Dorothy was behind her. "She wanted to come in." Dorothy's voice was apologetic[20].

Now she felt the accusation in Ray's eyes as he hurried over[21] to them[22]. "Ray, I'm sorry. I couldn't make her stay inside."

Ray pulled Nancy against him. "It's all right, Dorothy," he said briefly. His voice changed and became tender. "Honey, just relax. Nobody's going to hurt you."

Dorothy felt the dismissal in his tone[23]. He had counted on her to keep Nancy away while he spoke to the Chief, and she couldn't even do that much[24]. She was useless[25] here—useless. "Ray," she said stiffly[26]. "It's ridiculous to bother you about this, but the office just phoned to remind me that Mr. Kragopou-

1. ce sera le cas
2. se révèle être
3. dénicher les ragots
4. fixa
5. Il fait frais
6. portraits
7. tenta de déglutir malgré
8. boule brûlante
9. lui serrait la gorge
10. pivotèrent
11. arcade
12. menant à
13. mouluré
14. rassemblés en
15. chignon
16. nuque
17. tension
18. lui donnait un teint crayeux
19. gagnait
20. parlait d'un ton d'excuse
21. se hâtait
22. à leur rencontre
23. comprit qu'on la congédiait
24. même ça, elle n'avait pas pu
25. ne servait à rien
26. avec raideur

los, who wrote about the Hunt property, wants to see it at two o'clock. Shall I get someone else to take him up there?"

Ray looked over Nancy's head as he held her firmly against him. "I don't give a damn[1]," he snapped. Then quickly he said, "I'm sorry, Dorothy. I would appreciate it if you showed the place; you know The Lookout and can sell it if there's real interest. Poor old Mr. Hunt needs the money."

"I haven't told Mr. Parrish that we might be bringing people in today."

"His lease[2] clearly states[3] that we have the right to show the house at any time with simply a half hour's telephone notice[4]. That's why he has it so cheap[5]. Give him a call from the office and tell him you're coming."

"All right." Uncertainly[6], Dorothy waited, not wanting to go. "Ray..."

He looked at her, understanding her unspoken wish[7] but dismissing her[8]. "There's nothing you can do here now, Dorothy. Come back when you've finished at The Lookout."

She nodded and turned to go. She didn't want to leave them; she wanted to stay with them, sharing[9] their anxiety. Ever since that first day when she'd walked into Ray's office, he'd been a lifeline[10] for her. After nearly twenty-five years of planning her every activity[11] with Kenneth or around Kenneth's schedule[12], she'd been so rootless[13] and, for the first time in her life, frightened. But working with Ray, helping him to build the business, using her knowledge[14] of interior decorating to spark[15] people to buy the houses, then invest in renovating them had filled so much of the void[16]. Ray was such a fair, fine person. He'd given her such a generous profit-sharing arrangement[17]. She couldn't have thought more of him if[18] he'd been her own son. When Nancy had come, she'd been so proud that Nancy trusted her[19]. But there was a reserve in Nancy that didn't permit any real intim-

1. Je m'en fous complètement
2. bail
3. stipule
4. en le prévenant par téléphone même juste une demi-heure à l'avance
5. son loyer est si modeste
6. Indécise
7. souhait non formulé
8. la renvoyant
9. pour partager
10. planche de salut
11. la moindre de ses activités
12. emploi du temps
13. déracinée
14. connaissance
15. inciter
16. le vide de sa vie
17. mode de partage des bénéfices
18. ne l'aurait pas estimé davantage même si
19. lui donne sa confiance

acy, and now she felt like an unnecessary bystander[1]. Wordlessly[2] she left them, got her coat and scarf and went to the back door.

She braced herself against[3] the wind and sleet as she opened it. Her car was parked halfway[4] around the semicircular back driveway. She was glad she didn't have to go through the front drive. One of the networks[5] had a television van[6] parked in front of the house.

As she hurried toward her car, she saw the swing on the tree at the edge[7] of the property. That was where the children had been playing and where Nancy had found the mitten. How many times had she herself pushed the children on that swing? Michael and Missy... The awful possibility that something might have happened to them—that they might be dead—gave her a terrible choking sensation[8]. *Oh, please not that... almighty and merciful God[9], please not that.* She'd joked[10] once about being their surrogate[11] grandmother, and then the look of pain[12] had been so unmistakable[13] on Nancy's face that she had wanted to bite her tongue off[14]. It had been a presumptuous[15] thing to say.

She stared at the swing, lost in thought[16], unmindful of the[17] wet sleet stinging her face. Whenever Nancy stopped in the office, the children made a beeline for[18] her desk. She tried to always have a surprise for them. Just yesterday[19] when Nancy had come in with Missy, she'd had tollhouse cookies[20] she'd baked[21] the night before as the special treat[22]. Nancy had been on her way[23] to look at drapery material[24], and Dorothy had offered to mind[25] Missy and pick up[26] Michael at kindergarten. "It's hard to select material unless you can really concentrate," she'd said, "and I have to pick up some title-search papers[27] at the courthouse[28]. It will be fun to have company, and on the way back we'll get some ice cream, if that's all right[29]." Only twenty-four hours ago....

1. avait l'impression d'être là en spectateur inutile
2. Sans un mot,
3. se prépara à affronter
4. à mi-chemin
5. chaînes de télévision
6. camionnette
7. en bordure
8. sensation d'étouffement
9. Seigneur tout-puissant et miséricordieux
10. plaisanté
11. de substitution
12. expression de souffrance
13. visible
14. se mordre la langue
15. présomptueuse
16. perdue dans ses pensées
17. indifférente au
18. venaient tout droit à
19. Hier encore,
20. cookies aux pépites de chocolat
21. qu'elle avait cuits au four
22. tout spécialement
23. se disposait à
24. tissu pour des rideaux
25. s'occuper de
26. d'aller chercher
27. des actes de propriété [avec éventuels relevés d'hypothèque]
28. tribunal
29. si vous êtes d'accord

"Dorothy."

1. Surprise
2. coupé à travers bois
3. il les faisait largement

Startled[1], she looked up. Jonathan must have cut through the woods[2] from his house. His face was deeply creased today. She knew he must be nearly sixty years old, and today he looked every bit of it[3]. "I just heard about the Eldredge children," he said. "I've got to talk to Ray. Possibly I can help."

4. d'une voix mal assurée
5. inquiétude
6. curieusement réconfortante

"That's nice of you," Dorothy said unsteadily[4]. The concern[5] in his voice was oddly comforting[6]. "They're inside."

"No trace of the children yet?"

"No."

"I saw the article in the paper."

7. Avec retard
8. froideur
9. reproche
10. lui avait menti en affirmant
11. Avec lassitude
12. mit le moteur en marche
13. noyaient

Belatedly[7], Dorothy realized that sympathy was not being offered to her. There was a coolness[8] in Jonathan's tone, a reproof[9] that clearly reminded her that she had lied to him about[10] having known Nancy in Virginia. Wearily[11], she opened the door of her car. "I have an appointment," she said abruptly. Without giving him time to answer, she got in and started up the engine[12]. It was only when her vision blurred that she realized that tears were swimming in[13] her eyes.

13

The clatter[1] **of** the helicopters pleased him. It reminded him of the last time, when everyone for miles around the University had fanned out looking[2] for the children. He stared out the front window overlooking[3] the bay. The gray water was caked with[4] ice near the jetty[5]. Earlier the radio had spoken of gale warnings[6] and sleet or rain mixed with snow. For once, the weatherman[7] had been right. The wind was whipping[8] the bay into angry whitecaps. He watched as a flock of gulls[9] flew unsteadily in a futile[10] effort to make headway[11] against the wind.

He carefully consulted the indoor-outdoor[12] thermometer. Twenty-eight degrees out there[13] now—a drop of twenty degrees since the morning. The helicopters and search planes[14] wouldn't be up much longer[15] in this[16]. There wouldn't be many searchers out on land either.[17]

High tide was seven o'clock tonight. At that time he'd take the children up through the attic[18] to the outer[19] balcony they called the widow's walk[20]. The water at high tide covered the beach below, broke furiously against the retaining wall[21] and then, sucked[22] by the violent undertow[23], rolled back to sea. That would be

1. fracas saccadé
2. s'était déployé à la recherche
3. qui donnait sur
4. couverte de
5. jetée
6. avis de tempête
7. [présentateur de] la météo
8. fouettait
9. vol de mouettes
10. vain
11. avancer
12. intérieur-extérieur
13. Il faisait – 2 °C [=28 °F] dehors
14. avions de reconnaissance
15. ne resteraient pas en vol beaucoup plus longtemps
16. dans ces conditions
17. À terre non plus, les recherches ne mobiliseraient bientôt plus grand monde.
18. grenier
19. extérieur
20. promenade de la veuve
21. mur de soutènement
22. aspirée
23. reflux

the time to drop the children... over[1]... down... They might not be washed in for weeks.... But even if they were found in a few days, he'd prepared for that. He'd given them only milk and cookies. He wouldn't be fool enough to feed them anything[2] that would suggest that a person other than Nancy had fed them a real meal after breakfast. Of course, hopefully[3] they'd be beyond analysis[4] when they were found.

He chuckled[5]. In the meantime,[6] he had five hours: five long hours to look at the floodlights[7] that were being set up[8] near Nancy's house and the lake; five hours to be with the children. Even the boy, come to think of it[9], was a beautiful child... such soft skin, and that perfectly formed body.

But it was the little girl. She looked so much like Nancy... that silky, beautiful hair and small, well-formed ears. He turned from the window abruptly. The children were lying together on the couch. The sedative[10] he'd put in the milk had both of them sleeping. The boy's arm was protectively over his sister[11]. But he didn't even stir[12] when he picked up the little girl. He'd just take her inside and put her on the bed and undress her. She made no sound as he carefully carried her into the bedroom and laid her down. He went into the bathroom and turned on the faucets[13] in the tub[14], testing the gushing water[15] until it reached[16] the temperature he wanted. When the tub was filled, he tested the water again with his elbow[17]. A little hotter than it should be, but that was all right. It would cool in a few minutes.

He sucked in his breath[18]. He was wasting time[19]. Swiftly he opened the door of the medicine cabinet[20] and pulled out the can of baby powder he'd slipped into his coat pocket at Wiggins' Market this morning. As he was about to close the door, he noticed the little rubber duck[21] poked back[22] behind the shaving[23] cream. He'd forgotten about that... why[24] it had been used the last time... how appropriate[25]. Laughing soft-

1. balancer les enfants...
2. leur donner quoi que ce soit à manger
3. avec un peu de chance,
4. plus aucune analyse ne serait possible
5. ricana
6. En attendant,
7. projecteurs
8. qu'on installait
9. à la réflexion
10. sédatif
11. entourait sa sœur, d'un geste protecteur
12. ne remua pas du tout
13. robinets
14. baignoire
15. l'eau du robinet
16. atteigne
17. coude
18. aspira profondément
19. perdait du temps
20. armoire à pharmacie
21. canard en caoutchouc
22. caché
23. à raser
24. mais bien sûr,
25. exactement ce qu'il fallait

ly, he reached for the duck; ran it[1] under cold water, feeling the lack[2] of elasticity and the cracking[3] of the rubber; then tossed[4] it into the tub. It was a good idea to distract[5] children sometimes.

Grabbing the can of powder, he hurried back into the bedroom. Swiftly his fingers unbuttoned[6] Missy's jacket and pulled it off. Easily, he slipped the turtle-neck polo shirt over her head, bringing her undershirt[7] with it. He sighed—a lingering, groaning sound[8]—and picked up the little girl, hugging her limp body to him[9]. Three years old. Just a beautiful age. She stirred and started to open her eyes. "Mommy, Mommy..." It was a weak, lazy[10] cry—so dear, so precious.

The phone rang.

Angrily he tightened his grip[11] on the child, and she began to wail—a hopeless[12], lethargic cry.

He'd let the phone ring. He never, never got calls. Why now? His eyes narrowed[13]. It might be a call from the town, asking him to volunteer in the search. He'd better answer.[14] It might be suspicious not to answer. He tossed Missy back onto the bed and closed the bedroom door securely[15] before he picked up the phone in the sitting room. "Yes." He made his voice sound formal and cold.

"Mr. Parrish, I hope I haven't disturbed you[16]. This is Dorothy Prentiss of Eldredge Realty. I'm sorry to give you such short notice[17], but I'll be bringing a prospective buyer[18] for the house over in twenty minutes. Will you be there or shall I use my passkey[19] to show your apartment?"

1. le passa
2. manque
3. craquelures
4. jeta
5. distraire
6. déboutonnèrent
7. maillot de corps
8. un grognement prolongé
9. tenant son petit corps mou serré contre lui
10. sans énergie
11. resserra son étreinte
12. geignard
13. se rétrécirent
14. Il était préférable de répondre.
15. soigneusement
16. que je ne vous dérange pas
17. de vous prévenir si peu de temps à l'avance
18. je viens avec un acheteur potentiel
19. mon passe

14

Lendon Miles turned right off Route 6A onto[1] Paddock Path. All the way down on the trip[2] from Boston he'd kept his radio at a news station, and most of the news was about Nancy Eldredge and the missing Eldredge children.

According to the bulletins, Maushop Lake had been divided into sections, but it would take divers at least three days to search it properly[3]. Maushop Lake was filled with underwater ledges[4]. Police Chief Coffin of Adams Port was quoted as explaining[5] that at one point it was possible to walk halfway across the lake and still be in water only to the waist; a few yards away[6], only five feet from the shore, the water became forty feet deep. The underwater ledges caught and held[7] objects and made the search hazardous[8] and inconclusive[9]....

The bulletins announced that helicopters, small seaplanes[10] and ground search parties had been out[11] but gale warnings for the Cape were in effect[12] and the air search was being called off[13].

At the news that Nancy Eldredge was expected to be taken to Police Headquarters for questioning, Lendon unconsciously accelerated the car. He felt a

1. Lendon Miles quitta la 6A et tourna à droite dans
2. Depuis qu'il était parti
3. à fond
4. hauts-fonds
5. avait expliqué
6. mais quelques mètres plus loin
7. retenaient
8. risquées
9. peu concluantes
10. hydravions
11. avaient été à l'œuvre
12. étaient décrétés
13. annulé

desperate urgency about getting to Nancy.[1] But he quickly found that he had to reduce his speed. Sleet was glazing[2] the windshield[3] so rapidly that the defroster[4] was having trouble[5] melting[6] the crusting ice[7].

When at last he turned into Paddock Path, he had no trouble finding the Eldredge home. There was no mistaking[8] the center of activity on the street. Halfway up the road, a television van was parked across the street from a house[9] that had two police cars stationed in front of it. Private cars lined[10] the road near the television van. Many bore[11] special press identifications[12].

The entrance to the semicircular driveway was blocked by one of the police cars. Lendon stopped and waited for a policeman to come over to him. When one did, his tone was brusque. "State your business[13], please."

Lendon had anticipated the question and was ready. He handed out his card with a note scrawled[14] on it. "Please take this to Mrs. Eldredge."

The policeman looked uncertain. "If you'll wait here, Doctor... I'll have to check[15]." He returned promptly, his attitude subtly[16] less hostile. "I'll move the squad car out of the way. Park in the driveway and go into the house, sir."

From across the street, reporters had been watching the byplay[17], and they hurried over. One of them thrust[18] a microphone in front of Lendon's face as he got out of the car.

"Dr. Miles, may we ask you a few questions?"

Without waiting for an answer, he went on quickly, "Sir, you are a prominent psychiatrist[19] on the staff of[20] Harvard Medical School. Has the Eldredge family sent for you?[21]"

"No one has sent for me," Lendon replied sharply[22]. "I am a friend—was a friend—of Mrs. Eldredge's mother. I have come here because of personal friendship and that alone[23]."

1. Il lui fallait rejoindre Nancy au plus vite.
2. givrait
3. pare-brise
4. dégivreur
5. avait du mal
6. à faire fondre
7. le givre en formation
8. Impossible de manquer
9. de l'autre côté de la chaussée, face à une maison
10. étaient alignées le long de
11. arboraient
12. macarons de presse
13. Veuillez me dire ce que vous faites ici
14. griffonnée
15. vérifier
16. imperceptiblement
17. scène secondaire
18. brandit
19. éminent psychiatre
20. membre de la
21. Êtes-vous là à la demande de la famille Eldredge ?
22. sèchement
23. rien de plus

He tried to pass, but was blocked by the microphone-holding reporter. "You say you were a friend of Mrs. Eldredge's mother. Will you tell us this: Was Nancy Harmon Eldredge ever a patient of yours?"

"Absolutely not!" Lendon literally shoved his way through the reporters and onto[1] the porch. The front door was being held open by another policeman. "Right in there[2]," the man said, indicating the room to the right.

Nancy Eldredge was standing at the fireplace next to a tall young man, undoubtedly her husband. Lendon would have known her anywhere[3]. The finely chiseled[4] nose, the large midnight-blue[5] eyes that looked straight out from under thick lashes, the widow's peak at the hairline[6], the profile that was so like Priscilla's...

Ignoring the openly[7] hostile look of the police officer and the scrutiny[8] of the craggy-faced[9] man at the window, he went directly to Nancy. "I should have come before," he said.

The girl's eyes had a staring quality[10], but she knew what he meant[11]. "I thought you would come last time," she told him—"when Mother died. I was so sure you would come. And you didn't."

Expertly[12], Lendon measured[13] the symptoms of shock that he could see: the enlarged pupils[14]; the rigidity of her body; the low[15], monotone quality[16] of her voice. He turned to Ray. "I want to help if there's any possible way," he said.

Ray studied him intently[17] and instinctively liked what he saw. "Then as a doctor, try to persuade the Chief here that it would be a disaster to take Nancy to the police station," he said flatly.

Nancy stared into Lendon's face. She felt so detached—as though each minute she were slipping farther and farther away[18]. But there was something about this Dr. Miles. Mother had liked him so much;

1. dut écarter les reporters pour accéder au
2. De ce côté
3. l'aurait reconnue n'importe où
4. finement ciselé
5. bleu nuit
6. cheveux en V sur le front
7. ouvertement
8. regard scrutateur
9. au visage anguleux
10. quelque chose de fixe
11. voulait dire
12. En expert
13. évalua
14. pupilles dilatées
15. sourd
16. timbre
17. attentivement
18. de plus en plus loin

Mother's letters had sounded so happy; more and more often his name had been in them[1].

When her mother had come out to visit her at college she'd asked about the doctor; how important was he? But Carl was with them, and Mother didn't seem to want to talk about him then. She just smiled and said, "Oh, terribly[2] important, but I'll fill you in[3] later, dear."

She could remember that so clearly. She had wanted to meet Dr. Miles. Somehow she'd been sure that when he heard about[4] Mother's accident he would call her. She had needed to talk to someone who loved Mother too....

"You loved my mother, didn't you?" It was her voice asking that question. She wasn't even aware[5] that she had intended[6] to ask it.

"Yes, I did. Very much. I didn't know that she had told you about me. I thought you might resent me[7]. I should have tried to help you."

"Help me now!"

He took her hands in his, her terribly cold hands. "I'll try, Nancy, I promise." She sagged[8], and her husband put his arms around her.

Lendon liked the looks[9] of Ray Eldredge. The younger man's face was gray with anxiety, but he bore himself well[10]. His attitude toward his wife was protective. He obviously had a firm grip on[11] his own emotions. Lendon noticed the small framed picture on the table next to the sofa. It was an outdoor snapshot of Ray holding a little boy and girl.... The missing children. Of course. What a handsome[12] family. Interesting that nowhere[13] in this room could he see a single[14] picture of Nancy. He wondered if she ever allowed herself to be photographed[15].

"Nancy, come, honey. You've got to rest." Ray gently eased her down[16] onto the sofa and lifted her feet. "Now, that's better." She obediently[17] leaned back[18]. Lendon watched as her eyes focused[19] on the snap-

1. elle parlait de lui dans ses lettres
2. très
3. je t'expliquerai
4. aurait appris
5. ne se rendait même pas compte
6. avait eu l'intention
7. me rejeter
8. s'affaissa
9. allure
10. ne se laissait pas aller
11. contrôlait parfaitement
12. belle
13. nulle part
14. une seule
15. se laissait jamais photographier
16. l'installa
17. docilement
18. s'inclina en arrière
19. son regard se posait

shot of Ray and the children and then closed in pain. A shiver made her entire body tremble.

"I think we'd better stir up[1] this fire," he told Ray. He selected a medium-sized log[2] from the basket[3] on the fireplace and threw it onto the smoldering hearth[4]. A shower of flames sprayed up.[5]

Ray tucked a quilt around Nancy[6]. "You're so cold, darling," he said. For an instant he held her face between his hands. Tears trickled[7] from under her closed eyelids[8] and dampened[9] his fingers.

"Ray, have I your permission to represent Nancy as her legal counsel[10]?" Jonathan's voice had subtly altered[11]. It was infused with an authoritative crispness.[12] Calmly he met[13] the astonished stares. "I assure you I am well qualified[14]," he said drily[15].

"Legal counsel," Nancy whispered. From somewhere she could see the colorless, frightened face of the lawyer last time. Domes, that had been his name—Joseph Domes. He'd kept[16] saying to her, "But you must tell me the truth. You must trust me to help you." Even he hadn't believed her.

But Jonathan Knowles was different. She liked his bigness[17] and the courtly way he always spoke to her[18], and he was so attentive to the children when he stopped to speak.... Lowery's Market—that was it. A couple of weeks ago, he'd helped her and Mike to stack up[19] the cans that Mike had knocked over. He liked her, she was sure. Instinctively she knew it. She opened her eyes. "Please," she said, looking at Ray.

Ray nodded. "We'd be very grateful, Jonathan."

Jonathan turned to Lendon. "Doctor, may I have your medical opinion[20] as to the advisability[21] of allowing Mrs. Eldredge to[22] be taken to the police station for questioning?"

"It is highly[23] inadvisable[24]," Lendon said promptly. "I would urge that[25] any questioning be done here."

"But I can't remember." Nancy's voice was weary, as though she had said those same words too many

1. ranimer
2. bûche de taille moyenne
3. panier
4. braises
5. Une gerbe de flammes s'éleva.
6. recouvrit Nancy d'un édredon
7. coulèrent
8. paupières
9. mouillèrent
10. avocat
11. changé
12. Elle était maintenant claire et assurée.
13. soutint
14. que j'ai les compétences pour
15. sèchement
16. Il n'avait cessé de
17. grande taille
18. sa façon courtoise de lui parler
19. remettre en piles
20. avis
21. opportunité, ou non,
22. de laisser Mrs. Eldredge
23. tout à fait
24. déconseillé
25. J'insiste pour que

1. à partir du moment où
2. nous perdons simplement notre temps
3. ne permettrai pas
4. angoisse
5. Penthotal [dit sérum de vérité]
6. sous calmant
7. recevable
8. concours
9. se rappeler
10. On remontait dans le temps
11. J'étais à ce point la meilleure
12. dortoir
13. eut un mouvement de recul
14. Un appel longue distance

times. "You say I know where my children are. But I don't remember anything from when[1] I saw that paper in the kitchen this morning until I heard Ray calling me." She looked up at Lendon, her eyes clouded and staring. "Can you help me to remember? Is there any way?"

"What do you mean?" Lendon asked.

"I mean isn't there some way you can give me something so that if I know... or saw... or did... Even if I did something... I have to know... That isn't something you can hide. If there is some awful part of me that could hurt my children... we have to know that too. And if there isn't but if somehow I know where they might be, we're just wasting time[2] now."

"Nancy, I won't let[3]—" But Ray stopped when he saw the anguish[4] in her face.

"Is it possible to help Nancy to remember what happened this morning, Doctor?" Jonathan asked.

"Perhaps. She is probably suffering from a form of amnesia which is not uncommon after what to her was a catastrophic experience. In medical terms, it's a hysterical amnesia. Under an injection of sodium amytal[5], she would be relaxed and probably able to tell us what happened—the truth as she knows it."

"Answers given under sedation[6] would not be admissible[7] in court," Jed snapped. "I can't have you questioning Mrs. Eldredge like that."

"I used to have such a good memory," Nancy murmured. "Once at college we had a contest[8] to see who could recall[9] what she'd done every day. You just kept going backwards[10] day by day until you couldn't remember anymore. I won by so much[11] that it was a joke in the dorm[12]. Everything was so clear...."

The telephone rang and had the effect of a pistol exploding in the room. Nancy shrank back[13], and Ray covered her hands with his. They all waited silently until the policeman on duty at the phone came into the room. He said, "Long distance[14] for you, Chief."

"I can assure you[1] that this is the call I've been trying to place[2]," Jed told Nancy and Ray. "Mr. Knowles, I'd appreciate it if you'd come with me. You too, Ray."

"Be right back[3], darling," Ray murmured to Nancy. Then he looked into Lendon's face. Satisfied with what he saw, he followed the other men out of the room.

Lendon watched as relief drained from Nancy's expression[4]. "Every time it rings, I think somebody has found the children and they're safe," she murmured. "And then I think it will be like last time... when the call came[5]."

"Steady[6]," Lendon said. "Nancy, this is important. Tell me when you started having trouble[7] remembering specific events[8]."

"When Peter and Lisa died... but maybe even before that. It's so hard to remember the years I was married to Carl."

"That could be because you associate those years with the children and it's too painful to remember anything about them."

"But during those five years... I was so terribly tired so much... after Mother died... always so tired. Poor Carl... so patient. He did everything for me. He got up with the children at night—even when they were babies. Everything was such an effort for me[9].... After the children disappeared, I couldn't remember... like... like now... I just couldn't." Her voice had begun to rise[10].

Ray came back into the room. Something had happened. Lendon could see it in the taut lines[11] around Ray's mouth, the slight trembling of his hands. He found himself praying[12]: *Please, don't let it be bad news*[13].

"Doctor, could you speak with Jonathan for a minute, please?" Ray was making a determined effort[14] to keep his voice even[15].

1. Je parie
2. que j'ai essayé d'avoir
3. Je reviens tout de suite
4. observa l'apaisement quitter le visage de Nancy
5. quand le téléphone a sonné
6. Pas trop vite
7. à avoir du mal
8. des événements précis
9. La moindre chose me demandait un tel effort
10. s'était haussée d'un ton
11. plis contractés
12. Il se surprit à prier
13. faites que ce ne soit pas de mauvaises nouvelles
14. manifestement un effort
15. un ton calme

"Certainly." Lendon hurried toward the arched doorway that led into the family and dining room, sure that the phone call had badly upset[1] Ray.

When he got to the dining room, Chief Coffin was still on the phone. He was barking orders[2] to the lieutenant on duty at the station: "Get the hell down to that post office[3] and round up every clerk[4] who was on duty October thirtieth and don't stop questioning them until somebody remembers who picked up that letter from the *Community News* addressed to J. R. Penrose. I need a full description, and I need it now[5]." He slammed[6] the receiver into its cradle[7].

There was new tension in Jonathan too. Without preamble[8], he said, "Doctor, we can't lose any time in trying to break through Nancy's amnesia[9]. To fill you in[10], I have a very complete file on the Harmon case because of a book I'm writing. I've spent the last three hours studying that file and reading the article that appeared in today's paper. Something struck me[11] that seemed of the greatest possible importance, and I asked Chief Coffin to phone the District Attorney in San Francisco and check my theory. His assistant has just returned the call[12]."

Jonathan reached into his pocket for his pipe, clamped[13] his teeth on it without lighting it[14] and continued, "Doctor, as you may know, in cases of missing children where foul play is suspected[15], the police will often deliberately withhold[16] a piece of information so that they have some help in sifting through[17] the inevitable meaningless clues[18] they receive after a publicized disappearance[19]."

He began to speak more quickly, as though he felt he was letting too much time pass[20]. "I noticed that all the newspaper accounts seven years ago described the missing children as wearing red cardigan sweaters with a white pattern[21] when they disappeared. Nowhere in any of the extensive newspaper coverage[22] is there an exact description of what that pat-

1. secoué
2. aboyait des ordres
3. Bon sang, filez à ce bureau de poste
4. rassemblez tous les employés
5. tout de suite
6. reposa brutalement
7. support
8. préambule
9. dissiper l'amnésie de Nancy
10. Pour que vous soyez au courant
11. m'a frappé
12. vient de rappeler
13. serra
14. l'allumer
15. disparition d'enfants que l'on pense d'origine criminelle
16. il est fréquent que la police garde pour elle
17. qui peut aider à filtrer
18. renseignements sans intérêt
19. après qu'une disparition a été rendue publique
20. était trop long
21. motif
22. dans aucun de ces nombreux articles de journaux

tern was. I surmised[1]—correctly[2]—that the motif of the pattern had been deliberately withheld[3]."

Jonathan looked directly at Lendon, wanting him to understand immediately the importance of what he was about to tell him. "The article which appeared in the *Cape Cod Community News* clearly states[4] that when the Harmon children disappeared they were wearing red cardigan sweaters with an unusual white sailboat design[5], and that they were still wearing them when their bodies were washed ashore weeks later. Now, Nancy, of course, was aware of that sailboat design. She made those sweaters herself.[6] But only one other person outside of[7] the top people on the San Francisco investigative staff[8] knew about that design." Jonathan's voice rose in pitch[9]. "If we assume Nancy's innocence[10], that person was the one who kidnapped the Harmon children seven years ago—and who one month ago wrote the story that appeared in today's paper!"

"Then you mean[11]—" Lendon began.

"Doctor, I mean, as Nancy's lawyer and friend, if you can break through her amnesia, do it—quickly! I have persuaded Ray that it is worthwhile[12] to waive any immunity[13]. The overriding necessity is[14] to find out what Nancy may know; otherwise it will surely be too late to help her children."

"Can I telephone a drugstore[15] and get something delivered[16]?" Lendon asked.

"You call, Doctor," Jed ordered. "I'll send a squad car over to pick up whatever you need. Here[17]—I'll dial the drugstore for you."

Quietly Lendon phoned his instructions and when he had finished went into the kitchen for a glass of water. *Oh, the waste*[18], he thought—*the awful*[19] *waste.* The tragedy that had begun with Priscilla's accident... cause and effect[20]... cause and effect. If Priscilla had not died, she probably would have persuaded Nancy not to marry so young. The Harmon children would

1. J'ai supposé
2. et j'avais vu juste
3. n'avait été communiqué à la presse
4. précise clairement
5. ornés d'un bateau à voiles blanc peu courant
6. C'est elle qui avait tricoté ces pulls.
7. mis à part
8. principaux inspecteurs chargés de l'affaire
9. monta d'un ton
10. Si on présuppose que Nancy est innocente
11. Mais alors, vous voulez dire...
12. qu'il y avait un avantage
13. à renoncer à l'immunité [donc risquer de s'incriminer par son propre témoignage]
14. Il est primordial
15. pharmacie
16. pour faire livrer quelque chose
17. Tenez, laissez-moi faire
18. quel gâchis
19. terrible
20. un enchaînement de causes

never have been born. Sharply he pulled himself back from useless speculation.[1] The kitchen had obviously been gone over for fingerprints.[2] Grains of powder were still evident on the countertops[3], around the sink and on the stove. No one had wiped up[4] the stain[5] from where coffee had spilled.

He returned to the dining room to hear Chief Coffin say, "Remember, Jonathan, I may well be exceeding my authority as it is[6]. But I'm going to have a tape recorder on[7] in that room when that girl is questioned. If she confesses to[8] anything under sedation, we may not be able to use it directly, but I'll know what to ask her under regular[9] questioning later."

"She's not going to confess to anything," Jonathan said impatiently. "What concerns me[10] is that if we accept her innocence as a fact—not only about Michael and Missy's disappearance but also her innocence in the murder of the Harmon children—then our next supposition becomes this[11]: if the killer of the Harmon children wrote the article for the *Community News* and used a Hyannis post office, he has been here on the Cape for some time."

"And you are saying that he abducted[12] the Eldredge children this morning," Chief Coffin finished.

Jonathan relit[13] his pipe and puffed at it[14] vigorously before answering. "I'm afraid so[15]," he said. His tone of voice, deliberately devoid of expression[16], made Lendon understand what he meant. Jonathan believed that if the killer of the Harmon children had taken Michael and Missy Eldredge, they were probably dead.

"On the other hand[17]," Jed theorized[18], "if we remove[19] Mrs. Eldredge as a suspect, it is equally[20] possible that someone who never came forward[21] at the Harmon trial knew something about those murders, wrote that article and has now kidnapped the Eldredge children. A third possibility is that the two cases are unrelated[22] except that someone reading[23] that article and recognizing Nancy Eldredge has

1. Mais foin de ces spéculations stériles.
2. Les empreintes digitales avaient évidemment été relevées dans la cuisine.
3. plans de travail
4. essuyé
5. tache
6. j'outrepasse très certainement mes pouvoirs en faisant ça
7. faire installer un magnétophone
8. avoue
9. plus réglementaire
10. m'intéresse
11. alors notre hypothèse suivante est celle-ci
12. a enlevé
13. ralluma
14. tira dessus
15. C'est bien ce que je crains
16. volontairement neutre
17. Par ailleurs
18. argumenta
19. si nous ne retenons pas
20. également
21. resté dans l'ombre
22. indépendants
23. ayant lu

become involved in[1] the disappearance this morning. The children may have been taken by a frustrated[2] mother who feels[3] Nancy doesn't deserve them[4]. I've seen a lot screwier rationalizations than that in my day.[5]"

"Jed," snapped Jonathan, "what I'm trying to say is that no matter who else may have become involved[6], one fact is very clear: I don't believe there's any question but that[7] Nancy knew more than she told about the disappearance of her children seven years ago."

Lendon raised an eyebrow[8]. Jed frowned deeply[9]. At the expressions on the faces of the two men, Jonathan slapped[10] his hand impatiently on the table. "I'm not saying that that girl is guilty. I am saying that she knew more than she told; probably knew more than she was aware of knowing[11]. Look at the pictures of her on the witness stand. Her face is an absolute blank[12]. Read the testimony. For God's sake, man, read the trial testimony. That girl was out of it[13]. Her lawyer may have upset her conviction[14] on a technicality, but that doesn't mean that he didn't let that district attorney crucify her[15]. That entire setup stank[16], and you're trying to reenact it here[17]."

"I'm trying to get away from your theories... and that's all they are... and perform my job[18], which is to recover[19] those children—dead or alive—and find out who abducted them." Jed was clearly out of[20] patience. "In one breath[21] you tell me she's too sick to be questioned and in the next one[22] that she knows more than she ever let on[23]. Look, Jonathan, you said yourself that writing a book about questionable[24] verdicts is a hobby with you. But those lives aren't hobbies with me, and I'm not here to help you play chess[25] with the law[26]."

"Hold on[27]." Lendon put a restraining hand on the Chief's arm.[28] "Mr. Knowles... Jonathan... you believe that whatever knowledge Nancy has of the death

1. est mêlé à
2. en manque
3. considère
4. ne les mérite pas
5. J'ai déjà vu des justifications encore plus tordues que ça.
6. peu importe qui d'autre pourrait être impliqué
7. il ne fait aucun doute que
8. leva un sourcil
9. parut très soucieux
10. abattit
11. qu'elle n'avait conscience de savoir
12. totalement inexpressif
13. ne se sentait pas concernée
14. a peut-être fait casser la condamnation
15. la flinguer
16. Toute cette histoire puait
17. là, vous essayez de recommencer
18. de faire mon boulot
19. retrouver
20. à bout de
21. D'un côté
22. et de l'autre
23. que ce qu'elle a jamais reconnu
24. contestables
25. aux échecs
26. la police
27. Attendez
28. Posant la main sur son bras, Lendon arrêta le commissaire.

of her first family may help us find the Eldredge children."

"Exactly. But the problem is to extract[1] that knowledge, not drive it deeper[2] into her subconscious. Dr. Miles, you are considered an expert in the use of sodium amytal in psychiatry, are you not?"

"Yes, I am."

"Is it possible you might be able to have Nancy reveal not only what she knows of this morning's events—which I suspect will be nothing[3]—but also information about the past that she doesn't even know she has herself?"

"It's possible."

"Then unless she can tell us something tangible[4] about Michael and Missy's whereabouts[5], I beg you[6] to try."

When Dorothy was readmitted to the house an hour later, the family room and kitchen were deserted[7] except for[8] Bernie Miles, the policeman charged with answering the phones. "They're all in there," he said, jerking his head toward[9] the front parlor. "Something pretty queer going on.[10]"

Dorothy hurried down the hall, but stopped at the doorway of the room. The greeting she was about to utter[11] died on her lips as she took in[12] the scene before her.

Nancy was lying on the couch, a pillow[13] under her head, a quilt tucked around her. A stranger who looked like a doctor was sitting beside her, speaking softly. Nancy's eyes were closed. An anguished-looking[14] Ray and grim-faced Jonathan were side by side on the love seat[15]. Jed Coffin was sitting at a table behind the couch, holding a microphone pointed toward Nancy.

As Dorothy realized what was happening, she sank[16] into a chair, not bothering to take off her coat. Numbly she slipped her chilled fingers[17] into the deep side

1. d'arriver à lui soutirer
2. et non pas de l'enfoncer plus profond
3. c'est-à-dire rien, probablement
4. de concret
5. sur l'endroit où se trouvent Michael et Missy
6. vous supplie
7. désertes
8. à l'exception de
9. désignant d'un hochement brusque
10. C'est bizarre, ce qui se passe.
11. prononcer
12. découvrait
13. oreiller
14. angoissé
15. causeuse
16. se laissa tomber
17. Elle glissa tant bien que mal ses doigts gourds

pockets[1], unconsciously gripping the scrap[2] of damp, fuzzy wool that she felt in the right-hand pocket.

"How do you feel, Nancy? Are you comfortable?" Lendon's voice was tranquil.

"I'm afraid...."

"Why?"

"The children... the children..."

"Nancy. Let's talk about this morning. Did you sleep well last night? When you woke up did you feel rested[3]?"

Nancy's voice was reflective. "I dreamed. I dreamed a lot...."

"What did you dream about?"

"Peter and Lisa.... They'd be so grown up[4].... They're dead seven years...." She began to sob. Then, as Jonathan's iron grip[5] held Ray back, she cried, "How could I have killed them? They were my children! How could I have killed them...?"

1. poches latérales
2. morceau
3. reposée
4. si grands aujourd'hui
5. la poigne de fer

15

Before Dorothy had met John Kragopoulos at the office, she had tried to camouflage[1] her red-rimmed[2] eyes with a dusting powder[3]. She'd tried to convince herself that after all, showing the Hunt place would be an outlet[4], an action that could be concentrated on for a little while and keep her mind from its endless squirreling for[5] clues to the children's whereabouts[6]. What clues?

Normally she took prospective clients on a brief tour of the area before showing a property, to let them see the beaches and lakes and marina; the stately old homes[7] that were scattered[8] between Cranberry Highway[9] and the bay; the breathtaking[10] view from Maushop Tower; the old town landmarks[11].

But today, with the sleet beating a sharp tattoo[12] on the car roof and windows, with the sky filled with black fields of clouds[13] and with the cold sea air chilling the very marrow of the bones[14], she headed directly for[15] The Lookout.

It was so hard to keep her mind on what she was doing. She felt so distracted and shaken[16]. She who hadn't cried in years was having to bite her lips to keep tears back[17]. There was a crushing weight[18] on

1. camoufler
2. rougis
3. de la poudre [de maquillage]
4. dérivatif
5. la forcerait à faire autre chose que chercher sans cesse
6. un indice pour retrouver les enfants
7. vieilles demeures majestueuses
8. éparpillées
9. l'autoroute
10. à couper le souffle
11. monuments
12. qui tambourinait
13. trains de nuages
14. qui transperçait jusqu'à la moelle
15. se dirigea droit vers
16. secouée et l'esprit ailleurs
17. contenir ses larmes
18. poids écrasant

1. douleur
2. dangereusement
3. glissante
4. jetait de temps en temps un coup d'œil
5. au teint basané
6. avait dans les 45 ans
7. carrure
8. haltérophile
9. courtoisie naturelle
10. maintien
11. qui allait bien avec
12. léger accent
13. prévoyaient d'installer le prochain
14. se fixer
15. souhaitaient surtout
16. retraités aisés
17. et bénéficier du tourisme estival
18. horrible mélange
19. de pizzerias
20. un coin épouvantable
21. hôtel-restaurant
22. considérablement
23. transformé
24. ça n'a jamais marché
25. plus de 3 ha
26. en bord de mer
27. terrain
28. s'était déjà renseigné
29. capitaine de baleinier
30. dans les années 1690

her shoulders, a weight of grief[1] and fear that she could not hope to support alone.

As she drove the car along the treacherously[2] slick[3] road, she stole an occasional glance[4] at the swarthy-complexioned[5] man beside her. John Kragopoulos was somewhere in his mid forties[6]. He had the build[7] of a weight lifter[8], yet there was an innate courtliness[9] in his bearing[10] that complemented[11] his slightly accented manner of speaking[12].

He told Dorothy that he and his wife had just sold their restaurant in New York and agreed their next venture would be[13] in an area where they would want to settle permanently[14]. They were anxious[15] to be where well-to-do retired people[16] could be found for winter business, as well as the summer resort trade[17].

Mentally reviewing these points, Dorothy said, "I'd never recommend investing in a restaurant over on the other side of the Cape anymore; it's just one mass[18] of motels and pizza parlors[19] now—absolutely frightful zoning[20]—but this side of the Cape is still lovely. The Lookout has unlimited possibilities as a restaurant and inn[21]. During the thirties it was renovated extensively[22] and turned into[23] a country club. People didn't have money to join expensive country clubs at that time, and so it never caught on[24]. Eventually Mr. Hunt bought the house and grounds—nine acres[25] in all, including one thousand feet of waterfront[26] property[27] and one of the finest views on the Cape."

"The Lookout was originally a captain's house, was it not?"

Dorothy realized that John Kragopoulos had done some homework[28] on the place—a sure sign of real interest. "Yes, it was," she agreed. "It was built by a whaling captain[29] in the sixteen-nineties[30] as a gift for his bride. The most recent renovation, forty years ago, added two floors, but the original roof was put back on[1], including one of those charming little balconies near the peak[2] of the chimney—widow's walks they're called, because so many of the captains' wives used to watch in vain for their men to come back from a voyage."

"The sea can be treacherous," her passenger agreed. "By the way[3], is there a dock with the property[4]? If I relocate up here[5], I plan to buy a boat."

"A very good one," Dorothy assured him. "Oh, dear!" She gasped[6] as the car skidded[7] dangerously when she turned onto the narrow, winding[8] road that led up to The Lookout. She managed to straighten[9] the wheels and glanced anxiously at her passenger. But he seemed unperturbed[10], and remarked mildly[11] that she was a brave lady[12] to risk driving on such icy roads.

Like a surgeon's knife[13] the words penetrated to the core[14] of Dorothy's misery[15]. It was a frightful day. It would be a miracle if the car didn't skid right off this narrow road[16]. Whatever interest she had talked herself into[17] about showing the house vanished[18]. If the weather were only decent[19], the beaches and streets and woods would be filled with men and boys looking for Missy and Michael; but in this weather only the heartiest[20] would think of going out—especially since many felt it was a useless search.

"I don't mind driving," she said thickly[21]; "I'm just sorry Mr. Eldredge isn't with us. But I'm sure you understand."

"I understand very well," John Kragopoulos said. "What an agonizing experience[22] for the parents to have young children missing! I am only sorry to take your time today. As a friend and coworker, you must be concerned."

Determinedly, Dorothy did not let herself reply to the sympathy in the man's voice and manner. "Let me tell you more about the house," she said. "All the windows to the front look over the water[23]. The front

1. remis en place
2. sommet
3. À propos
4. la propriété a-t-elle son embarcadère
5. viens m'installer ici
6. s'écria
7. dérapait
8. sinueuse
9. redresser
10. n'avait pas l'air inquiet
11. avec douceur
12. courageuse
13. scalpel
14. cœur
15. souffrance
16. restait sur la route étroite sans déraper
17. Tout l'intérêt qu'elle était parvenue à prendre
18. s'évanouit
19. convenable
20. seuls les plus résolus
21. d'une voix sourde
22. Quel supplice
23. ont vue sur la mer

1. très raffinée
2. imposte
3. caractéristique
4. cheminées sur pignon
5. privent le virage
6. apparut dans sa totalité
7. désolée
8. surgissant ainsi
9. derrière le talus noyé dans la brume
10. marqués par les intempéries
11. bardeaux
12. d'un gris austère
13. cruellement
14. volets écaillés
15. affaissées
16. marches extérieures
17. des courses [alimentaires]
18. en rentrant
19. chance
20. vaste
21. courir jusqu'à
22. auvent
23. sermonna
24. résistant
25. allons-y en vitesse
26. leur mitrailla le visage
27. tira sur
28. Contrariée
29. fermée à double tour
30. prévenant
31. s'emporta-t-elle
32. fouilla dans
33. coup sec

door has an exquisite[1] fan-light[2], which was a feature[3] on the finer houses of that period. The large downstairs rooms have wonderful gable-end fireplaces[4]. On a day like this many people would enjoy going to a restaurant where they can watch the storm while they enjoy a good drink and good food and a warm fire. Here we are."

They rounded the curve[5], and The Lookout was in full view[6]. To Dorothy it seemed strangely bleak and dreary[7] as it loomed[8] against the shrouded embankment[9]. The weather-beaten[10] shingles[11] were stark gray[12]. The sleet slapping against the windows and porches seemed to reveal mercilessly[13] the peeling shutters[14] and sagging[15] outside steps[16].

She was surprised to see that Mr. Parrish had left the garage doors open. Maybe he had been carrying groceries[17] his last trip in[18] and had forgotten to come out again to pull the door down. But it was a break[19] for them. She'd drive right into the roomy[20] garage and park her car beside his old station wagon, and they'd be able to make a run for[21] the house with some protection from the garage overhang[22].

"I've got a key to the back door," she told John Kragopoulos after they'd gotten out of the car. "I'm so sorry I didn't think to bring Ray's golf umbrella. I hope you don't get too wet."

"Don't worry about me," he chided[23]. "I'm pretty rugged[24]. Don't I look it?"

She smiled faintly and nodded. "All right, let's make a dash for it[25]." They ran out of the garage and kept close to the wall as they covered the fifty feet to the kitchen door. Even so, the sleet pelted their faces[26] and the wind pulled at[27] their coats.

To her annoyance[28], Dorothy found that the door was double-locked[29]. Mr. Parrish might have been more considerate[30], she fumed[31]. She rummaged through[32] her bag for the key to the top lock and found it. She gave a quick yank[33] at the bell to let

Mr. Parrish know they had arrived. She could hear the ringing sound echoing upstairs as she pushed the door in.

Her prospective buyer seemed unperturbed as he brushed sleet from his coat and dried his face with a handkerchief. He was a low-keyed person[1], Dorothy decided. She had to will herself[2] not to sound either nervous or overly talkative[3] showing the place[4]. Every fiber of her being made her want to[5] rush this man through the house[6]. *See this... and this... and this... Now let me go back to Ray and Nancy, please; maybe there's been some news of the children.*

She did notice[7] that he was carefully studying the kitchen. Deliberately she reached for her own handkerchief to dab at her[8] face, aware suddenly that she was wearing her new suede winter coat. This morning she'd decided to wear it because of this appointment. She knew it was becoming[9] and that the gray shade complemented[10] her pepper-and-salt-colored hair. The big deep pockets were what made her conscious that she wasn't wearing her old storm coat[11]—but the storm coat would certainly have been a better choice today.

And there was something else. Oh, yes. When she had put on the coat, she had wondered if Jonathan Knowles would stop into the office this afternoon and maybe notice it. Maybe this would be the day when he'd suggest they might have dinner together. She had daydreamed like that[12] only hours ago. How could everything change so quickly, so terribly...?

"Mrs. Prentiss?"

"Yes. Oh, I'm sorry. I guess I'm a bit distracted today." To her ears she sounded falsely cheery[13]. "As you can see, this kitchen needs modernizing, but it is very well laid out[14] and roomy[15]. That fireplace is large enough to cook for a crowd[16]—but I'm sure you'd settle for[17] modern ovens[18]."

1. quelqu'un de posé
2. devrait prendre sur elle
3. trop bavarde
4. en faisant visiter
5. De tout son être, elle aurait voulu
6. expédier la visite
7. remarqua toutefois
8. se tamponner le
9. seyant
10. s'accordait bien avec
11. parka
12. Voilà à quoi elle avait rêvé
13. enjouée
14. agencée
15. spacieuse
16. pour un régiment
17. que vous préféreriez
18. un four moderne

Unconsciously she'd lifted her voice. The wind was howling[1] around the house with a harsh, mournful sound[2]. From somewhere upstairs she heard a door slam[3] and, just for a second, a wailing sound[4]. It was her nerves; this house upset her[5] today. The kitchen was freezing, too.

Quickly she led the way[6] into the front rooms. She was anxious that[7] Mr. Kragopoulos have the important first impression of the water view.

The savagery of the day[8] only enhanced[9] the breathtaking panorama that met their eyes when they stood at the windows. Angry whitecaps churned, lifted, fell, crashed on the rocks, pulled back[10]. Together they stared at the tumultuous beating[11] of the water on the rocks at the base of the cliff[12] below.

"At high tide these rocks are completely covered," she said. "But just down a little to the left, past[13] the jetty, there's a beautiful big sandy beach that is part of the property, and the dock is just past that."

She took him from room to room, pointing out[14] the magnificent wide oak floors, the massive fireplaces, the leaded pane windows, the way the overall layout lent itself to[15] a fine restaurant. They went up to the second floor, and he examined the large rooms that could be rented to overnight guests[16].

"During the renovation, they changed the small bedrooms into baths[17] and connected them with the[18] large rooms," Dorothy explained. "As a result, you've got really beautiful units that only need painting and papering[19]. The brass beds alone[20] are worth[21] a fortune. Really, most of the furniture[22] is very good—look at that highboy[23], for example. I used to have an interior decorator's shop, and a house like this is my idea of a dream to work on[24]. The possibilities are endless[25]."

He was interested. She could tell by the way he took time to open closet doors[26], pound[27] walls and turn on water taps[28].

1. hurlait
2. une plainte lugubre
3. claquer
4. un couinement plaintif
5. la mettait mal à l'aise
6. montra le chemin
7. Elle tenait à ce que
8. temps déchaîné
9. ne faisait que rehausser
10. battaient en retraite
11. martèlement
12. falaise
13. après
14. signalant
15. dont l'agencement des pièces se prêtait à l'aménagement d'
16. louées pour la nuit
17. salles de bains
18. les ont reliées aux
19. qu'il suffit de peindre ou de tapisser
20. À eux seuls, les lits en cuivre
21. valent
22. la plupart des meubles
23. commode haute
24. j'aurais adoré aménager une maison comme celle-ci
25. infinies
26. les portes des placards
27. tapoter
28. les robinets

"The third floor[1] has more bedrooms, and then Mr. Parrish's apartment is on the fourth floor[2]," she said. "That apartment was designed for the resident manager[3] of the country club. It's quite spacious and has a wonderful view of the town as well as the water."

He was pacing off[4] the room and did not answer. Feeling pushy[5] and garrulous[6], Dorothy walked over to the window. She should give him a chance[7] to consider[8] the house quietly and come up with any[9] questions that might occur to him[10]. *Hurry*[11], *hurry*, she thought. She wanted to get out of here. The insistent need to be back with Ray and Nancy, to know what was happening, was overwhelming[12]. Suppose[13] the children were out somewhere, exposed to this weather? Maybe she should take the car and cruise up and down[14]; maybe they had just wandered away[15]. Maybe if she tried to look in the woods, if she called them... She shook her head. She was being so foolish.

When Nancy had left Missy at the office with her yesterday, she'd said, "Please make her keep her mittens on[16] when you go out. Her hands get so cold." Nancy had laughed as she handed[17] Dorothy the mittens, saying, "As you can see, they don't match[18]—and I'm not trying to set a style[19]. This kid is always losing mittens." She'd given her one red mitten with a smile face and a blue-and-green-checked one[20].

Dorothy remembered the cheerful smile with which Missy had held up her hands when they'd gone for their drive. "Mommy said don't forget my mittens, Aunt Dorothy," she'd warned[21] reproachfully[22]. Later on, when they'd picked up Mike and stopped for ice cream, she'd asked, "Is it all right if I take my mittens off when I eat my cone?" Blessed little baby.[23] Dorothy dabbed at the tears that rushed to her eyes[24].

Determinedly she composed herself[25] and turned back to John Kragopoulos, who had just finished making notes on the size of the room. "You don't get

1. Le 2e étage
2. au 3e
3. prévu pour être le logement de fonction du gérant
4. arpentait
5. insistante
6. trop volubile
7. le laisser
8. explorer
9. formuler toutes les
10. qui lui viendraient à l'esprit
11. Vite
12. irrésistible
13. Et si
14. sillonner le pays
15. s'étaient juste égarés
16. garder ses moufles
17. en tendant
18. elles sont dépareillées
19. lancer une mode
20. une à carreaux bleus et verts
21. rappelé
22. sur un ton de reproche
23. Adorable petite.
24. lui montaient au yeux
25. reprit contenance

high ceilings like these anymore except in these wonderful old houses," he exulted[1].

She couldn't tolerate being here like this[2] any longer. "Let's go upstairs now," she said abruptly. "I think you'll like the view from the apartment." She led the way back into[3] the hall and to the front staircase. "Oh, did you notice that there are four heat zones[4] in this house? It saves a lot on[5] fuel bills[6]."

They walked up the two flights of stairs[7] quickly. "The third floor[8] is exactly like the second floor[9]," she explained as they passed it. "Mr. Parrish has been renting the apartment on and off for six or seven years, I guess. His rent is quite minimal; but Mr. Eldredge felt that the presence of a tenant[10] discourages vandals. Here we are—just down the hall[11]." She knocked at the door of the apartment. There was no answer. "Mr. Parrish," she called. "Mr. Parrish."

She began to open her handbag. "That's strange. I can't imagine where he'd go without his car. But I've got a key here somewhere." She started to rummage through her bag, feeling unreasonable annoyance[12]. Over the phone Mr. Parrish had obviously been unhappy[13] that she was bringing someone over. If he had been going out, he might have told her. She hoped the apartment was tidy[14]. There weren't that many people[15] looking for a three-hundred-fifty-thousand-dollar investment. They hadn't had even a nibble on[16] the property in nearly a year.

Dorothy did not realize that the handle was being turned from the inside. But when the door was pulled open abruptly, she looked up and gasped[17] and stared into the searching eyes and perspiring[18] face of the fourth-floor tenant, Courtney Parrish.

"What a dreadful[19] day for you to have to come." Parrish's tone was courteous[20] as he stepped aside[21] to let them pass. By holding the door back and getting out of the way[22], he reasoned[23], he might be able

1. jubila
2. supporter de rester là
3. Passant devant, elle regagna
4. la maison est divisée en quatre parties pour le chauffage
5. Ça fait une économie appréciable sur
6. la facture de fuel
7. volées d'escalier
8. 2e étage
9. 1er étage
10. locataire
11. au bout du couloir
12. exagérément agacée
13. mécontent
14. bien rangé
15. tellement de gens
16. Personne n'avait même été tenté par
17. sursauta
18. en sueur
19. horrible
20. courtois
21. s'écartait
22. en s'effaçant
23. s'était dit

to avoid shaking hands[1]. He could feel that his hands were drenched in perspiration[2].

His eyes darted[3] from one to the other. Had they heard the little girl—that one cry[4]? He was such a fool... getting too eager[5]. After the phone call, he'd had to hurry so much. Picking up the children's clothing, in his excitement he'd almost missed the little girl's undershirt. Then the can of baby powder had spilled[6]. He'd had to wipe that up[7].

He'd taped[8] the children's hands and feet and mouths and hidden them in that secret room behind the fireplace downstairs that he'd discovered months ago in wandering[9] through the house. He knew those hidden rooms were peculiar to[10] many old Cape houses. The early settlers used to hide in them during Indian attacks. But then he'd panicked. Suppose that fool of a real estate woman[11] knew about[12] that room and decided to show it? It was reached by a spring[13] in the built-in bookcase in the main room downstairs.

Suppose she knew about it; just suppose. Even as[14] Dorothy's Buick sedan pulled up and[15] into the garage, he had dashed from[16] his watching point at the window and rushed down[17] to get the children. He'd carried them up and thrown them into one of the deep closets in the bedroom. Better... much better. He could say that he used that closet for storage[18] and couldn't find the key. Since he had put a new lock on[19], that fool of a real estate woman couldn't possibly have a duplicate[20]. Besides, the other closet in the room was practically the same size. She could show that one. That was where he could make a mistake... by getting complicated.

They'd dallied[21] downstairs long enough for him to make one last inspection of the apartment; he hadn't missed anything[22], he was sure. The tub was still full, but he'd decided to leave it. He knew he'd sounded too annoyed[23] over the phone. Let Dorothy think that

1. éviter d'avoir à serrer la main
2. moites
3. Son regard passait rapidement
4. cet unique cri
5. trop impatient
6. s'était renversé
7. essuyer
8. attaché avec du ruban adhésif
9. flânant
10. une des particularités de
11. idiote de l'agence immobilière
12. connaisse l'existence de
13. Pour y accéder, on actionnait un ressort
14. Au moment où
15. venait s'arrêter
16. quitté en urgence
17. s'était précipité en bas
18. comme rangement
19. changé la serrure
20. double
21. s'étaient attardés
22. rien oublié
23. trop contrarié

that was the reason; he'd been just about to bathe[1]. That would justify annoyance[2].

He wanted so much to get back to the little girl that it was painful[3]. From deep in his loins[4] he felt frantic[5] desire. Right now, there she was, just a few feet from them all, behind that door, her little body half-naked[6]. Oh, he couldn't wait! Be careful. Be careful. He tried to pay attention to[7] the voice of reason that kept cautioning him[8], but it was so hard....

"John Kragopoulos." That damn fellow was insisting on shaking his hand. Clumsily[9] he tried to dry his palm[10] on his trouser leg before grasping[11] the outstretched[12] hand that he could not ignore. "Courtney Parrish," he said sullenly[13].

He could see the fleeting[14] expression of distaste[15] come over the other man's face when their hands touched. Probably a damned fag[16]. Half the restaurants on this side of the Cape were run by[17] fags. Now they wanted this house too. Well, fine.[18] After today he wouldn't need it.

Suddenly he realized that if this house were sold, no one would ever find it suspicious if as[19] Courtney Parrish he didn't come back to the Cape. Then he could lose weight[20] and let his hair grow and totally change his appearance again, because he would want to be here for Nancy's trial, after they found the children's bodies and accused her. Why, this wasn't a problem at all. Fate was playing into his hands.[21] This was meant to be.[22]

He shuddered as a wave of exhilaration surged through his body[23]. Why[24], he could even ask about[25] Nancy. It would be only neighborly.[26] Feeling suddenly confident[27], he said courteously, "I am pleased to meet you, Mr. Kragopoulos, and rue the weather[28] in which you first observe this wonderful house." Miraculously, the dampness was leaving his hands and armpits and groin[29].

1. sur le point de prendre un bain
2. sa contrariété
3. douloureux
4. Au creux de ses reins,
5. éperdu
6. à moitié nu
7. prêter attention à
8. ne cessait de le mettre en garde
9. Maladroitement
10. paume
11. prendre
12. tendue
13. d'un air renfrogné
14. brève
15. dégoût
16. un de ces pédés
17. tenus par
18. Bof, après tout !
19. sous le nom de
20. perdre du poids
21. La chance était de son côté.
22. C'était écrit.
23. en sentant monter une bouffée d'euphorie
24. Mais oui
25. prendre des nouvelles de
26. Simple affaire de bon voisinage.
27. en confiance
28. je déplore ce mauvais temps
29. son entrejambe

The tension in the small foyer[1] relaxed tangibly. He realized that most of it was emanating from[2] Dorothy anyway. Why not? He'd seen her countless times[3] in these past years, in and out[4] of the Eldredge house, pushing the children on the swing, taking them in her car. He had her number[5]: one of those dreary[6] middle-aged[7] widows trying to be important to someone; a parasite. Husband dead. No children. A miracle she didn't have a sick old mother. Most of them did. That helped them to be[8] martyrs to their friends. So nice to Mother. Why? Because they needed to be nice to someone. They had to be important. And if they had children, they concentrated on them. The way Nancy's mother had.

"I have been listening to the radio," he said to Dorothy, "and am so disturbed[9]. Have the Eldredge children been found yet?"

"No." Dorothy felt all her nerve endings tingling[10]. From inside she could hear that the radio was on. She caught[11] the word "bulletin." "Excuse me," she cried, and hurried into the living room and over to the radio. Swiftly she turned up the volume[12]. "... storm increasing. Gale winds from fifty to sixty miles an hour are predicted[13]. Driving is hazardous.[14] The air and water search for the Eldredge children has been suspended indefinitely[15]. Special patrol cars will continue cruising[16] in Adams Port and vicinity[17]. Chief Coffin of Adams Port urges that anyone who[18] believes he or she may have any information report it[19] at once. He urges that any untoward[20] incident be discussed with[21] the police, such as a strange vehicle that may have been seen in the neighborhood of the Eldredge home; any unfamiliar person or persons in the area. Call this special number: KL five, three eight hundred. Your privacy will be respected[22]."

The commentator's voice continued. "Despite the urgent appeal for clues to the missing children, we have it on good authority[23] that Mrs. Nancy Harmon

1. entrée
2. provenait
3. à d'innombrables reprises
4. toujours à vaquer aux abords
5. Il connaissait le genre
6. ternes
7. dans la cinquantaine
8. à se poser en
9. inquiet
10. se sentait les nerfs à vif
11. entendit
12. monta le son
13. annoncés
14. Il est dangereux de prendre sa voiture.
15. pour une durée indéterminée
16. à patrouiller
17. dans les environs
18. invite instamment quiconque
19. à le faire savoir
20. insolite
21. signalé à
22. identité ne sera pas divulguée
23. savons de source sûre

Eldredge will be taken to Police Headquarters for questioning."

She had to go to Nancy and Ray. Dorothy turned to John Kragopoulos abruptly. "As you can see, this is a charming apartment quite suitable[1] for two people. The view from both the front and back windows in this room is really spectacular."

"You are an astronomer, perhaps?" John Kragopoulos spoke to Courtney Parrish.

"Not really. Why do you ask?"

"It is just that magnificent[2] telescope."

Belatedly,[3] Parrish realized that the telescope was still positioned facing[4] the Eldredge house. Seeing that John Kragopoulos was about to look through it he gave it an abrupt push so that it tilted upward[5].

"I enjoy studying the stars," he volunteered hastily[6].

John Kragopoulos squinted as he looked through the lens. "Magnificent equipment," he cried. "Simply magnificent." Carefully he manipulated the telescope until it was pointing in the same direction as it had been when he had first noticed it[7]. Then, sensing the other man's antagonism[8], he straightened up[9] and began to study the room. "This is a well-laid-out apartment," he commented to Dorothy.

"I have been most comfortable[10] here," Parrish volunteered. Inwardly[11] he was fuming at himself[12]. Once more he had suspiciously overreacted[13]. The moisture was pouring from his body again.[14] Had he forgotten anything else? Was there any sign of the children around? Frantically[15] his eyes darted around the room. Nothing.

Dorothy said, "I'd like to show the bedroom and bath if it's all right."

"Of course."

He'd straightened[16] the coverlet[17] on the bed and shoved[18] the can of baby powder into the night-table drawer.

1. parfait
2. superbe
3. Trop tard,
4. pointé vers
5. l'orienter vers le haut
6. justifia-t-il promptement
7. l'appareil avait attiré son regard la première fois
8. hostilité
9. se redressa
10. J'ai toujours été très bien
11. Intérieurement,
12. pestait contre lui-même
13. curieusement surréagi
14. Son corps ruisselait à nouveau de sueur.
15. Fébriles,
16. arrangé
17. couvre-lit
18. fourré

"The bathroom is as large as most of today's second bedrooms," Dorothy told John Kragopoulos. Then, as she glanced around it, she said, "Oh, I'm so sorry." She stared down at the filled[1] tub. "We did catch you at an inconvenient time.[2] You were just about to bathe."

"I have no rigid schedule[3] to follow." Despite the words, he managed to leave the impression that she had indeed[4] inconvenienced[5] him.

John Kragopoulos stepped back into the bedroom hastily. He realized that this man obviously resented their coming[6]. Leaving the tub like that was a clumsy[7] way of making the point[8]. And that duck floating in the tub. A child's toy. He winced, disgusted. His hand touched the closet door. The satiny quality[9] of the wood intrigued him. Really, this house was beautifully constructed. John Kragopoulos was a hardheaded[10] businessman, but he also believed in instinct. His instinct told him that this house would be a good investment. They wanted three hundred and fifty thousand for it.... He'd offer two ninety-five and come up to[11] three twenty. He was sure he could get it for that.

The decision finalized[12] in his mind, he began to take a proprietary[13] interest in the apartment. "May I open this closet?" he asked. The question was perfunctory[14]. He was already turning the handle.

"I'm sorry. I changed the lock on that closet and can't seem to find the key. If you'll look in this other closet... they're practically identical."

Dorothy looked sharply at the new handle and lock. Both were run-of-the-mill[15] low-priced[16] hardware-store items[17]. "I do hope you kept the original handle," she said. "All the doorknobs[18] were specially cast solid brass[19]."

"Yes, I have it. It needs fixing.[20]" God, would that woman insist on turning the handle? Suppose the new lock gave[21]? It wasn't a very tight fit[22] into the old wood. Suppose it slid open?

1. pleine [d'eau]
2. Nous tombons mal en effet.
3. d'emploi du temps strict
4. effectivement
5. dérangé
6. n'appréciait pas leur venue
7. maladroite
8. le faire savoir
9. douceur satinée
10. à la tête froide
11. puis remonterait jusqu'à
12. Une fois parvenu à cette décision
13. de propriétaire
14. de pure forme
15. ordinaire
16. et bon marché
17. de la quincaillerie
18. poignées
19. des pièces moulées en laiton massif
20. Il faut que je la répare.
21. cédait
22. Elle était mal fixée

Dorothy relaxed her grip on the handle[1]. The slight flare of annoyance[2] she'd felt vanished as quickly as it had come. What, in the name of heaven, difference did it make if all the brass handles all over the universe were changed? Who cared[3]?

Parrish had to clamp his lips together[4] to keep from ordering that nosy woman and her prospective buyer out[5]. The children were just on the other side of the door. Had he tightened their gags[6] enough? Would they hear the familiar voice and try to make some kind of sound? He had to get rid of[7] these people.

But Dorothy wanted to go too. She was aware of an indefinably familiar scent[8] in the bedroom—one that made her acutely aware of[9] Missy. She turned to John Kragopoulos. "Perhaps we should start... if you're ready."

He nodded. "I'm quite ready, thank you." He started to leave, this time obviously avoiding shaking hands. Dorothy followed him. "Thank you, Mr. Parrish," she said hastily over her shoulder. "I'll be in touch with you.[10]"

She led the way down the stairs to the main floor in silence. They went through the kitchen, and when she opened the back door she could see why the gale warnings were in effect[11]. The wind had heightened sharply[12] in the brief time they'd been in the house. Oh, God, the children would die of exposure[13] if they were outside all this time.

"We'd better make a dash for the garage," she said. John Kragopoulos, looking preoccupied, nodded and took her arm. Together they ran, not bothering to stay under the overhang. With the increased wind velocity[14] there was simply no protection from the sleet, which was now finely blended with snow[15].

In the garage, Dorothy walked between the station wagon and her car and opened the door on the driver's side. As she began to slide into her car, she glanced down[16]. A bright red scrap of material[17] on

1. lâcha la poignée
2. agacement
3. s'en souciait
4. prendre sur lui
5. s'empêcher de dire à cette petite curieuse et à son client de s'en aller
6. bâillons
7. Il fallait qu'il se débarrasse
8. percevait une odeur vaguement familière
9. qui lui rappelait vivement
10. Je vous ferai signe.
11. on avait émis un avis de tempête
12. avait beaucoup forci
13. allaient mourir de froid
14. force accrue du vent,
15. mêlé de neige
16. regarda par terre
17. bout de tissu

the garage floor caught her eye[1]. Getting out of the car again, she bent down, picked it up, then slumped back[2] into the car seat holding the object against her cheek. John Kragopoulos, sounding alarmed[3], asked, "My dear Mrs. Prentiss, what is wrong?"

"It's the mitten!" Dorothy cried. "It's Missy's. She was wearing it yesterday when I took her out for ice cream. She must have left it in the car. I guess I kicked it out[4] when I got out of the car before. She was always losing her mittens. She never had two on that matched[5]. We always joked about that.[6] And this morning, they found the mate of this one[7] on the swing." Dorothy began to sob—a dry, hacking sound[8] that she tried to stifle[9] by holding the mitten against her lips.

John Kragopoulos said quietly, "There is little that I can say except to remind you[10] that a merciful and loving God is aware of your pain and the agony of the parents. He will not fail your need.[11] Somehow I am confident of that.[12] Now, please, wouldn't you like me to drive?"

"Please," Dorothy said in a muffled[13] voice. She pushed the mitten deep into her pocket as she slid over[14]. She wouldn't want Nancy or Ray to see it; it would be too heartbreaking[15]. Oh, Missy, Missy! She'd taken it off when she started to eat the cone yesterday. She could see her dropping it on the seat. Oh, the poor little kids.

John Kragopoulos was glad to be driving. A great restlessness[16] had come over him[17] in the room with that hideous[18] man. There was something too slimy[19] and sour-smelling[20] about him. And that scent of baby powder in the bedroom and that incredible toy in the tub. How could a grown man[21] need such trappings[22]?

Upstairs, Parrish stood to one side and watched from the window until the car had disappeared around the bend in the lane. Then, with trembling fingers, he drew out the key from his pocket and unlocked the closet door.

1. attira son regard
2. se laissa tomber
3. visiblement inquiet
4. J'ai dû la pousser du pied
5. ne portait jamais la paire
6. C'était devenu une plaisanterie.
7. l'autre moufle
8. un bruit sec, haché
9. d'étouffer
10. si ce n'est vous rappeler
11. Il ne vous décevra pas dans votre attente.
12. J'en suis convaincu.
13. étouffée
14. en se glissant sur le siège voisin
15. cela leur briserait le cœur
16. nervosité
17. l'avait envahi
18. affreux
19. visqueux
20. fétide
21. adulte
22. accessoires

The boy was conscious. His sandy hair fell on his forehead, and his large blue eyes were filled with terror as he stared mutely[1] up. His mouth was still securely taped and his hands and legs still firmly tied.

Roughly he pushed the child aside and reached past him for the little girl. He lifted out her limp body and laid her on the bed—then shrieked[2] in outrage and despair[3] as he stared down at her closed eyes and pinched blue face[4]....

1. en silence
2. poussa un cri perçant
3. de rage et de désespoir
4. visage bleui et les traits tirés

16

Nancy's hands were clenching and unclenching[1], pulling at the coverlet. Gently, Lendon covered her fingers with his own strong, well-shaped[2] hands. Anxiety and agitation were causing her to breathe in harsh, labored breaths.[3]

"Nancy, don't worry. Everyone here knows that you couldn't hurt your children. That's what you meant, isn't it?"

"Yes... yes... people think I could hurt them. How could I kill them? They are me. I died with them...."

"We all die a little death when we lose the people we love[4], Nancy. Think back[5] with me before all the trouble started[6]. Tell me what it was like when you were growing up in Ohio."

"Growing up?" Nancy's voice trailed off into a whisper[7]. The rigidity of her body began to relax.

"Yes, tell me about your father. I never knew him."

Jed Coffin moved restlessly, and the chair he was sitting on made a creaking sound against[8] the wooden floor. Lendon shot him a warning glance[9]. "I have reason for this[10]," he said quietly. "Please bear with me.[11]"

1. se serraient et se desserraient tour à tour
2. belles
3. Anxieuse, agitée, Nancy respirait difficilement, par à-coups.
4. La perte de ceux que nous aimons est un avant-goût de notre propre mort
5. Reportez-vous en arrière
6. avant que ne débutent tous ces ennuis
7. se perdit dans un chuchotement
8. grinça sur
9. lui lança un regard d'avertissement
10. J'ai mes raisons pour lui poser ces questions
11. Un peu de patience.

"Daddy?" A lilt came into Nancy's voice.[1] She laughed softly. "He was such fun[2]. Mother and I used to drive to the airport to pick him up when he came in from a flight. In all those years he never came back from a trip without something for Mother and me. We used to go all over the world on his vacations[3]. They always took me with them. I remember one trip[4]..."

Ray could not take his eyes off Nancy. He had never heard her speak in that tone of voice—animated, amused, a ripple of laughter running through her words[5]. Was this what he had been blindly[6] trying to find in her? Was it more than being tired of living with the fear of discovery? He hoped so.

Jonathan Knowles listened intently to Nancy, approving of the technique Lendon Miles was using to gain her confidence[7] and relax her before asking about the details of the day the Harmon children had vanished. It was agonizing[8] to hear the soft ticking[9] of the grandfather clock[10]... a reminder that time was passing[11]. He realized that he was finding it impossible not to look at Dorothy. He knew he had been harsh[12] when he spoke to her as she was getting into her car. It was his disappointment that had reacted to her deliberate falsehood[13]—the fact that she had made a point of[14] telling him personally about knowing Nancy as a child.

Why had she done that? Was it perhaps that he had indicated somehow that Nancy looked familiar[15]? Had it been simply an attempt[16] to keep him from the truth[17] because she couldn't trust him with the truth[18]? Had he perhaps been displaying what Emily used to call his "Your witness, Counsel" manner[19]?

In any event,[20] he felt that he owed Dorothy an apology[21]. She didn't look well. The strain was telling on her.[22] She still was wearing her heavy coat, and her hands were jammed in[23] her pockets. He decided that he wanted to talk to her at the first opportunity.

1. La voix de Nancy se fit plus animée.
2. si amusant
3. pendant ses congés
4. voyage
5. le ton rieur
6. inconsciemment
7. confiance
8. très angoissant
9. tic-tac
10. grande horloge
11. rappelant sans cesse que le temps s'écoulait
12. dur
13. mensonge
14. avait tenu à
15. Nancy lui rappelait quelqu'un
16. tentative
17. de lui celer la vérité
18. la lui dire en toute confiance
19. son air de dire « Le témoin est à vous, cher confrère »
20. Quoi qu'il en soit,
21. devait des excuses à Dorothy
22. Elle accusait le coup.
23. fourrées au fond de ses

She needed calming down. She certainly thought the world of those children.[1]

The lights in the room flickered[2], then went off[3]. "That figures.[4]" Jed Coffin propped the microphone[5] on the table and searched for matches. Quickly Ray lighted the antique gas lamps on either side of the mantel. They threw a yellow glow[6] that melted and blended[7] with the vivid red flames of the fireplace, bathing the couch where Nancy was lying in a rosy glow and throwing deep shadows on the corners of the dark room.

It seemed to Ray that the steady[8] tattooing of the sleet against the house and the moaning[9] of the wind through the pines had intensified. Suppose the children were out somewhere in this weather...? Last night he'd awakened hearing Missy cough[10]. But when he went into her room, she'd been settled again in deep sleep[11], her cheek cupped in[12] her palm. As he bent over to pull up her covers, she'd murmured, "Daddy" and stirred, but at the touch of his hand on her back she'd settled down again[13].

And Michael. He and Mike had gone for milk[14] to Wiggins' Market—was it just yesterday morning? They'd arrived just as that tenant at The Lookout, Mr. Parrish, was leaving. The man had nodded pleasantly, but when he got into that old Ford wagon of his, Michael's face had wrinkled with distaste[15]. "I don't like him," he'd said.

Ray almost smiled at the memory. Mike was a rugged[16] little guy, but he had something of Nancy's distaste for ugliness[17], and no matter how you sliced it[18], Courtney Parrish was a clumsy, slow-moving[19], unattractive[20] man.

Even the Wigginses had commented on him[21]. After he left, Jack Wiggins said drily, "That fellow's about the slowest-moving human being I ever bumped into[22]. He meanders around shopping[23] like he's got all the time in the world."

1. Aucun doute, elle était très attachée à ces enfants.
2. vacillèrent
3. s'éteignirent
4. Tu m'étonnes !
5. cala le micro
6. lueur
7. se confondait
8. régulier
9. mugissement
10. tousser
11. dormait à nouveau profondément
12. calée au creux de
13. s'était rendormie
14. partis chercher du lait
15. avait grimacé de dégoût
16. costaud
17. laideur
18. il n'y avait pas à tortiller
19. lourdaud
20. déplaisant
21. fait des réflexions à son sujet
22. rencontré
23. Quand il fait ses courses, il tournicote

Michael had looked reflective[1]. "I never have enough time," he said. "I'm helping my dad refinish[2] a desk for my room, and every time I want to keep working on it, I have to get ready for school."

"You've got quite an assistant there[3], Ray," Jack Wiggins had remarked. "I'll give him a job anytime[4]; he sounds like a worker[5]."

Mike had picked up the package. "I'm strong, too," he'd said. "I can carry things. I can carry my sister for a long time."

Ray ground his hands into fists[6]. This was unreal, impossible. The children missing. Nancy sedated[7]. What was she saying?

Her voice still had that eager lilt.[8] "Daddy used to call Mother and me his girls...." Her voice faltered.[9]

"What is it, Nancy?" Dr. Miles asked. "Your father called you his little girl? Did that upset you?"

"No... no... no... he called us his girls. It was different... it was different... not like that at all...." Her voice rose sharply in protest[10].

Lendon's voice was soothing[11]. "All right, Nancy. Don't worry about that. Let's talk about college. Did you want to go away to school[12]?"

"Yes... I really did... except... I was worried about[13] Mother...."

"Why did you worry about her?"

"I was afraid she'd be lonely[14]—because of Daddy... and we'd sold the house; she was moving into an apartment. So much had changed for her. And she'd started a new job. But she liked working.... She said she wanted me to go.... She liked to say that today... today..."

"Today is the first day of the rest of your life," Lendon finished quietly. Yes, Priscilla had said that to him too. The day she came into the office after she'd put Nancy on the plane for school. She told him about still waving goodbye[15] after[16] the plane had taxied away toward the runway[17]. Then her eyes had filled[18], and

1. pensif
2. remettre en état
3. C'est un bon adjoint que tu as là
4. Je lui donne un boulot quand tu veux
5. c'est un bosseur, on dirait
6. serra les poings
7. sous sédatif
8. Son ton était toujours enjoué.
9. Elle balbutia.
10. s'éleva brusquement en signe de protestation
11. apaisante
12. l'université
13. Je me faisais du souci pour
14. qu'elle ne se sente seule
15. qu'elle faisait encore au revoir de la main
16. alors que
17. rejoignait déjà la piste d'envol
18. s'étaient emplis de larmes

she'd smiled apologetically[1]. "Look how ridiculous I am," she'd said, trying to laugh; "the proverbial mother hen[2]."

"I think you're doing fine[3]," Lendon had told her.

"It's just that when you think how your life can change... so incredibly. All of a sudden, a whole part, the most important part... is ended. But on the other hand[4], I think when you've had something quite wonderful... so very much happiness[5]... you can't look back and regret. That's what I told Nancy today.... I don't want her worrying about me. I want her to have a wonderful time in school. I said that we should both remember that motto[6]: 'Today is the first day of the rest of our lives.' "

Lendon remembered that a patient had come into the office. At the time, he'd considered it a blessing[7]; he'd been dangerously close[8] to putting his arms around Priscilla.

"... but it was all right," Nancy was saying, her voice still hesitant and groping[9]. "Mother's letters were cheerful. She loved her job. She wrote a lot about Dr. Miles.... I was glad...."

"Did you enjoy school, Nancy?" Lendon asked. "Did you have many friends?"

"At first, I liked the girls, and I dated a lot[10]."

"How about your schoolwork? Did you like your subjects[11]?"

"Oh, yes. They all came pretty easily[12]... except bio...."

Her tone changed—subtly became troubled[13]. "That was harder. I never liked science but the college required it[14]... so I took it...."

"And you met Carl Harmon."

"Yes. He... wanted to help me with bio. He had me come[15] to his office and he'd go over the work[16] with me. He said I was dating too much and that I must stop or I'd be sick. He was so concerned[17]... he even started giving me vitamins. He must have been right...

1. en manière d'excuse
2. mère poule caricaturale
3. que vous vous débrouillez très bien
4. d'un autre côté
5. tant de bonheur
6. devise
7. bénédiction
8. sur le point
9. peu assurée
10. je sortais souvent avec des garçons
11. les différentes matières
12. Je me débrouillais plutôt bien
13. s'altéra
14. c'était une matière obligatoire
15. me faisait venir
16. repassait les cours
17. inquiet

because I was so tired... so much... and started to feel so depressed.... I missed Mother[1]...."

"But you knew you would be home over Christmas."

"Yes... and it didn't make sense.... All of a sudden... it got so bad... I didn't want to upset her[2]... so I didn't write about it... but I think she knew.... She came out for a weekend[3]... because she was worried about me... I know it.... And then she was killed... because she came out to see me.... It was my fault... my fault...." Her voice rose in a shriek of pain[4], then broke into a sob[5].

Ray started out[6] of his chair, but Jonathan pulled him back. The oil lamp flickered on Nancy's face. It was contorted with pain[7]. "Mother!" she cried, "Oh, Mother... please don't be dead... live! Oh, Mother, please, please live.... I need you.... Mother, don't be dead... Mother..."

Dorothy turned her head, trying to bite back tears[8]. No wonder[9] Nancy had resented her remarks about being a surrogate grandmother[10] to Missy and Michael. Why was she here? No one was even conscious or caring of[11] her presence. She'd be more useful if she went out and made coffee. Nancy might want some later too. She should take off her coat. She couldn't. She felt too cold; so alone. She stared down for a moment at the hooked rug and watched as the pattern blurred[12] before her eyes. Lifting her head, she met the inscrutable[13] gaze of Jonathan Knowles and knew that he'd been watching her for some time.

"... Carl helped you when your mother died. He was good to you[14]?" Why was Lendon Miles dragging out this agony[15]? What point was there[16] in making Nancy relive[17] this too? Dorothy started to her feet[18].

Nancy's answer was quiet. "Oh, yes. He was so good to me.... He took care of everything."

"And you married him."

"Yes. He said he'd take care of me. And I was so tired. He was so good to me...."

1. Maman me manquait
2. l'inquiéter
3. est venue me voir un week-end
4. s'éleva en un cri de douleur
5. se brisa dans un sanglot
6. s'élança
7. déformée par la douleur
8. refouler ses larmes
9. Rien d'étonnant à ce que
10. ait mal pris qu'elle ait dit être un peu une grand-mère de substitution
11. ni ne se souciait
12. se brouillait
13. impénétrable
14. gentil avec vous
15. faisait-il durer ce calvaire
16. À quoi cela servait-il
17. revivre
18. se leva

"Nancy, you mustn't blame yourself for[1] your mother's accident. That wasn't your fault."

"Accident?" Nancy's voice was speculative[2]. "Accident? But it wasn't an accident. It wasn't an accident...."

"Of course it was." Lendon's voice stayed calm, but he could feel the tightness of his throat muscles[3].

"I don't know... I don't know...."

"All right; we'll talk about it later. Tell us about Carl."

"He was good to me...."

"You keep saying that[4], Nancy. How was he good to you?"

"He took care of me. I was sick; he had to do so much for me...."

"What did he do for you, Nancy?"

"I don't want to talk about that."

"Why, Nancy?"

"I don't. I don't...."

"All right. Tell us about the[5] children. About Peter and Lisa."

"They were so good...."

"They were well behaved, you mean.[6]"

"They were so good... too good..."

"Nancy you keep saying 'good.' Carl was so good to you. And the children were good. You must have been very happy."

"Happy? I was so tired..."

"Why were you so tired?"

"Carl said I was so sick. He was so good to me."

"Nancy, you must tell us. How was Carl good to you?"

"He made sure I was getting better.[7] He wanted me to get better. He said I had to be a good little girl."

"How did you feel sick, Nancy? What hurt you?"

"So tired... always so tired.... Carl helped me...."

"Helped you how?"

"I don't want to talk about that."

"But you must, Nancy. What did Carl do?"

1. vous sentir responsable de

2. pensive

3. sa gorge se serrer

4. ne cessez de répéter cela

5. Parlez-nous des

6. Ils étaient bien élevés, vous voulez dire.

7. Il veillait à ce que je me rétablisse.

"I'm tired... I'm tired now...."

"All right, Nancy. I want you to rest for a few minutes; then we'll talk some more. Just rest... just rest...."

Lendon got up. Chief Coffin immediately took his arm and jerked his head[1] toward the kitchen. As soon as they were out of the room, Chief Coffin spoke abruptly. "This isn't leading us anywhere.[2] This could take hours and you're not going to find anything out[3]. The girl blames herself for her mother's accident because the mother had made the trip to see her. It's that simple.[4] Now, if you think you can find out anything else about the Harmon murders, get to it[5]. Or else[6] I question her at Headquarters."

"You can't force... She's starting to talk.... There's a great deal[7] that even her subconscious[8] doesn't want to face[9]."

The Chief snapped: "And I don't want to face myself[10] if there's any chance[11] those kids are still alive[12] and I've wasted precious time here[13]."

"All right, I'll get to[14] questioning her about this morning. But first, please, let me ask her about the day the Harmon children disappeared. If there is any link[15] between the two, she may reveal it."

Chief Coffin looked at his watch. "God, it's almost four already. Whatever visibility there was all day will be gone[16] in half an hour. Where is a radio? I want to hear the newscast."

"There's one in the kitchen, Chief." Bernie Mills, the patrolman[17] on guard in the house, was an earnest[18], dark-haired man in his early thirties. He'd been on the force[19] twelve years, and this was by far[20] the most sensational case he'd ever known. Nancy Harmon. Nancy Eldredge was Nancy Harmon! Ray Eldredge's wife. It showed.[21] You never knew what was going on inside people. Bernie had played on the same ball team summers with[22] Ray Eldredge when they were little kids. Then Ray had gone to one of those fancy prep schools[23] and Dartmouth College. He had never

1. fit un mouvement de la tête
2. Tout ça ne nous mène nulle part.
3. il n'en sortira rien
4. C'est aussi simple que ça.
5. venez-en au fait
6. Sinon,
7. Il y a beaucoup d'éléments
8. que même son subconscient
9. affronter
10. je ne pourrai plus me regarder en face
11. s'il y a la moindre chance
12. que ces enfants soient encore en vie
13. et que je reste ici à perdre un temps précieux
14. je vais commencer à
15. un quelconque lien
16. Le peu de visibilité qu'on a eu dans la journée aura disparu
17. l'agent
18. sérieux
19. dans la police
20. de loin
21. Ça se voyait
22. L'été, Bernie jouait dans les mêmes équipes de baseball que
23. écoles haut de gamme

expected Ray would settle on the Cape when he finished service. But he did. When he married the girl who'd rented this house, everybody said that she was some looker[1]. A few people commented[2] that she kind of reminded you of someone[3].

Bernie remembered his own reaction to that talk. Lots of people look like someone else. His own uncle, a deadbeat[4] and drunk[5] who made his aunt's life miserable[6], was a dead ringer for[7] Barry Goldwater. He glanced quickly out the window. The television news guys were all still out there, with their trucks and all their gear[8]. Looking for a story. He wondered what they'd think if they knew Nancy Eldredge was injected with truth serum right now. Now, there was a story.[9] He was anxious to get home to tell Jean about it. He wondered how she was doing[10]. The baby had been teething[11] last night; kept both of them up[12].

For a single, terrible minute Bernie wondered how it would feel if the little guy was missing on a day like this... out there somewhere... and he not knowing[13]. The prospect[14] was so awful, so breathtaking[15], so mindshattering[16] that he rejected it. Jean never took her eyes off Bobby[17]. Sometimes she bugged[18] Bernie the way she was always fussing about the kid[19]. Right now[20] her need to never take her eyes off their baby reassured him, assuaged[21] his apprehensions. The little guy was fine—trust[22] Jean.

Dorothy was in the kitchen filling the coffeepot. Bernie reflected that Dorothy bugged him a little. She had such a—well, guess you'd call it reserved—way.[23] She could be nice and friendly—but, well[24], Bernie didn't know. He decided that Dorothy was just a little too highfalutin[25] for his thinking[26].

He turned on the transistor radio, and instantly the voice of Dan Phillips, the newscaster for WCOD in Hyannis, filled the room. "The case of the missing Eldredge children has just taken a new twist[27]," Phillips said, and his voice was pulsing with[28] somewhat

1. vraiment canon
2. avaient ajouté
3. qu'elle leur rappelait quelqu'un
4. bon à rien
5. un ivrogne
6. avait gâché la vie de sa tante
7. ressemblait comme deux gouttes d'eau à
8. tout leur matériel
9. Ça, c'était un scoop.
10. ça allait
11. faisait ses dents
12. aucun des deux n'avait dormi
13. qu'il ne sache pas où
14. Cette perspective
15. incroyable
16. accablante
17. ne quittait jamais Bobby des yeux
18. énervait
19. tellement elle était autour du gosse
20. Mais à présent
21. calmait
22. faites confiance à
23. Elle était tellement – eh bien, disons, réservée.
24. en fait
25. faisait un peu trop la chichiteuse
26. à son goût
27. tournure
28. vibrait d'

unprofessional[1] excitement[2]. "A mechanic[3], Otto Linden from the Gulf Station on Route Twenty-eight in Hyannis, has just phoned us to say that he can positively state[4] that this morning at nine a.m. he filled the gas tank of[5] Rob Legler, the missing witness in the Harmon murder case of seven years ago. Mr. Linden said that Legler appeared nervous and volunteered the information[6] that he was on his way to Adams Port to visit someone who probably wouldn't be glad to see him. He was driving a late-model[7] red Dodge Dart."

Jed Coffin swore[8] softly. "And I'm wasting my time here listening to this claptrap[9]." He started for[10] the phone and picked it up just as it rang. After the caller identified himself, he said impatiently, "I heard it. All right. I want a roadblock[11] on the bridges going to the mainland. Check with the FBI deserter file[12]—find out what they may know about the latest whereabouts of Rob Legler. Put out a bulletin about[13] a red Dodge." He slammed the receiver back onto the hook[14] and turned to Lendon. "Now I've got a simple, direct question for you to ask Mrs. Eldredge. It's whether or not[15] Rob Legler got here this morning... and what he said to her."

Lendon stared. "You mean..."

"I mean that Rob Legler is the person who could dump Nancy Eldredge back[16] into the middle of a murder trial. The Harmon case has never been closed. Now, suppose he's been hiding out in Canada for six years or so. He needs money. Didn't it come out[17] at the Harmon trial that Nancy had inherited a fair amount of money[18] from her parents?—some hundred and fifty thousand dollars. Now, suppose Rob Legler knows about that money and somehow finds out where Nancy is. The District Attorney's staff[19] in San Francisco know where she's been. Now, suppose Legler decides he's sick of[20] Canada and wants to come back here and needs a stake[21]. How about[22]

1. assez peu professionnelle
2. une excitation
3. garagiste
4. est sûr et certain
5. a fait le plein de la voiture de
6. a annoncé
7. d'un modèle récent
8. jura
9. blabla
10. se dirigea vers
11. barrage
12. fichier FBI des déserteurs
13. Passez un communiqué concernant
14. raccrocha violemment
15. Est-ce que, oui ou non,
16. replonger Nancy Eldredge
17. N'est-il pas apparu
18. hérité une somme conséquente
19. les services
20. qu'il en a marre du
21. qu'il a besoin de fric
22. Pourquoi ne pas

going to Nancy Eldredge and promising to change his testimony if he's ever caught[1] and there's a new trial? That's the same as making her give him a blank check[2] for the rest of her life. He gets here. He sees her. The deal sours.[3] She doesn't go for it[4]... or he changes his mind[5]. She knows that at any moment he may be caught or turn himself in[6] and she's back in San Francisco on a murder charge, and she cracks...."

"And murders her Eldredge children?" Lendon's voice was scornful[7]. "Have you thought about the possibility that this student who nearly put Nancy in the gas chamber[8] was in the vicinity[9] when both sets of children disappeared[10]?"

"Give me one more chance," Lendon pleaded[11]. "Just let me ask her about the day the Harmon children disappeared. I want her to describe the events of that day[12] first."

"You have thirty minutes—no more."

Dorothy began pouring[13] coffee into cups that she'd already placed on a tray[14]. Quickly she cut up a coffee cake that Nancy had baked[15] the day before. "Perhaps coffee will help everyone[16]," she said.

She carried the tray into the front room. Ray was sitting in the chair Lendon had drawn next to the couch. He was holding Nancy's hands in his[17], gently massaging them[18] . She was very still[19]. Her breathing was even[20], but as the others came into the room, she stirred[21] and moaned[22].

Jonathan was standing by the mantel, staring into the fire. He had lighted his pipe, and the warm smell of the good tobacco he used had begun to penetrate the room. Dorothy breathed it in deeply[23] as she set the coffee tray on the round pine table by the fireplace. A wave of pure nostalgia washed over her[24]. Kenneth had smoked a pipe, and that had been his brand of tobacco[25]. She and Kenneth used to love stormy[26] winter afternoons like this. They would make a roaring fire[27] and get out wine and cheese and books and

1. si jamais on l'attrape
2. Ce qui revient à lui soutirer un chèque en blanc
3. L'affaire tourne à l'aigre.
4. ne marche pas dans la combine
5. d'avis
6. se livrer à la police
7. pleine de dédain
8. fait condamner Nancy à mort
9. dans les environs
10. à chacune des doubles disparitions
11. implora
12. déroulement de cette journée
13. à verser
14. plateau
15. cuit au four
16. fera du bien à tout le monde
17. dans les siennes
18. les massant
19. ne bougeait pas d'un pouce
20. régulière
21. s'agita
22. gémit
23. en inspira une grande bouffée
24. la submergea
25. il prenait la même marque
26. orageux
27. une bonne flambée

1. passaient un bon moment
2. Les regrets l'envahirent.
3. n'êtes pas maître de
4. ainsi
5. Bientôt.
6. frigorifiée
7. se servaient du
8. remplit
9. frissonna
10. Elle ouvrit brusquement les yeux
11. leva le bras
12. heurtant la tasse, qui s'échappa des mains de Ray
13. faisant gicler
14. peignoir
15. Des éclaboussures tachèrent
16. tressaillirent
17. pris au piège

sit contently together[1]. Regret swept over her.[2] Regret because you really can't control[3] your life. Most of the time you don't act; you react.

"Will you have coffee and cake?" she asked Jonathan.

He looked at her thoughtfully. "Please."

She knew he took cream and one sugar. Without asking, she prepared the coffee that way[4] and handed it to him. "Shouldn't you take your coat off?" he asked her.

"In a little while.[5] I'm still so chilled[6]."

Dr. Miles and Chief Coffin had followed her in and were helping themselves to the[7] coffee. Dorothy poured[8] another cup and carried it over to the couch. "Ray, please have some."

He looked up. "Thank you." As he reached for it, he murmured to Nancy, "Everything is going to be all right, little girl."

Nancy shuddered[9] violently. Her eyes flew open[10] and she threw up her arm[11], knocking the cup from Ray's hand[12]. It fell and broke on the floor, spewing[13] hot liquid over her robe[14] and the blanket. Splashes of it spattered on[15] Ray and Nancy. Simultaneously they winced[16] as Nancy cried out in the desperate tone of a trapped[17] animal, "I am not your little girl! Don't call me your little girl!"

17

Courtney Parrish turned from the small unmoving[1] figure on the bed, sighing heavily. He'd taken the adhesive from Missy's mouth and the cords from her wrists[2] and ankles[3], and they made an untidy pile on the quilt. Her fine, silky hair was matted[4] now. He'd been planning to brush it when he bathed her, but now there was no point[5]. He needed her response[6].

The little boy, Michael, was still on the floor of the closet. His large blue eyes were terrified as Courtney picked him up and hugged him[7] against his massive chest.

He laid Michael on the bed, undid the bindings[8] on his ankles and wrists and with a quick pull yanked the adhesive off his mouth[9]. The boy cried out in pain[10], then bit his lip[11]. He seemed more responsive[12]—infinitely wary[13], apprehensive[14], but with some of the courage of the trapped animal.

"What did you do to my sister?" The belligerent[15] tone made Courtney realize that the boy hadn't drunk all the milk with the sedative he'd given him just before the meddling fools[16] came along.

"She's asleep."

1. inerte
2. poignets
3. chevilles
4. tout emmêlés
5. cela n'avait aucun sens
6. réaction
7. le serra
8. liens
9. d'un coup sec retira l'adhésif de sa bouche
10. poussa un cri de douleur
11. se mordit la lèvre
12. réactif
13. méfiant
14. sur la défensive
15. agressif
16. enquiquineurs

1. nous avez cachés
2. l'incurva
3. en forme de gant [de baseball]
4. gifla Michael
5. Sous la douleur, Michael partit en arrière
6. roula hors de portée
7. perdit l'équilibre
8. lourdement en travers du lit
9. emmêlés
10. son attention fut détournée
11. Essayant de se relever
12. debout
13. s'accroupissant pour bondir sur
14. reculait
15. traversa en courant
16. se précipita
17. cliquetis
18. vers
19. marches nues
20. obscurité protectrice
21. course éperdue
22. dégringola
23. en saisissant
24. rampe
25. retrouver ses esprits
26. se releva
27. aiguë
28. Les bruits de pas avaient cessé.
29. tout son temps
30. allait d'abord fermer

"Let us go home. We want to go home. I don't like you. I told my daddy I didn't like you, and Aunt Dorothy was here and you hid us[1]."

Courtney lifted his right hand, curved it[2] into the mitt-like shape[3] and slapped Michael across the cheek[4]. Michael jerked back in pain[5] and then rolled out from under the man's grasp[6]. Courtney reached for him, lost his balance[7] and fell clumsily across the bed[8]. His mouth touched Missy's tangled[9] yellow hair, and for an instant he was distracted[10]. Pulling himself up[11], he turned and was on his feet[12], crouching to spring at[13] Michael. But Michael was backing away[14] toward the bedroom door. With a swift movement he opened it and raced through[15] the adjoining sitting room.

Courtney lunged[16] after him, realizing that he hadn't locked the apartment door. He hadn't wanted Dorothy to hear the distinct ping[17] of the lock turning as she went downstairs.

Michael threw open the door and raced for the[18] staircase. His shoes clattered on the uncarpeted stairs[19]. He moved swiftly, a slim shadow that darted down into the protecting gloom[20] of the third floor. Courtney hurried after him, but in his frantic rush[21] lost his balance and fell. He hurtled down[22] six steps before he managed to stop the fall by grasping[23] the heavy wooden banister[24]. Shaking his head to clear it[25], he picked himself up[26], aware of a sharp[27] pain in his right ankle. He had to make sure the kitchen door was locked.

There was no further sound of footsteps.[28] The boy was probably hiding in one of the third-floor bedrooms, but he had plenty of time[29] to look for him. First the kitchen door. The windows were no problem. They were all double-locked, and too heavy anyhow. The double lock on the front door was too high for the child. He'd just secure[30] the kitchen door, then search for the boy—room by room. He'd call to him and warn him[1]. The boy was so frightened. His eyes had been so terrified and wary. He looked more than ever like Nancy this way. Oh, this was so unexpectedly wonderful[2]. But he had to hurry. He had to make sure the boy couldn't get out of the house.

"I'll be right back, Michael," he called. "I'll find you. I'll find you, Michael. You're a very bad boy. You must be punished, Michael. Do you hear me, Michael?"

He thought he heard a noise in the bedroom on his right and rushed in, favoring[3] his ankle. But the room was empty. Suppose the boy had run through this hallway and used the front stairs? Suddenly panicking, he lumbered down[4] the remaining two flights. From outside he could hear the waves from the bay crashing against the rocks. He raced into the kitchen and over to the door. This was the door he always used going into and out of the house. This one had not only a double lock[5] but a high bolt[6]. His breath came in quick furious gasps.[7] With thick, trembling fingers, he shoved the bolt into place[8]. Then he pulled over[9] a heavy wooden kitchen chair and wedged it under the knob[10]. The boy would never be able to move this. There was no other way out of the house.

The heavy storm had almost obliterated[11] the remaining daylight[12]. Courtney switched on[13] the overhead light[14], but an instant later it flickered and went off. He realized that the storm had probably pulled down some wires[15]. It would make it harder to find the boy. All the upstairs bedrooms were fully furnished[16]. They all had closets, too—deep ones—and cupboards[17] that he might hide in[18]. Courtney bit his lip in fury as he reached for the hurricane lamp[19] on the table, struck the match[20] and lighted the wick[21]. The glass was red, and the light cast an eerie reddish glow against[22] the fireplace wall and faded planked floor[23] and thick-beamed ceiling[24]. The wind wailed[25] against the shutters as Courtney

1. le menacerait
2. tout cela était si merveilleusement imprévu
3. tout en prenant garde à
4. descendit pesamment
5. serrure à double tour
6. verrou
7. Il haletait rageusement.
8. poussa la tige du verrou
9. tira
10. la coinça sous la poignée
11. caché
12. ce qui restait de la lueur du jour
13. alluma
14. plafonnier
15. endommagé des câbles
16. pleines de meubles
17. des armoires
18. où se cacher
19. lampe-tempête
20. grattait l'allumette
21. mèche
22. une inquiétante lueur rougeâtre sur
23. le plancher défraîchi
24. les poutres épaisses du plafond
25. gémit

called, “Michael... it’s all right, Michael. I’m not angry anymore. Come out, Michael. I’ll take you home to your mother.”

18

THE CHANCE TO BLACKMAIL[1] Nancy Harmon was the break[2] Rob Legler had been needing for over six years—from the day he'd gotten on a plane to Canada after carefully shredding[3] his embarkation orders[4] for Vietnam. During those years, he'd worked as a farmhand[5] near Halifax. It was the only job he'd been able to get, and he loathed[6] it. Not for a minute did he regret his decision to bolt the Army[7]. Who in the hell wanted to go to a filthy, hot hole[8] to be shot at[9] by a bunch of pint-sized bastards[10]? He didn't.[11]

He'd worked on the farm in Canada because he didn't have any alternative[12]. He'd left San Francisco with sixty bucks[13] in his pocket. If he went back home, he'd be tossed in jail[14]. A conviction for desertion wasn't his idea of the way to spend the rest of his life. He needed a good stake[15] to cut out for[16] some place like Argentina. He wasn't just one of the thousands of deserters who eventually[17] might be able to slip back[18] into the States with faked identification[19]. Thanks to that blasted[20] Harmon case, he was a hunted[21] man.

If only that conviction hadn't been upset[22]... that case would be finished. But that bastard of a D.A.[23]

1. La possibilité de faire chanter
2. chance
3. déchiré
4. ordre d'embarquement
5. ouvrier agricole
6. détestait
7. déserter
8. Qui diable était prêt à aller dans un trou pourri
9. se faire tirer dessus
10. par une bande de minus
11. Pas lui !
12. d'autre solution
13. dollars
14. jeté en prison
15. paquet de fric
16. pour se tirer
17. un jour
18. rentrer en douce
19. sous une fausse identité
20. fichu
21. traqué
22. cassée
23. salaud de proc'

1. qu'il mettrait peut-être
2. mais qu'il rouvrirait le procès de
3. fournissait le mobile
4. Déjà que
5. autre chose dans ce meurtre qu'une accusée voulant se soustraire à des ennuis familiaux
6. rendraient jalouses
7. de nombreuses jeunes femmes
8. attachement
9. pour tous
10. étudiant-réparateur
11. subir
12. un désagrément temporaire
13. avances
14. élever des enfants, c'est pas son truc
15. méprise
16. s'est joué de
17. adultère
18. rapporte
19. accablantes
20. prononcées par Nancy Harmon
21. Qu'il aille se faire mettre.
22. une peur panique
23. au ventre
24. un complice du meurtre
25. Tout ça
26. n'avait pas pour habitude de
27. proposer
28. de la belle nana
29. ce vieux craignos

had said if he spent[1] twenty years he'd retry[2] Nancy Harmon for the murder of those kids. And Rob was the witness, the witness who supplied the motive[3].

Rob couldn't let that scene happen again. As it was,[4] the D.A. last time had told the jury that there was probably more to the killing than Nancy Harmon wanting to get out of a home situation[5]. "She was probably in love," he'd said. "We have here a very attractive young woman who since the age of eighteen has been married to an older man. Her life might well be the envy[6] of many a young woman[7]. Professor Harmon's devotion[8] to his young wife and family was an example for the community[9]. But is Nancy Harmon satisfied? No. When a student-repairman[10] comes in, sent by her husband so that she will not have to endure[11] even a few hours' discomfort[12], what does she do? She follows him around, insists he have coffee, says it's nice to talk to someone young... says she has to get away... responds passionately to his overtures[13]... and then when he tells her that 'raising kids isn't his bag[14]' she calmly promises him that her children are going to be smothered.

"Now, ladies and gentlemen of the jury, I despise[15] Rob Legler. I believe that he toyed with[16] this foolish young woman. I don't for a minute believe that their unholy[17] passion ended with a few kisses... but I do believe him when he quotes[18] the damning[19] phrases that fell from Nancy Harmon's lips[20]."

Frig him.[21] Rob felt sick fear[22] in the pit of his stomach[23] whenever he remembered that speech. That bastard would have given anything to have made him an accessory to murder[24]. All[25] because he'd been in old Harmon's office the day his wife phoned to tell him the heater had gone off. Rob wasn't usually given to[26] volunteering[27] his services. But he'd never seen a machine or engine or piece of equipment he couldn't fix, and he'd heard some guys talk about what a doll[28] that creepy old drag[29] had for a wife.

That piece of intriguing information[1] had made him[2] volunteer his services. At first Harmon had turned him down[3], but then when he couldn't get his regular maintenance man[4] he'd said okay. He said he didn't want his wife taking the kids to a motel. That was what she'd suggested.

So Rob had gone over[5]. Everything the guys had said about Nancy Harmon was true. She was a real looker.[6] But she sure didn't seem to know it. She was kind of[7] hesitant... unsure of herself[8]. He'd gotten over about noon[9]. She was just feeding the two little kids... a boy and a girl. Quiet kids, both of them. She didn't pay much attention to him, just thanked him for coming and turned back to the kids.

He realized that the only way to get her attention was through[10] the kids and started talking to them. It was always easy for Rob to turn on the charm[11]. He liked gals[12] older than himself, too. Not that this one was older by much[13]. But he'd learned from the time he was sixteen and screwing[14] his next-door neighbor's wife that if you're nice to a woman's kids, she thinks you're A-okay[15] and all the guilt[16] goes down the drain[17]. Boy[18], Rob could write a book on the whole mother-complex rationalization.

In a couple of minutes he'd had the kids laughing[19] and Nancy laughing, and then he'd invited the little boy down to be his helper fixing[20] the furnace. Just as he expected, the little girl asked to go too, and then Nancy said she'd come along to make sure they didn't get in the way[21]. There wasn't much wrong with the furnace[22]—just a clogged[23] filter—but he said it needed a part[24] and he could get it working but he'd be back and do the job right[25].

He got out fast the first day. No point in[26] getting old Harmon upset. Went straight back to his office. Harmon looked annoyed[27] and worried when he opened the door, but when he saw Rob he gave a

1. L'info avait éveillé sa curiosité
2. et l'avait incité à
3. décliné son offre
4. réparateur habituel
5. y était donc allé
6. C'était vraiment une beauté.
7. plutôt
8. pas très sûre d'elle
9. vers midi
10. par le biais des
11. faire du charme
12. [girls]
13. Non que celle-ci soit tellement plus vieille.
14. qu'il baisait
15. un type bien
16. sa culpabilité
17. s'envole
18. Vrai,
19. il avait fait rire les enfants
20. à venir l'aider à réparer
21. qu'ils ne dérangeaient pas
22. La chaudière n'avait pas grand-chose
23. encrassé
24. qu'une pièce de rechange était nécessaire
25. finirait le boulot correctement
26. Inutile de
27. contrarié

big, relieved smile[1]. "So soon? You must be a whiz[2]. Or couldn't you take care of it[3]?"

Rob said, "I got it going[4]. But you need a new part, sir, that I'll be glad to pick up[5]. It's one of those little things that if you call in a regular service, they'll make a big production over[6]. I can get the part for a couple of bucks. Be glad to do it.[7]"

Harmon fell for it[8], of course. Probably glad to save the money[9]. And Rob went back the next day and the next day. Harmon warned him that his wife was very nervous and rested a lot and to please keep out of her way[10]. But Rob didn't see where she acted nervous[11]. Timid, maybe, and scared. He got her talking.[12] She told him that she'd had a nervous breakdown[13] after her mother died. "I guess I've been terribly depressed," she said. "But I'm sure I'm getting better. I've even stopped taking most of my medicine[14]. My husband doesn't realize that. He'd probably be annoyed. But I feel better without it."

Rob had told her how pretty she was, kind of feeling his way[15]. He'd begun to suspect that she might be a pushover[16]. It was obvious she was pretty bored[17] with old Harmon and getting restless. He said maybe she should get out more. She'd said, "My husband doesn't believe in company[18]. He feels that at the end of the day he doesn't need to see any more people—not after all the students he has to contend with[19]."

That was when he'd known he'd try to make a pass at her[20].

Rob had an airtight[21] alibi for that morning the Harmon kids had disappeared. He'd been in a class of only six students. But the D.A. had told him that if he could find one shred of evidence[22] that would help him hang an accessory charge on Rob[23], it would be his pleasure to do it. Rob had hired a lawyer[24]. Plenty scared[25], he didn't want the D.A. poking into his background[26] and finding out about the time he'd been named in a paternity suit[27] in Cooperstown. The

1. eut un grand sourire de soulagement
2. as
3. À moins que vous n'ayez pas réussi
4. Je l'ai fait redémarrer
5. je peux me procurer, si vous le souhaitez
6. ils en feront toute une affaire
7. Ce sera avec plaisir.
8. y avait cru
9. faire une économie
10. ne pas la déranger
11. en quoi elle était nerveuse
12. Il la fit parler.
13. dépression nerveuse
14. mes médicaments
15. histoire de tâter le terrain
16. femme facile
17. s'ennuyait ferme
18. n'aime pas recevoir des gens
19. auxquels il a affaire
20. lui faire du plat
21. en béton
22. un seul élément de preuve
23. à accuser Rob de complicité
24. pris un avocat
25. Paniqué
26. fouille dans son passé
27. impliqué dans une affaire de recherche en paternité

lawyer had told him that his posture had to be that he was the[1] respectful student of a distinguished professor; had been anxious to do a favor for him; had tried to stay away from the wife, but she had kept following him around. That he never took it seriously[2] when she talked about the children being smothered. Actually, he'd thought she was just nervous and sick, the way the Professor had warned him[3].

But on the stand it didn't work like that. "Were you attracted to this young woman?" the D.A. asked smoothly[4].

Rob looked at Nancy sitting at the defendant's table[5] next to her lawyer, looking at him through blank, unseeing eyes[6]. "I didn't think in those terms, sir," he replied. "To me Mrs. Harmon was the wife of a teacher I admired greatly. I simply wanted to fix the furnace as I'd volunteered to do and get back to my room. I had a paper[7] to write, and anyhow a sick woman with two children simply isn't my bag[8]." It was that elaboration[9], that last damned phrase that the D.A. had pounced on[10]. By the time he was finished with him[11], Rob was wringing with[12] perspiration.

Yes, he'd heard the Professor's wife was a doll.... No, he wasn't given to volunteering his help.... Yes, he'd been curious to get a look at her[13].... Yes, he had made a pass at her....

"But it stopped there!" Rob had shouted from the stand[14]. "With two thousand coeds[15] on campus, I didn't need problems." Then he'd admitted that he had told Nancy that she turned him on[16] and he'd like to hustle her[17].

The D.A. had looked at him contemptuously[18], then read into the record[19] the time Rob had been beaten up[20] by an irate[21] husband—the episode in Cooperstown when he'd been named in the paternity suit.

The D.A. said, "This philanderer[22] was no willing volunteer. He went into that house to size up[23] a beautiful young woman whom he'd heard about. He

1. qu'il devait se poser en
2. ne l'avait pas prise au sérieux
3. tout comme le professeur le lui avait signalé
4. d'une voix suave
5. banc des accusés
6. sans le voir
7. un devoir
8. c'est vraiment pas mon truc
9. C'est de cet ajout
10. que le proc' s'était emparé
11. Quand il en eut fini avec lui
12. trempé de
13. de voir quelle tête elle avait
14. le box
15. étudiantes
16. l'excitait
17. se la faire
18. d'un air méprisant
19. avait lu à la cour
20. la fois où Rob avait été rossé
21. en colère
22. coureur de jupons
23. se faire son idée sur

made a play for her[1]. It succeeded beyond his wildest dreams.[2] Ladies and gentlemen of the jury, I am not suggesting that Rob Legler was part of the scheme to murder[3] Nancy Harmon's children. At least, in the legal sense he wasn't.[4] But I am convinced that morally, before God, he is guilty. He let this gullible, ungrateful[5] young woman know that he'd—and I use his words—'hustle her' if she were free, and she chose a freedom[6] that is repugnant to[7] the basic instincts of mankind. She murdered her children to be free of them."

After Nancy Harmon was sentenced to die in the gas chamber, Professor Harmon had committed suicide. He drove his car to the same beach where one of the kids had been found and left it by the shore. He pinned a note[8] to the wheel[9] saying that it was all his fault. He should have realized how sick his wife was. He should have taken his children from her. He was responsible for their deaths and her action. "I tried to play God[10]," he wrote. "I loved her so dearly[11] that I thought I could cure her[12]. I thought bearing children[13] would turn her mind from[14] the grief of her mother's death. I thought love and care would heal her[15], but I was wrong; I meddled beyond my depth[16]. Forgive me, Nancy."

There hadn't been any roar of approval[17] when the conviction was overturned. It happened because two women jurors[18] had been heard discussing the case in a bar midway through the trial and saying she was guilty as sin[19]. But by the time a new trial was ordered Rob had graduated[20], been drafted[21], given Vietnam orders and bolted[22]. Without him, the D.A. had no case and had to let Nancy—but swore he'd retry her the day he could get hold of Rob again.

Over the years in Canada, Rob had thought of that trial often. There was something that bothered him about the whole setup. Taking himself out of it[23], he didn't buy Nancy Harmon as a murderess[24]. She'd

1. lui avait fait des avances
2. Cela avait marché au-delà de ses rêves les plus fous.
3. ait trempé dans le projet d'assassinat
4. Pas aux yeux de la loi, tout du moins.
5. crédule et ingrate
6. forme de liberté
7. contraire à
8. laissé un mot
9. sur le volant
10. Je me suis pris pour Dieu
11. Elle m'était si chère
12. la guérir
13. qu'avoir des enfants
14. lui ferait oublier
15. pouvoir la guérir à force d'amour et de soins
16. j'ai touché à quelque chose qui me dépassait
17. cris d'approbation
18. jurées
19. tout ce qu'il y a de coupable
20. fini ses études
21. appelé sous les drapeaux
22. pris la tangente
23. En prenant du recul
24. ne voyait pas Nancy Harmon en meurtrière

been like a clay pigeon[1] in court. Harmon certainly hadn't helped her, breaking down[2] on the stand when he was supposed to be in the midst of saying what a great mother she was.

In Canada, Rob was something of a celebrity[3] among the draft evaders[4] he hung out with[5] whom he'd told about the case. They'd asked about Nancy, and Rob told them what a dish she was[6]... hinting that he'd had a little action[7]. He showed them the press clippings[8] of the trial and Nancy's pictures.

He told them that she had to have some dough[9]—that it came out at the trial that her folks left her over a hundred and fifty grand[10]; that if he could find her he'd put the arm on her for money[11] to split[12] to Argentina.

Then he got his break[13]. One of his buddies[14], Jim Ellis, who knew about his connection with[15] the Harmon case, slipped home to visit his mother, who had terminal cancer. The mother lived in Boston, but because the FBI was watching the house hoping to pick up[16] Jim, she met him in Cape Cod in a cottage she had hired on Maushop Lake. When Jim got back to Canada, he was bursting with news[17]. He asked Rob what it would be worth to him[18] to know where he could find Nancy Harmon.

Rob was skeptical until he saw the picture Jimmy had managed to snap of Nancy on the beach. There was no mistaking her.[19] Jim had done some digging, too[20]. The background checked.[21] He'd found out that her husband was pretty prosperous[22]. Quickly they worked out a deal[23]. Rob would get to see Nancy. Tell her that if she'd stake him to[24] fifty thousand bucks, he'd split to Argentina and she'd never have to worry about him testifying against her. Rob reasoned[25] that she'd go for it[26], especially now that she was remarried and had more kids. It was a cheap price for her to know that someday she wouldn't be haul-assed[27] back to California to stand trial.

1. cible facile
2. en s'effondrant
3. connu
4. réfractaires
5. qu'il fréquentait
6. ce qu'elle était canon
7. sous-entendant la partie de jambes en l'air
8. coupures de presse
9. du pognon
10. dollars
11. il la taxerait
12. pour se tirer
13. l'occasion s'était présentée
14. potes
15. implication dans
16. coincer
17. avait plein de nouvelles
18. combien il était prêt à mettre
19. C'était bien elle.
20. avait aussi fait des recherches
21. Tout correspondait.
22. à l'aise
23. combinèrent un plan
24. lui filait
25. se disait
26. accepterait
27. ramenée d'urgence

1. tout bonnement
2. part
3. dégoterait
4. de faux passeports canadiens
5. des papiers
6. Tout ça se trouvait si on y mettait le prix.
7. dès que
8. tous ces satanés flics
9. fichues
10. vous choper avec leurs radars
11. d'une seule traite
12. prévoyait d'arriver à Cape Cod
13. Il n'avait plus beaucoup d'essence en arrivant à Cape Cod.
14. Il risquait moins de se faire remarquer.
15. À tous les coups il saurait
16. si elle retirait un paquet de liquide
17. pompiste
18. serviable
19. fut pris au dépourvu
20. payait
21. venait
22. C'est là qu'il en avait trop dit, racontant

Jim wanted a flat[1] twenty percent for his share[2]. While Rob was seeing Nancy, Jim would arrange for[3] phony Canadian passports[4], identification[5] and reservations to Argentina. They were available for a price.[6]

They laid their plans carefully. Rob managed to rent a car from an American kid who was in school in Canada. He shaved his beard and cut his hair for the trip. Jim warned him that the minute[7] you looked like a hippie, every damn cop[8] in those crappy[9] New England towns was ready to clock you with radar[10].

Rob decided to drive straight through[11] from Halifax. The less time he spent in the States, the less chance of getting picked up. He timed his arrival at the Cape for[12] early in the morning. Jim had found out that Nancy's husband always opened his office about nine-thirty. He'd get to her house around ten. Jim had made a map of her street for him, including that driveway through the woods. He could hide the car there.

He was running low on gas when he hit the Cape.[13] That was why he got off at Hyannis to refuel. Jim had told him that even out of season there were a lot of tourists there. He'd be less likely to be noticed.[14] All the way down he'd been nervous, trying to decide if he should offer his deal to Nancy and her husband together. Likely he'd have to know about[15] her getting a bundle of cash[16]. But suppose this guy called the cops? Rob would be convicted of desertion and blackmail. No, it was better to talk directly to Nancy. She must still remember sitting at that defendant's table.

The attendant[17] at the gas station was helpful[18]. Checked everything over, cleaned the windows, put air in the tires without being asked. That was why Rob was off guard[19]. When he was settling the bill[20], the attendant asked if he was down[21] for some fishing. That was when he babbled[22] that he was actually doing some hunting—going to Adams Port to see an old girlfriend who might not be glad to see him.

Then, cursing his talkiness[1], he bolted, stopping at a nearby diner[2] for some breakfast.

He drove into Adams Port at quarter of ten. Slowly cruising around[3], studying the map Jim had drawn for him, he got a feel of the layout[4]. Even so[5] he almost missed the dirt road leading to the woods behind her property. He realized that after he slowed up for that old Ford wagon pulling out from it. Backing up, he turned into the dirt road, parked the car and started walking to the rear door of Nancy's house. That was when she'd come running out like a madwoman[6] shrieking those names. Peter, Lisa, those were the dead kids. He followed her through the woods to the lake and watched when she threw herself into the water. He was just about to go after her[7] when she dragged herself out[8] and fell on the beach. He knew she looked in his direction. He wasn't sure if she saw him, but he did know that he had to get out of there[9]. He didn't know what was happening, but he didn't want to get involved[10].

Back in the car, he'd cooled off[11]. Maybe she'd turned into a drunk.[12] If she was still screaming for the dead kids, chances were[13] that she'd jump at the chance[14] to know she didn't have to worry about a new trial. He decided to check[15] into some motel in Adams Port and try to see her again the next day.

In the motel, Rob promptly[16] went to bed and fell asleep. He awakened late in the afternoon and switched on the television set to catch the news. The screen focused[17] in time for him[18] to see a picture of himself[19] and a voice describing him[20] as the missing witness in the Harmon murder case. Numbly[21], Rob listened as the announcer recapped[22] the disappearance of the Eldredge children. For the first time in his life he felt trapped. Now that he'd shaved off his beard and shortened his hair, he looked exactly the way he had in the picture.

1. se maudissant d'avoir bavardé
2. cafétéria
3. Roulant lentement de-ci de-là
4. il repéra la disposition des lieux
5. Malgré ça
6. folle
7. Il s'apprêtait à aller à la rescousse
8. s'était traînée hors de l'eau
9. ce qui était sûr, c'est qu'il fallait qu'il gicle
10. se retrouver impliqué
11. s'était calmé
12. Peut-être s'était-elle mise à boire.
13. il y avait de fortes chances
14. saute sur l'occasion
15. prendre une chambre
16. vite
17. L'image devint nette
18. juste à temps
19. pour se voir à l'écran
20. entendre une voix le présentant
21. Hébété
22. faisait le point sur

If Nancy Eldredge had actually killed her new family, who would believe that he hadn't had something to do with it? It must have happened just before he got there. Rob thought of the old Ford wagon that had backed out from the dirt road just before he turned in. Massachusetts license[1], first two numbers 8-6... heavyset[2] guy behind the wheel.

But he couldn't talk about that even if he got caught. Couldn't admit being[3] at the Eldredge house this morning. Who would believe him if he told the truth? Rob Legler's instinct for self-preservation[4] told him to get off Cape Cod, and it was a cinch he couldn't go in[5] a bright red Dodge that every cop was looking for.

He packed his bag and slipped out the back door of the motel. A Volks Beetle[6] was parked in the stall[7] next to the Dodge. Through the window he'd noticed the couple who had left it. They'd checked in[8] just before he turned on the news. Chances were, if he was any judge, they were good for a couple of hours.[9] No one else was outside braving the sleet and wind.

Rob opened the engine lid[10] of the Volks, connected[11] a few wires and drove away. He'd use Route 6A heading for the bridge[12]. With any luck, in half an hour he'd be off the Cape.

Six minutes later, he ran a red light[13]. Thirty seconds after that, he glanced in the rearview mirror[14] and saw a flashing red light reflected there. He was being chased by a police car.[15] For an instant he considered surrendering himself[16]; then the overwhelming need to bolt from trouble[17] overcame him[18]. As he rounded a corner, Rob slipped open the door, wedged the accelerator down[19] with his suitcase[20] and jumped out. He was disappearing into the wooded area behind stately Colonial homes when the police car, its siren now screaming, chased[21] the wildly careening[22] Volkswagen down the sloping road[23].

1. Une plaque d'immatriculation du
2. costaud
3. reconnaître qu'il était
4. Son instinct de conservation
5. bien sûr, il n'était pas question qu'il prenne
6. Coccinelle
7. box
8. étaient arrivés au motel
9. Ils en auraient certainement pour deux bonnes heures.
10. capot
11. relia
12. Son idée était de prendre la 6A en direction du pont
13. brûla un feu rouge
14. rétroviseur
15. Une voiture de police l'avait pris en chasse.
16. envisagea de se rendre
17. fuir les ennuis
18. prit le dessus
19. coinça l'accélérateur
20. valise
21. coursait
22. en proie à de folles embardées
23. dans la pente

19

When Michael began to run down the stairs, he was sure that Mr. Parrish would catch him. But then he heard the terrible thumping[1] that meant Mr. Parrish had fallen down the stairs. Michael knew that if he wanted to get away from Mr. Parrish he mustn't make any noise. He remembered the time Mommy had had the carpet on the stairs at home taken off[2]. "Now, until the new treads go down[3], you kids have to play a new game," she'd said. "It's called civilized walking[4]." Michael and Missy had made a game of walking down the side of the stairs near the banister[5] on tiptoe[6]. They got so good at it[7] they used to sneak down[8] and scare each other[9]. Now, walking lightly that same way, Michael slipped noiselessly[10] down to the first floor[11]. He heard Mr. Parrish calling his name, saying he would find him.

He knew he had to get out of this house. He had to run down the winding[12] road to the long road that led to Wiggins' Market. Michael hadn't decided whether he'd go into Wiggins' Market or run past it[13] across Route 6A up the road that led to his house[14]. He had to get Daddy and bring him back here for Missy.

1. vacarme
2. avait fait enlever le tapis de l'escalier
3. tant que les marches ne seront pas recouvertes
4. marcher sur des œufs
5. près de la rampe
6. sur la pointe des pieds
7. étaient devenus si adroits,
8. qu'il arrivait à l'un de se glisser jusqu'en bas
9. de faire peur à l'autre
10. sans bruit
11. au rez-de-chaussée
12. en lacets
13. s'il rentrerait dans le supermarché ou s'il continuerait en courant,
14. traverserait la 6A et remonterait la route allant chez lui

Yesterday in Wiggins' Market he had told Daddy he didn't like Mr. Parrish. Now he was afraid of him. Michael felt the choking fear[1] as he ran through the dark house. Mr. Parrish was a bad man. That was why he had tied them up and hidden them in the closet. That was why Missy was so scared she couldn't wake up. Michael had tried to touch Missy in the closet. He knew she was scared. But he couldn't get his hands free[2]. From inside the closet, he could hear Aunt Dorothy's voice. But she hadn't asked for them[3]. She was right there[4] and didn't guess[5] that they were there. He was very angry that Aunt Dorothy didn't know they needed her. She should have guessed.

It was getting so dark. It was hard to see.[6] At the bottom of the stairs, Michael looked around, confused[7], then darted toward the back of the house. He was in the kitchen. The outside door was over there[8]. He rushed to it and reached for the knob. He was just about[9] to turn the lock when he heard the footsteps approaching. Mr. Parrish. His knees trembled. If the door stuck[10], Mr. Parrish would grab him[11]. Quickly, noiselessly, Michael raced out the other kitchen door, across the small foyer and into the little back parlor[12]. He heard Mr. Parrish bolt[13] the kitchen door. He heard him drag the chair over to it. The light in the kitchen was snapped on[14], and Michael shrank[15] behind the heavy overstuffed couch. Crouching quietly[16], he barely fitted into the space between the couch and the wall[17]. Dust[18] from the couch tickled his nose[19]. He wanted to sneeze[20]. The light in the kitchen and hallway went out suddenly, and the house was black dark[21]. He heard Mr. Parrish walking around, striking a match.

A moment later there was a reddish glow in the kitchen, and he heard Mr. Parrish call, "It's all right, Michael. I'm not angry anymore. Come out, Michael. I'll take you home to your mother."

1. la peur lui serrer la gorge
2. n'avait pu se libérer les mains
3. à les voir
4. là, tout près
5. deviné
6. On ne voyait plus grand-chose.
7. désorienté
8. par là
9. sur le point de
10. ne s'ouvrait pas
11. s'emparerait de lui
12. salon à l'arrière
13. verrouiller
14. allumée
15. se fit tout petit
16. Recroquevillé sans un bruit,
17. il tenait à peine, coincé entre le canapé et le mur
18. La poussière
19. lui chatouillait le nez
20. éternuer
21. plongée dans le noir

20

John Kragopoulos had intended to drive directly to New York after leaving Dorothy, but a vague sense of depression[1] coupled with[2] a headache[3] over the bridge of his nose[4] made the five-hour trip seem suddenly insurmountable. It was the frightful weather, of course, and the intense distress[5] Dorothy was suffering couldn't help transmitting itself[6]. She had shown him the picture she carried in her wallet[7], and the thought of those beautiful children having met with[8] foul play[9] left a sickening feeling[10] in the pit of[11] his stomach.

But what an incredible thought, he mused[12]. There was still the possibility the children had simply wandered away[13]. How could anyone hurt a child? John thought of his own twenty-eight-year-old twin sons[14]—one an Air Force pilot, the other an architect. Fine young men, both of them. A source of pride[15] for a father. Long after he and their mother were gone, they would live. They were a part of his immortality. Suppose when they were babies, he had lost them[16]....

He was driving down Route 6A toward the mainland. Ahead on the right an attractive restaurant

1. abattement
2. associé à
3. mal de tête
4. qui lui tenaillait le bas du front
5. angoisse
6. avait été contagieuse
7. sac à main
8. victimes d'un
9. acte crapuleux
10. impression d'écœurement
11. au creux de
12. songeait-il
13. se soient simplement égarés
14. fils jumeaux
15. fierté
16. Et s'il les avait perdus tout bébés

was set back from the road[1]. The lighted sign[2], THE STAGEWAY[3], was a welcoming beacon[4] in the afternoon gloom[5]. Instinctively[6], John swung off[7] the road and into the parking lot. He realized that it was nearly three o'clock and he had had exactly[8] one cup of coffee and one piece of toast all day. The bad weather had made the driving up from New York so slow he had been forced to skip lunch[9].

He rationalized that it was common sense to have a decent meal[10] before he attempted the trip[11]. And it was good business sense[12] to try to strike up[13] a conversation with the personnel of a large restaurant in a vicinity he was considering[14]. He might be able to garner[15] some useful information on the probable trade[16] in the area.

Subconsciously approving of the rustic interior of the restaurant, he went directly to the bar. There were no customers[17] at it, but that wasn't unusual before five o'clock in a town like this. He ordered a Chivas Regal on the rocks; then, when the bartender[18] brought it, he asked if it would be possible to get something to eat.

"No problem." The bartender was about forty, dark-haired, with exaggerated muttonchops[19]. John liked both his obliging[20] answer and the way he kept the bar immaculately neat[21]. A menu was produced.[22] "If you feel like steak, the special sirloin[23] is great," he volunteered. "Technically,[24] the kitchen is closed between two-thirty and five, but if you don't mind eating right here[25]..."

"Sounds perfect." Quickly John ordered the steak rare[26] and a green salad. The Chivas warmed his body, and some of his depression began to lift[27]. "You make a good drink," he said.

The bartender smiled. "It takes real talent[28] to put together a Scotch on the rocks[29]," he said.

"I'm in the business. You know what I mean." John decided to be candid[30]. "I'm thinking of buying the

1. situé en retrait de la route
2. L'enseigne lumineuse
3. L'ÉTAPE
4. fanal engageant
5. cet après-midi morose
6. Sans réfléchir
7. quitta
8. en tout et pour tout
9. sauter le déjeuner
10. Le bon sens lui dictait de faire un repas convenable
11. de faire le voyage
12. cela participait du bon sens commercial
13. que d'engager
14. près de là où il comptait s'établir
15. recueillir
16. nombre de clients auquel s'attendre
17. pas de clients
18. barman
19. favoris
20. aimable
21. la propreté irréprochable de son bar
22. On lui passa la carte.
23. faux-filet
24. En principe,
25. de manger au bar
26. saignant
27. s'estomper
28. C'est tout un art
29. de verser du scotch sur des glaçons
30. franc

place they call The Lookout for a restaurant. What's your top-of-the-head opinion?[1]"

The other man nodded emphatically[2]. "Could work. A real class restaurant, I mean. Here we do fine, but we get the middle-buck crowd[3]. Families with kids. Old ladies on pensions[4]. Tourists heading for the beach or antique shops. We're right on the main drag[5]. But a place like The Lookout overlooking the bay... good atmosphere[6], good booze[7], a good menu... you could charge top dollar[8] and keep it packed[9]."

"That's my feeling."

"Of course, if I was you, I'd get rid of[10] that old creep[11] on the top floor."

"I was wondering about him. He seems to be somewhat odd.[12]"

"Well, he's supposed to be up here every year around this time for the fishing. I know because Ray Eldredge happened to mention it[13]. Nice guy, Ray Eldredge. He's the one whose kids are missing."

"I heard about that."

"Damn shame.[14] Nice little kids. Ray and Mrs. Eldredge bring them in here once in a while[15]. Some looker, Ray's wife. But like I was saying, I'm not a native[16]. I quit bartending in New York ten years ago after the third time I was mugged[17] going home late. But I always been crazy for[18] fishing. That's how I ended here.[19] And one day just a few weeks ago, this big guy comes in and orders a drink. I know who he is, I seen him around. He's the tenant at The Lookout. Well, I try to make anybody relax, get his beefs off his chest[20], so just to make conversation, I ask him if he was here in September when the blues were running[21]. You know what that stupe[22] said?"

John waited

"Nothing. Blank.[23] Zero. He didn't have a clue.[24]" The bartender stood with his hands on his hips. "Do you believe anyone can come fishing to the Cape seven years and not know what I meant?"

1. Vous en pensez quoi, comme ça, sans trop réfléchir ?
2. énergiquement
3. les revenus moyens
4. à la retraite
5. route principale
6. ambiance
7. bonne cave
8. faire payer un max
9. il y aura toujours du monde
10. je me débarrasserais
11. drôle de type
12. Il est plutôt bizarre.
13. m'en a parlé, une fois
14. Quelle misère !
15. de temps en temps
16. je ne suis pas d'ici
17. agressé
18. dingue de
19. C'est comme ça que j'ai atterri ici.
20. que le client se détende un peu
21. au moment du passage du bleu [poisson très prisé à Cape Cod]
22. andouille
23. Néant.
24. Il ne savait pas de quoi je parlais.

The steak arrived. Gratefully John began to eat. It was delicious. As the taste[1] of the prime meat[2] combined with the warm glow[3] of the drink, he relaxed perceptibly and began to think about The Lookout.

What the bartender had told him had confirmed his decision to make an offer on the place.

He had enjoyed going through the house. The sense of discomfort[4] he'd experienced[5] had begun only on the top floor. That was it.[6] He had been uneasy[7] in the apartment of the tenant, Mr. Parrish.

John finished the steak thoughtfully and rather abstractedly[8] paid his bill, remembering to tip the bartender generously[9]. Turning up[10] his collar, he left the restaurant and headed for his car. Now he should turn right and keep toward the mainland? But for minutes he sat irresolutely[11] in the car. What was the matter with him? He was acting like a fool. What crazy impulse[12] was forcing him[13] to return to The Lookout?

Courtney Parrish had been nervous. John had been too many years in the business of sizing people up[14] not to know nervous tension when he saw it[15]. That man had been worried... desperately anxious for them to leave. Why? There had been a heavy, sour, sweaty smell[16] on him... the smell of fear... but fear of what? And that telescope. Parrish had rushed over to change the direction it was pointing in when John bent over it. John remembered that when he put it back to approximately where it had been, he'd been able to see the police cars around the Eldredge home. Such an incredibly powerful telescope. If it was directed into the windows of homes in the town, anyone looking into it could become a peeping tom[17]... a voyeur.

Was it possible that Courtney Parrish had been looking through the telescope when the children disappeared from behind their home... that he had seen

1. saveur
2. viande de premier choix
3. la chaleur ambrée
4. malaise
5. ressenti
6. C'est ça.
7. Il s'était senti mal à l'aise
8. distraitement
9. donner un pourboire généreux au barman
10. Remontant
11. resta assis, indécis
12. impulsion folle
13. le poussait à
14. avait trop l'habitude de jauger les gens
15. pour ne pas déceler la nervosité des autres
16. odeur de transpiration
17. indiscret

something? But if he had, of course he would have called the police.

The car was cold. John turned the ignition key[1] and waited for the engine to warm up[2] before switching on the heater[3]. He reached for a cigar and lighted it with the small gold Dunhill lighter[4] that had been his wife's anniversary present to him: an extravagant, deeply cherished[5] gift. He puffed at the cigar until the tip[6] began to glow[7].

He was a fool. A suspicious[8] fool. What did one do?[9] Phone the police and say that a man seemed nervous and they should look into it[10]? And if they did, Courtney Parrish would probably say, "I was about to take my bath and disliked[11] having such short notice[12] of the house being shown." Perfectly reasonable[13]. People who lived alone tended to[14] become precise in their habits[15].

Alone. That was the word. That was what was nagging[16] John. He had been surprised not to see someone else in the apartment. Something had made him sure that Courtney Parrish was not alone.

It was the child's toy in the tub. That was it. That incredible rubber duck. And the cloying scent[17] of baby powder...

A suspicion so absurd that it would be impossible to vocalize[18] took shape in John Kragopoulos' mind.

He knew what he had to do. Deliberately he took his gold lighter from his pocket and hid it in the glove compartment[19] of his car.

He would drive back to The Lookout unannounced[20]. When Courtney Parrish answered the door, he would ask permission to look for his valuable[21] lighter, which he must have dropped somewhere in the house during his inspection. It was a plausible request[22]. It would give him a chance to look around carefully and either allay[23] what was probably a ridiculous suspicion or have something more than suspicion to discuss with the police.

1. clé de contact
2. laissa tourner le moteur
3. d'enclencher le chauffage
4. briquet
5. très précieux à ses yeux
6. bout
7. devienne incandescent
8. soupçonneux
9. Que faire ?
10. aller vérifier
11. je n'ai pas apprécié
12. d'être prévenu si peu de temps à l'avance
13. normal
14. avaient tendance à
15. tenir à leurs habitudes
16. tracassait
17. cette odeur écœurante
18. inexprimable
19. boîte à gants
20. sans prévenir
21. précieux
22. demande
23. dissiper

1. Sa décision prise
2. appuya
3. Des images d'un canard en caoutchouc décoloré, râpé
4. lui traversaient l'esprit
5. mitraille de grésil

Having made up his mind[1], John stepped[2] on the accelerator and swung the car left on Route 6A, back toward the center of Adams Port and the curving, hilly road that led to The Lookout. Visions of a faded, peeling rubber duck[3] bobbed in his head[4] as he drove through the steadily pelting sleet[5].

21

She didn't want to remember... there was only pain in going back. Once when she was very little, Nancy had reached up and pulled the handle of a pot[1] on the stove. She could still remember how great torrents of bright red tomato soup had gushed over on her[2]. She'd been in the hospital for weeks and still had faint scars[3] on her chest.

... Carl had asked her about those scars... stroked them[4]... "Poor little girl, poor little girl...." He liked her to tell him about the incident[5] over and over[6]. "Did it hurt very much?" he would ask.

Remembering was like that[7].... Pain... only pain.... Don't remember... forget... forget.... Don't want to remember....

But the questions, persistent[8], far away[9]... asking about Carl... about Mother... Lisa... Peter... Her voice. She was talking. Answering.

"*No*, please, I don't want to talk about it."

"But you must. You must help us." That persistent voice. Why? Why?

"Why were you afraid of Carl, Nancy?"

She had to answer, if only to[10] stop the questions.

1. poignée d'une casserole
2. s'étaient déversés sur elle
3. de légères cicatrices
4. les avait effleurées
5. lui faire raconter l'accident
6. encore et encore
7. Il en était de même du souvenir
8. insistantes
9. lointaines
10. ne serait-ce que pour

She heard her voice, far away, trying to answer.... It was like watching herself in a play[1].... Scenes were taking shape[2].

Mother... the dinner... the last time she saw Mother... Mother's face so troubled[3], looking at her, at Carl. "Where did you get that dress, Nancy?" She could tell[4] Mother didn't like it.

The white wool dress. "Carl helped me pick it out[5]. Do you like it?"

"Isn't it a bit... young?[6]"

Mother left to make a call. Was it to Dr. Miles? Nancy hoped so. She wanted Mother to be happy.... Maybe she should go home with Mother.... Maybe she would stop feeling so tired.[7] Did she say that to Carl?

Carl left the table. "Excuse me, dear."... Mother back[8] before him...

"Nancy, you and I must talk tomorrow... when we're alone. I'll pick you up[9] for breakfast."

Carl came back....

And Mother... kissing her cheek... "Good night, darling. I'll see you at eight." Mother getting in the rented car, waving goodbye[10], driving down the road...

Carl drove her back to school. "I'm afraid your mother doesn't approve of me yet[11], dear."

The call... "There's been an accident... Steering mechanism[12]..."

Carl... "I'll take care of you, my little girl...."

The funeral[13]...

The wedding. A bride[14] should wear white[15]. She'd wear the white wool dress. It would do[16] for just going to the Mayor's office[17].

But she couldn't wear it... grease stain[18] at the shoulder.... "Carl, where could I have gotten grease on this dress? I only wore it to have dinner with Mother."

"I'll have it cleaned[19] for you." His hand, familiar, patting[20] her shoulder...

"No... no... no...."

The voice. "What do you mean, Nancy?"

1. Il lui semblait se voir jouer dans une pièce
2. Des scènes prenaient forme
3. inquiète
4. voyait bien que
5. à la choisir
6. Ça ne fait pas un peu trop petite fille ?
7. Peut-être cette impression de fatigue cesserait-elle alors.
8. de retour
9. Je viendrai te chercher
10. faisant au revoir de la main
11. n'a pas encore une très bonne opinion de moi
12. La direction [de la voiture]
13. L'enterrement
14. Une mariée
15. être en blanc
16. Cela ferait l'affaire
17. à la mairie
18. tache de graisse
19. Je la ferai nettoyer
20. tapotant

"I don't know.... I'm not sure.... I'm afraid...."

"Afraid of Carl?"

"No... he is good to me.... I'm so tired... always so tired.... Drink your medicine[1].... You need it.... The children... Peter and Lisa... all right for a while.... Carl was good.... Please, Carl, close the door.... Please, Carl, I don't like that.... Don't touch me like that.... Leave me alone.[2]"

"How should he leave you alone, Nancy?"

"*No*... I don't want to talk about it...."

"Was Carl good to the children?"

"He made them obey.... He wanted them to be good[3].... He made Peter afraid[4]... and Lisa.... 'So my little girl has a little girl'..."

"Is that what Carl said?"

"Yes. He doesn't touch me anymore.... I'm glad[5].... But I mustn't have medicine after dinner... I get too tired.... There's something wrong.... I must get away.... The children... Get away..."

"From Carl?"

"I'm not sick.... Carl is sick[6]...."

"How is he sick, Nancy?"

"I don't know...."

"Nancy, tell us about the day Lisa and Peter disappeared. What do you remember about that?"

"Carl is angry."

"Why is he angry?"

"The medicine... last night.... He saw me pour it out[7]... got more[8]... made me drink it.... So tired... so sleepy[9].... Lisa is crying... Carl... with her.... I must get up... must go to her.... Crying so hard.... Carl spanked her[10]... said she wet the bed[11].... I have to take her away[12]... in morning.... My birthday... I'll tell Carl...."

"Tell him what?"

"He knows... he's beginning to know...."

"Know what, Nancy?"

"I'm going away... take the children.... Have to go away...."

1. Bois ton médicament
2. Laisse-moi tranquille.
3. qu'ils soient sages
4. Il faisait peur à Peter
5. contente
6. un malade
7. jeter le médicament
8. m'en a redonné
9. tellement sommeil
10. lui a donné une fessée
11. avait fait pipi au lit
12. Il faut que je l'emmène loin d'ici

"Didn't you love Carl, Nancy?"

"I should. He said, 'Happy birthday.'… Lisa so quiet[1]. I promised her we'd make a birthday cake for me... She and Peter and I.... We'd go out and get candles and chocolate for it. It's a bad day[2]... starting to rain.... Lisa may be getting sick[3]...."

"Did Carl go to school[4] that day?"

"Yes.... He phoned.... I said we were going to shopping center... that after that I was going to stop at the doctor's to let him see[5] Lisa.... I was worried. I said I'd go to the Mart[6] at eleven... after the children's television program...."

"What did Carl say when you told him you were worried about Lisa?"

"He said it was a bad day... if Lisa was getting a cold, he didn't want her out[7]. I said I'd leave them in the car while I shopped.... They wanted to help with the cake.... They were excited about my birthday. They never had fun[8].... I shouldn't have let Carl be so strict... my fault.... I'll talk to doctor... have to ask doctor... about Lisa... about me.... Why am I always so tired?... Why do I take so much medicine?... Rob made children laugh.... They were so different around him[9].... Children should laugh...."

"Were you in love with Rob, Nancy?"

"No.... I was in cage[10]... had to get out... wanted to talk to someone.... Then Rob said what I said to him.... Wasn't like that... wasn't like that.... Her voice began to rise.

Lendon's voice became soothing. "Then you took the children to the store at eleven."

"Yes. It's raining.... I told children to stay in car.... They said they would.... Such good little children... I left them in back seat of car[11].... Never saw them again... never... never..."

"Nancy, were there many cars in the lot[12]?"

"No.... No one I knew in store.... So windy... cold... not many people...."

1. Lisa qui ne dit rien
2. Il ne fait pas beau
3. Peut-être Lisa couve-t-elle quelque chose
4. Carl a-t-il donné ses cours
5. pour qu'il examine
6. au centre commercial
7. si Lisa était enrhumée, il ne voulait pas qu'elle sorte
8. Ils ne s'amusaient jamais
9. avec lui
10. prisonnière
11. sur la banquette arrière
12. parking

"How long were you in the store?"

"Not long... ten minutes.... Couldn't find birthday candles.... Ten minutes.... Hurry back to car[1].... The children gone." Her voice was incredulous.

"What did you do, Nancy?"

"Don't know what to do.... Maybe they went to buy present for me[2].... Peter has money.... They wouldn't leave except for that[3].... They're so good.... That might make them leave[4].... Maybe in other store... the dime store[5].... Look in candy store[6]... look in gift shop[7]... hardware store[8]... look back at car.... Look, look for children...."

"Did you ask anyone if they'd been seen?"

"*No*.... Mustn't let Carl know.[9] He'll be angry.... Don't want him to punish children...."

"So you checked[10] all the stores in the shopping center."

"Maybe they came looking for me[11]... got lost.... Look in parking lot.... Maybe they couldn't find car again[12].... Begin calling them.... Frightened.... Someone said we'll call police and your husband.... I said, 'Don't tell my husband, please.'... Woman told about that at trial[13].... I just didn't want Carl to be angry...."

"Why didn't you tell this at your trial?"

"Mustn't.... Lawyer said, Don't say Carl was angry.... Don't say you argued on phone[14].... Lisa didn't wet the bed... bed dry...."

"What do you mean?"

"Bed dry.... Why did Carl hurt her? Why? Doesn't matter[15].... Nothing matters.... Children gone.... Michael... Missy gone too.... Look for them... have to look for them...."

"Tell us about looking for Michael and Missy, this morning."

"I must look at the lake[16].... Maybe they went to the lake.... Maybe they fell into the water.... Hurry, hurry.... Something is in the lake.... Something is underwater[17]...."

1. Revenir vite à la voiture
2. m'acheter un cadeau
3. Il n'y a que ça qui les aurait fait sortir
4. C'est peut-être ça qui les a fait sortir
5. supérette
6. Aller voir à la confiserie
7. magasin de cadeaux
8. quincaillerie
9. Il ne faut pas que Carl le sache.
10. Et donc vous avez cherché dans
11. venus me chercher
12. n'ont pas retrouvé la voiture
13. Une femme l'a dit au procès
14. que vous avez eu une dispute au téléphone
15. Pas d'importance
16. Il faut que j'aille voir vers le lac
17. Il y a quelque chose dans l'eau

1. l'attraper
2. bondit, fébrile
3. leva la main pour le retenir
4. elle battit des paupières et rouvrit les yeux
5. pâlit
6. liées
7. L'effet du Penthotal s'atténue.
8. va revenir à elle
9. se releva en grimaçant,
10. les genoux et les cuisses endoloris
11. sur la réserve
12. recommanda
13. d'un instant à l'autre
14. ça doit durer encore combien de temps
15. continuer d'interroger Nancy
16. Qu'avons-nous appris,
17. à part
18. le regarda, sidéré
19. Mais bon Dieu
20. Vous n'avez pas compris ce que vous venez d'entendre ?
21. un seul élément m'ôtant la

"What was underwater, Nancy?"

"Red, something red.... Maybe it's Missy's mitten... I must get it.... Water is so cold.... I can't reach it[1].... It's not a mitten.... It's cold, cold...."

"What did you do?"

"Children aren't here.... Get out... get out of water.... So cold... the beach... I fell on the beach.... He was there... in the woods... watching me.... I saw him there... watching me...."

Jed Coffin stood up. Ray jumped forward convulsively[2]. Lendon held up a warning hand[3]. "Who was there, Nancy?" he asked. "Tell us who was there."

"A man... I know him.... It was... it was... Rob Legler.... Rob Legler was there.... He was hiding... looking at me." Her voice rose, fell; her eyelids fluttered open[4], then closed again slowly. Ray paled[5]. Dorothy inhaled sharply. So the two cases were linked[6].

"The amytal's about worn off.[7] She'll be coming to[8] soon." Lendon stood up, grimacing[9] against the cramped sensation in his knees and thighs[10].

"Doctor, may I speak with you and Jonathan outside?" Jed's voice was noncommittal[11].

"Stay with her, Ray," Lendon cautioned[12]. "She'll probably wake up any minute[13]."

In the dining room, Jed faced Lendon and Jonathan. "Doctor, how long is this to go on[14]?" Jed's face was impenetrable.

"I don't think we should attempt to question Nancy any further[15]."

"What have we gotten from all this[16] other than[17] the fact that she was afraid of her husband; that she obviously did not love him and that Rob Legler may have been at the lake this morning?"

Lendon stared[18]. "Good God[19], didn't you hear what that girl was saying? Don't you know what you were listening to?[20]"

"I only know that I haven't heard one thing that will help me discharge my[21] responsibility to find the Eldredge children. I heard Nancy Eldredge blaming herself for[1] her mother's death, which is natural in a case where a visit to a child in school results in[2] a parent's death. Her reactions to her first husband sound pretty hysterical. She's trying to blame him for the fact that she wanted out of their marriage[3]."

"What impression did you get of Carl Harmon?" Lendon asked quietly.

"One of those possessive guys who marries a younger girl and wants the upper hand[4]. Hell[5], he isn't any different than half the men on the Cape. I can cite you[6] examples of guys who won't let their wives handle a dime except for food money[7]. I know one who won't let his wife drive the family car. Another never lets his wife go out at night by herself[8]. This kind of thing is common all over the world. Maybe that's why that Women's Lib bunch[9] have something to beef about[10]."

"Chief, do you know what pedophilia is?" Lendon asked quietly.

Jonathan nodded. "That's what I've been thinking," he said.

Lendon didn't give Jed time to answer. "In laymen's terms[11], it's a sexual deviation[12] involving[13] sexual activity of any type[14] with a child who has not yet reached puberty[15]."

"How does that fit in here?[16]"

"It doesn't... not completely[17]. Nancy was eighteen when she married. But in appearance she could look quite childish[18]. Chief, is there any way you can run a check[19] on Carl Harmon's background[20]?"

Jed Coffin looked incredulous. When he answered, his voice was trembling with repressed fury[21]. He pointed to the sleet that was beating a steady, sharp staccato against the window. "Doctor," he said, "do you see and hear that? Somewhere out there two kids are either wandering around freezing or they're in the hands of God knows what kind of kook[22] and may-

1. se sentant responsable de
2. se solde par
3. se séparer de lui
4. veut la dominer
5. Bon sang
6. vous citer
7. ne laissent pas un sou à leur femme à part l'argent des courses
8. toute seule
9. cette bande du MLF
10. a de quoi râler
11. En termes simples
12. perversion
13. impliquant
14. un acte sexuel
15. non pubère
16. Quel est le rapport avec cette affaire ?
17. Il n'y en a pas... pas directement
18. elle pouvait faire très gamine
19. faire des recherches
20. les antécédents
21. de fureur contenue
22. Dieu sait quel dingue

be they're dead. But it's my job to find them and find them now[1]. We have one distinct lead to all this[2]. That is that both Nancy Eldredge and a gasoline attendant[3] have placed[4] Rob Legler, a pretty unsavory character[5], in the immediate vicinity[6]. That's the kind of information I can do something about[7]." His voice bit off[8] the words scornfully[9]. "And you're asking me to waste my time running a check on a dead man to prove some cockeyed[10] theory."

The telephone rang. Bernie Mills, who'd been standing unobtrusively[11] in the room, hurried to answer it. Now they were talking about running a check on Nancy's first husband. Wait till he told this to Jean. He picked up the phone quickly. It was the station house. "Put the Chief on.[12]" Sergeant Poler at the desk spat the words.[13]

Lendon and Jonathan watched while Chief Coffin listened, then asked quick, short questions. "How long ago? Where?"

The men looked at each other silently. Lendon realized he was praying[14]—an inarticulate, fervent prayer[15] that the message was not bad news about the children.

Jed slapped the receiver back into the cradle and turned to them. "Rob Legler checked into the Adams Port Motel right here in town[16] around ten-thirty this morning. A car we believe he stole[17] has just been smashed up on Route 6A, but he got away[18]. He's probably heading for the mainland. We've got an all-out search[19] for him and I'm going over to direct it. I'll leave Officer Mills here. We'll get that Legler bird[20], and when we do, I think we'll really have the answer to what happened to those kids."

After the door had closed behind the Chief, Jonathan spoke to Lendon. "What do you make of this so far[21]?" he asked.

Lendon waited a long minute before answering. *I am too close to this*[22], he thought. *I see Priscilla at that*

1. tout de suite
2. une piste précise dans toute cette affaire
3. pompiste
4. localisé
5. personnage peu reluisant
6. voisinage immédiat
7. que je peux exploiter
8. proférait
9. avec dédain
10. farfelue
11. discrètement
12. Passez-moi le commissaire.
13. Le sergent Poler, de l'accueil, avait braillé dans le téléphone.
14. priait
15. une prière rudimentaire, fervente
16. en ville
17. qu'il a probablement volée
18. a filé
19. Un avis de recherche générale a été émis
20. On va choper ce Lengler
21. Quel est votre avis pour l'instant
22. Je n'ai pas le recul

phone... calling me. Carl Harmon left the table after her. Where did he go? Did he overhear[1] *what Priscilla said to me? Nancy said her dress was smeared with*[2] *grease. Hadn't she been saying in effect*[3] *that she believed Carl's hand must have been smeared and when he put his hand on her shoulder, her dress got dirty? Hadn't she been trying to say that she believed Carl Harmon might have done something to Priscilla's car?* Lendon saw a violent pattern forming[4]. But what purpose would this knowledge serve[5] with Carl Harmon in his grave[6]?

Jonathan said, "If your mind is running in the same direction as mine[7], going back to the disappearance of the Harmon children won't help us. You're thinking of the father."

"Yes," Lendon said.

"And since he is dead, we turn to Rob Legler, the man sent into the home by Carl Harmon and the one witness[8] whose testimony convicted Nancy. How accurate is her statement[9] about this morning under the amytal?"

Lendon shook his head. "I can't be sure. It's been known that[10] even under sedation, some patients can resist and suppress[11]. But I believe that she saw—or believes she saw—Rob Legler at Maushop Lake."

Jonathan said, "And at ten-thirty this morning he checked into a motel *alone*."

Lendon nodded.

Without speaking again, the two men turned and looked out the window in the direction of the lake.

1. surpris
2. tachée
3. Est-ce qu'elle ne cherchait pas à dire
4. se dessiner un scénario macabre
5. quel intérêt de savoir ça
6. maintenant que Carl Harmon était mort
7. Si vous êtes en train de faire le même raisonnement que moi
8. seul témoin
9. Quelle valeur accorder à ce qu'elle a dit
10. On sait que
11. taire des informations

22

The five-o'clock television news gave little coverage to the Mideastern crisis[1], spiraling inflation[2], the automobile workers' threatened strike[3] or the dismal standing[4] of the New England Patriots[5]. Most of the half hour broadcast[6] was devoted to[7] the disappearance of the Eldredge children and old film clips from[8] the sensational Harmon murder case.

The pictures that had appeared in the *Cape Cod Community News* were reproduced. Special attention was focused on[9] the one of Rob Legler leaving the San Francisco courthouse with Professor Carl Harmon after Nancy Harmon's conviction for the willful murder[10] of her children.

The commentator's voice was especially urgent[11] when that picture was shown. "Rob Legler has been positively identified as being in the vicinity of the Eldredge home this morning. If you believe you have seen this man, please call this special number at once: KL five, three eight hundred. The lives[12] of the Eldredge children may be at stake[13]. If you believe you have any information which may lead to[14] the person or persons responsible for the children's disappearance, we urge you[15] to call this number: KL five, three

1. crise au Moyen-Orient
2. l'inflation galopante
3. menace de grève des ouvriers de l'automobile
4. classement lamentable
5. [équipe de football américain]
6. journal
7. consacré à
8. à des images d'archives de
9. était donnée à
10. homicide volontaire
11. se fit particulièrement insistante
12. La vie
13. est peut-être en jeu
14. mettre sur la piste de
15. nous vous engageons instamment

eight hundred. Let me repeat it again: KL five, three eight hundred."

The Wigginses had closed their store when the power failed[1] and were home in time to catch the broadcast on their battery-operated[2] television set.

"That fellow looks kind of familiar[3]," Mrs. Wiggins said.

"You'd say that anyhow[4]," her husband snorted[5].

"No... not really. There's something about him... the way he bends forward[6]... Certainly is nothing to look at.[7]"

Jack Wiggins stared at his wife. "I was just thinking he's the type that might turn a young girl's head[8]."

"Him? Oh, you mean the young one. I'm talking about the other fellow[9]—the professor."

Jack looked at his wife condescendingly[10]. "This is why I say women don't make good witnesses and never should be jurors. Nobody's talking about that Professor Harmon. He committed suicide. They're talking about the Legler fellow."

Mrs. Wiggins bit her lip[11]. "I see. Well, guess you're right[12]. It's just... oh, well[13]..."

Her husband got up heavily. "When'll dinner be ready?"

"Oh, not long. But it's hard to worry about food when you think about little Michael and Missy... God knows where.... You think you just want to help them.[14] I don't care what they say about Nancy Eldredge. She never came in the store much[15], but when she did, I liked to watch her with her kids. She had such a nice way with them—never upset[16], never cranky[17], the way half these young mothers are[18]. It makes our little annoyances[19] so unimportant[20], you know."

"What little annoyances do we have?" His tone was sharply suspicious.

"Well..." Mrs. Wiggins bit her lip. They'd had so much trouble with shoplifters[21] this past summer. Jack got so upset even discussing it.[22] That was why,

1. lors de la coupure de courant
2. à piles
3. Ce type me dit quelque chose
4. Tu dis ça à chaque fois
5. grogna
6. sa façon de se pencher
7. Pas très séduisant.
8. qui pourrait tourner la tête à une jeune fille
9. l'autre
10. avec condescendance
11. se mordit la lèvre
12. je suppose que tu as raison
13. bon, enfin
14. On se demande comment on pourrait les aider.
15. ne venait pas souvent au magasin
16. fâchée
17. grincheuse
18. comme le sont la moitié des jeunes mères
19. tracas
20. insignifiants
21. voleurs à l'étalage
22. Rien que d'en parler, ça énervait Jack.

all day[1], it just hadn't seemed worthwhile to tell him[2] that she was absolutely certain that Mr. Parrish had stolen a large can of baby powder from the shelf this morning.

1. depuis ce matin
2. elle avait préféré ne pas lui dire

23

The five o'clock news was on in a modest home down the block from[1] St. Francis Xavier Church in Hyannis Port. The family of Patrick Keeney was about to start dinner[2]. All eyes were glued on[3] the small portable set[4] in the crowded[5] junior-size[6] dining room.

Ellen Keeney shook her head as the picture of Michael and Missy Eldredge filled the screen. Involuntarily, she glanced at her own children—Neil and Jimmy, Deirdre and Kit... one... two... three... four. Whenever she took them to the beach, that was the way it was[7]. She never stopped counting[8] heads. *God, don't let anything happen to them, ever*[9], *please.* That was her prayer.

Ellen was a daily communicant[10] at St. Francis Church and usually went to the same Mass as Mrs. Rose Kennedy. She remembered the days after the President[11] and then Bobby were killed when Mrs. Kennedy would come into the church, her face lined with[12] grief but still serene[13] and composed[14]. Ellen never watched her during Mass. Poor lady, she had a right to some privacy somewhere[15]. Often Mrs. Kennedy would smile and nod and sometimes say, "Good morning" if they happened to[16] walk out after Mass

1. à une rue de
2. allait passer à table
3. rivés sur
4. poste portatif
5. encombrée
6. petite
7. c'est ce qu'elle faisait
8. passait son temps à compter
9. faites que rien ne leur arrive jamais
10. allait à la messe tous les jours
11. [JFK]
12. marqué par
13. serein
14. posé
15. il fallait bien que l'on respecte sa vie privée quelque part
16. s'il leur arrivait de

at the same moment. *How does she stand it*[1]*?* Ellen wondered. *How can she stand it?* Now she was thinking the same thing. *How can Nancy Eldredge stand it?... especially when you think that it happened to her before.*

The commentator was talking about the article in the *Community News*—that the police were trying to track down[2] the author. His words barely registered on[3] Ellen's mind as she decided that Nancy was not responsible for the death of her children. It simply wasn't possible. No mother murdered her flesh and blood[4]. She saw Pat looking at her and smiled at him faintly—a communication that said, *We are blessed*[5]*, my dear; we are blessed.*

"He got awful fat[6]," Neil said.

Startled,[7] Ellen stared at her oldest child. At seven, Neil worried her. He was so daring[8], so unpredictable[9]. He had Pat's dark-blond hair and gray eyes. He was small for his age, and she knew that worried him a little, but from time to time, she reassured him. "Daddy's tall and your Uncle John's tall, and someday you will be too." Still[10], Neil did look younger than anyone else in his class[11].

"Who got fat, dear?" she asked absently[12], turning her back to gaze at the screen[13].

"That man, the one in front. He's the one who gave me the dollar to ask for his mail[14] at the post office last month. Remember, I showed you the note he wrote[15] when you wouldn't believe me."

Ellen and Pat stared at the screen. They were looking at the picture of Rob Legler following Professor Carl Harmon out of the courtroom.

"Neil, you're mistaken[16]. That man has been dead for a long time."

Neil looked aggrieved[17]. "See.[18] You never believe me. But when you kept asking me[19] where I got[20] that dollar and I told you, you didn't believe me either. He's a lot fatter[21] and his hair's all gone, but when

1. tient-elle le coup
2. retrouver
3. s'inscrivaient à peine
4. la chair de sa chair
5. avons beaucoup de chance
6. Il a drôlement grossi
7. Surprise,
8. audacieux
9. imprévisible
10. Mais tout de même
11. faisait nettement plus jeune que tous ceux de sa classe
12. distraitement
13. pour regarder la télé
14. pour que j'aille relever son courrier
15. Tu te souviens, je t'avais montré le papier qu'il a écrit
16. te trompes
17. prit un air vexé
18. Tu vois !
19. t'arrêtais pas de me demander
20. comment j'avais eu
21. beaucoup plus gros

he leaned out of[1] the station wagon, he had his head kind of pulled down[2] on his neck like that man."

The anchorman[3] was saying, "... any piece of information, no matter how irrelevant you may consider it[4]."

Pat scowled[5].

"Why do you look mad[6], Daddy?" five-year-old Deirdre asked anxiously.

His face cleared[7]. Neil had said, "like that man." "I guess because sometimes I realize how hard it is to raise a bunch like you[8]," he answered, running his hand through her short curly hair, grateful that she was here within his touch. "Turn off the television, Neil," he ordered his son. "Now, children, before we say grace[9], we will pray that God sends the Eldredge children safely[10] home."

Through[11] the prayer that followed, Ellen's mind was far away. They had pleaded for any information[12], no matter how irrelevant it seemed, and Neil had gotten that dollar tip[13] to pick up[14] a letter at General Delivery[15]. She remembered the day exactly: Wednesday, four weeks ago. She remembered the date because there was a parents' meeting at school that night and she was annoyed[16] that Neil was late for the early dinner. Suddenly she remembered something.

"Neil, by any chance, do you still have[17] the note the man gave you to show the post office?" she asked. "Didn't I see you put it in your bank[18] with the dollar?"

"Yes, I saved it[19]."

"Will you get it[20], please?" she asked him. "I want to see the name on it."

Pat was studying her. When Neil left, he spoke over the heads of the other children. "Don't tell me you put any stock[21]..."

She suddenly felt ridiculous. "Oh, eat up[22], dear. I guess I just have a case of nerves[23]. It's people like me who are always wasting policemen's time[24]. Kit, pass me your plate. I'll cut up the end piece[25] of the meat loaf[26] just the way you like it."

1. il s'est penché à la vitre du
2. on aurait dit qu'il avait la tête enfoncée
3. présentateur
4. même si elle vous paraît sans aucun rapport
5. se renfrogna
6. en colère
7. s'éclaircit
8. d'élever une brochette comme vous
9. de dire les grâces
10. sains et saufs
11. Pendant
12. insisté pour que toute information leur soit transmise
13. reçu ce dollar en récompense
14. pour aller chercher
15. poste restante
16. mécontente
17. est-ce que par hasard tu aurais toujours
18. tirelire
19. je l'ai gardé
20. Peux-tu aller me le chercher
21. que tu accordes le moindre crédit...
22. finis de manger
23. suis un peu à cran
24. font toujours perdre leur temps aux policiers
25. bout
26. pain de viande

24

It was all going so badly. Nothing was working as he'd expected. That foolish woman coming here and then the little girl; having to wait till she woke up, if she woke up, so that he could feel her twisting and pulling from him[1]. Then the boy squirming away from him, hiding[2]. He'd have to find him.

Courtney had a feeling of everything slipping away from him. His sense of pleasure and expectation[3] had changed to disappointment and resentment[4]. He wasn't perspiring anymore, but the heavy sweat still clung to[5] his clothes and made them unpleasantly sticky[6] against his body. The thought of the boy's big blue eyes, so like Nancy's, didn't give him anticipatory[7] pleasure.

The boy was a threat[8]. If he escaped, it would be the end. Better to finish with them both[9]; better to do what he'd done before. In an instant he could remove[10] the threat—seal off air so that lips and nostrils and eyes were covered[11]—and then in a few hours—when the tide was high toss their bodies into the churning surf. No one would know. Then he'd be here safe again with nothing to threaten him; here to enjoy her torment[12].

1. se tortiller pour lui échapper
2. qui lui avait glissé entre les doigts, et se cachait
3. expectative
4. rancune
5. collait à
6. poisseux
7. anticipé
8. menace
9. Mieux valait en finir avec les deux
10. éliminer
11. boucher leurs lèvres, leurs narines et leurs yeux
12. jouir de son tourment

1. la tombée de la nuit
2. prise
3. en avoir fini
4. pénible
5. ingrat
6. fines bandes d'adhésif doux
7. marque
8. l'appliquerait
9. sans attendre non plus
10. développait toujours son intuition
11. cette petite route d'accès pour les fournisseurs
12. Personne en vue.
13. Aussitôt,
14. obéissants
15. surpris
16. torsadés bien serré
17. de gigoter
18. Absent moins de 8 minutes en tout
19. plongés dans
20. leurs expériences de labo
21. personne ne l'avait cherché
22. Une salle entière de témoins
23. pour témoigner de
24. si cela était nécessaire
25. jeté

And tomorrow night, with all the threat gone, he'd drive to the mainland. He'd go around dusk[1], and probably some little girl would be walking alone and he'd tell her he was the new teacher.... It always worked.

His decision made[2], he felt better. Now all he wanted was to be finished[3] with this threat. That child, recalcitrant like Nancy... troublesome[4]... ungrateful[5].... wanting to escape... he would find him. He'd tie him and then get the thin sheets of velvety plastic[6]. He'd made sure to have a brand[7] that Nancy could have bought at Lowery's. Then he'd seal it[8] on the boy first, because the boy was so troublesome. And then... the little girl... right away too[9]. It was too dangerous to even keep her.

The sense of danger always heightened his perception[10]. Like last time. He hadn't really known what he would do when he had slipped across the campus to the shopping center. He'd only known that he couldn't let Nancy take Lisa to the doctor. He'd been there before she arrived, parked on that little supply road[11] between the shopping center and the campus. He'd seen her drive in, speak to the children, go into the store. No cars nearby. Not a soul around.[12] In a moment[13] he'd known what to do.

The children had been so obedient[14]. They'd looked startled[15] and frightened when he opened the car door, but when he said, "Now, quickly—we're going to play a game on Mommy for her birthday," they'd gotten into the trunk and in an instant it was over. The plastic bags slipped over their heads, twisted tight[16], his hands holding them till they stopped squirming[17]; the trunk shut and he back in school. Less than eight minutes gone in all[18]; the students intent on[19] their lab experiments[20], no one had missed him[21]. A roomful of witnesses[22] to testify to[23] his presence if need be[24]. That night he'd simply driven the car to the beach and dumped[25] the bodies into the ocean.

Opportunity seized[1], danger averted[2] that day seven years ago, and now danger to be averted again[3]. "Michael, come out, Michael. I'll take you home to your mother."

He was still in the kitchen. Holding the hurricane lamp up, he looked around. There was no place to hide here. The cupboards were all high. But finding the boy in this dark, cavernous house with only this lamp to see by[4] would be infinitely difficult. It would take hours, and where should he begin?

"Michael, don't you want to go home to your mother?" he called again. "She didn't go to God[5]... she's all better[6]... she wants to see you."

Should he try the third floor and look in those bedrooms first? he wondered.

But the boy would probably have tried to get to this outside door. He was smart[7]. He wouldn't have stayed upstairs. Would he have gone to the front door? Better to look there.[8]

He started into the little hall[9], then thought of the small back parlor. If the boy had tried the kitchen and heard him coming, that would be the logical place to hide.

He walked to the doorway[10] of the room. Was that breathing he was hearing[11], or only the wind sighing[12] against the house? He walked a few steps farther[13], into the room, holding the kerosene lamp high above his head. His eyes darted, picking objects out of the gloom[14]. He was about to turn around when he swung the lamp to his right.

Staring at what he was seeing, he let out a high-pitched, hysterical whinny[15]. The shadow of a small figure huddled[16] behind the couch was silhouetted[17] like a giant crouched[18] rabbit across the faded oak floor. "I found you, Michael," he cried, still giggling[19], "and this time you won't get away."

1. L'occasion avait été saisie
2. écarté
3. devait à nouveau être écarté
4. s'éclairer
5. n'est pas partie au ciel
6. elle va beaucoup mieux
7. intelligent
8. Il valait mieux chercher par là.
9. vestibule
10. s'avança jusqu'à l'entrée
11. Était-ce un bruit de respiration qu'il entendait
12. se lamentant
13. Il fit quelques pas de plus
14. scrutaient l'obscurité
15. émit un hennissement aigu, hystérique
16. silhouette blottie
17. se découpait
18. accroupi
19. riant toujours nerveusement

25

The power failure[1] **began** as John Kragopoulos turned off Route 6A onto the road that led to The Lookout. Instinctively, he pressed the button under his foot to turn on the bright headlights[2]. Vision was still poor[3], and he drove carefully, feeling the slick road[4] under the tires and the tendency of the car to skid[5] at the turns.

He wondered how he could possibly justify looking through that cavernous house for a small lighter. Mr. Parrish could reasonably[6] suggest that he return in the morning or offer to search for it himself and give it to Dorothy if it was found.

John decided he would go to the door with his flashlight[7]. He'd say that he was quite sure he remembered hearing something drop[8] when he was bending over the telescope. He had meant to check[9] to see if something had slipped out of his pocket. That was reasonable[10]. It was the fourth-floor apartment that he wanted to see anyhow.

The hilly ascent[11] to The Lookout was treacherous. At the last bend[12] in the road, the front end of the car swayed precariously[13]. John gripped the wheel[14] as the tires grabbed and held the road[15]. He had been

1. coupure de courant
2. pour se mettre en pleins phares
3. La visibilité restait mauvaise
4. prenant garde à la route glissante
5. déraper
6. à juste titre
7. lampe torche
8. sûr d'avoir entendu tomber quelque chose
9. voulait vérifier
10. plausible
11. La montée très pentue
12. virage
13. dérapa dangereusement
14. se cramponna au volant
15. les pneus réadhéraient à la chaussée et maintenaient la trajectoire

within inches[1] of veering[2] onto the sloping embankment[3] and would surely have hit the massive oak tree less than six feet away. A few minutes later, he turned the car into the back driveway of The Lookout, rejecting the alternative of[4] pulling into the comparative shelter[5] of the garage as Dorothy had done. He wanted to be casual, open[6]. If anything[7] his manner should be a bit irritated[8] as though he were being inconvenienced too[9]. He would say that since he had discovered his loss[10] at dinner and was still in town, he'd decided to come right back rather than phone.

As he got out of the car, he was struck by the foreboding blackness of[11] the big house. Even the top floor was completely dark. Surely the man had hurricane lamps. Power blackouts[12] on the Cape in bad storms couldn't be unusual[13]. Suppose Parrish had fallen asleep and didn't realize the electricity had failed[14]? Suppose—just suppose—there'd been a woman visiting him who had not wanted to be seen. It was the first time the possibility had occurred to[15] John.

Suddenly feeling foolish[16], he debated about[17] getting back into the car. The sleet stung his face. The wind whipped it under[18] the collar and sleeves of his coat, and the warm satisfaction of the dinner was dispelled[19]. He realized he was chilled and tired and had a long, difficult drive[20] ahead of him. He would look like a fool with his contrived story[21]. Why hadn't he thought about the possibility that Parrish had a visitor who would be embarrassed at being seen? John decided he was a fool, a suspicious idiot. He and Dorothy had probably interrupted a liaison[22] and nothing more. He'd get away from here[23] before he made a further nuisance of himself[24].

He was about to get behind the wheel when he saw a glimmer of light[25] from the far-left kitchen window. It moved swiftly, and a few seconds later he could see it reflected in the windows to the right of the kitchen

1. à deux doigts
2. de virer
3. droit sur le talus
4. écartant la possibilité de
5. se mettre à l'abri relatif
6. avoir l'air dégagé, franc
7. Tout au plus
8. laisserait-il percer un léger agacement
9. comme si lui aussi était contrarié
10. la perte de son briquet
11. comme tout était noir dans
12. Les pannes d'électricité
13. devaient être fréquentes
14. était coupée
15. venait à l'esprit de
16. ridicule
17. hésita à
18. en glissait sous
19. dissipant la chaleur et la satisfaction de son repas
20. trajet
21. histoire tirée par les cheveux
22. troublé une rencontre galante
23. Le mieux était de s'en aller
24. avant de se montrer encore plus importun
25. lueur

door. Someone was walking around the kitchen with a lamp.

Carefully John closed the car door so that it made no slamming sound[1], only a soft click. Gripping the flashlight, he edged across[2] the driveway to the kitchen window and peered in[3]. The light seemed to be coming from the hall now. Mentally, he reviewed the layout of the house.[4] The back staircase was reached through that hall, and so was the small parlor on the other side. Sheltering against[5] the weathered shingles[6], he moved quickly along the back of the house, past the kitchen door, to the windows that should be[7] those of the small parlor. The glow from the lamp was muted[8], but as he watched it grew stronger. He shrank back as the lamp became visible, held by an outstretched arm. He could see Courtney Parrish now. The man was searching for something... for what? He was calling to someone. John strained to hear[9]. The wind smothered sound, but he could make out[10] the name "Michael." Parrish was calling, "Michael!"

John felt chilling fear race along his spinal column[11]. He had been right. The man was a maniac[12], and those children were somewhere in the house. The lamp he was arching in circles[13] was a spotlight[14] that illuminated the solid thickness of Parrish's bulk[15]. John felt totally inadequate[16], aware that he was no physical match for[17] this man. He had only the flashlight as a weapon. Should he go for help? Was it possible Michael had gotten away from Parrish? But if Parrish found him, even a few minutes might make a difference.

Then, before his horrified eyes, John saw Parrish swing the lamp over to the right and reach behind the couch to pull out a small figure who tried desperately to escape. Parrish put down the lamp and, as John watched, closed both hands around[18] the child's throat.

1. sans la faire claquer
2. se glissa le long de
3. regarda à l'intérieur
4. Il essaya de se rappeler la disposition des lieux.
5. S'abritant contre
6. bardeaux patinés
7. qui devaient être
8. voilée
9. tendit l'oreille
10. discerna
11. un effroi glacé le parcourir
12. déséquilibré
13. brandissait en cercles
14. projecteur
15. masse épaisse, corpulente de Parrish
16. se sentit totalement impuissant
17. ne faisait pas le poids face à
18. enserra de ses mains

Acting as instinctively as he had when he'd been on combat duty[1] in World War II[2], John pulled his arm back and smashed the window[3] with his flashlight. As Courtney Parrish spun around[4], John reached his hand in[5] and forced the lock open. With superhuman strength, he pushed the window up and vaulted over the sill[6] into the room. He dropped the flashlight as his feet hit the floor, and Parrish grabbed for it[7]. Still holding the hurricane lamp in his left hand, Parrish raised the flashlight in his right hand, holding it over his head like a weapon.

There was no way to escape the inevitable blow[8]. But John ducked[9] and weaved back against the wall[10] for time[11]. Shouting, "Run away, Michael.... Call help[12]," he managed to kick the kerosene lamp from Parrish's hand an instant before the flashlight crashed down on his skull[13].

1. en service commandé
2. pendant la Seconde Guerre mondiale
3. fit voler la fenêtre en éclats
4. pivotait
5. introduisit sa main
6. entra d'un bond [en franchissant le rebord]
7. s'en saisit
8. coup
9. esquiva
10. recula vers le mur
11. pour gagner du temps
12. Va chercher de l'aide
13. ne s'abatte sur son crâne

26

It had been a mistake to ditch[1] the car. It had been an act of sheer, stupid panic[2]. Rob believed in making your own luck[3]. Today he had made every blunder in the book[4]. When he saw Nancy at the lake, he should have gotten the hell off Cape Cod[5]. Instead, he'd figured that she might be on a trip[6] or stoned[7] and all he had to do was lie low[8] for a day and then go see her and her husband and get some money. Now he'd made a point of placing himself in the vicinity[9], and her kids were missing.

Rob had never really believed that Nancy had anything to do with the other kids' disappearance; but now, who could know? Maybe she did go haywire[10], just as Harmon used to tell him.

When he left the car, Rob had headed south toward the main expressway that ran through the center of[11] the Cape. But when a police car whipped past him[12], he'd doubled back[13]. Even if he could hitch a ride[14], the odds were they'd have[15] a roadblock[16] at the bridge. It would be better to head toward the bay. There had to be plenty of closed-up summer cottages[17] there. He'd break into[18] one of them and hole up[19] for a while. Most of them probably had some

1. abandonner
2. geste d'affolement stupide
3. qu'on avait les chances qu'on se donnait
4. toutes les gaffes possibles
5. aurait dû se tirer de Cape Cod, et vite
6. défoncée
7. bourrée
8. se planquer
9. il avait fallu qu'il aille se fourrer dans les parages
10. avait complètement débloqué
11. traversait
12. était passée devant lui à toute allure
13. avait vite fait demi-tour
14. faire du stop
15. il y aurait certainement
16. barrage
17. résidences secondaires fermées
18. s'introduirait
19. se planquerait

1. provisions
2. les choses se seraient calmées
3. camion
4. temps de merde
5. rencontrer
6. non plus
7. eut à peine le temps
8. haies
9. l'ait dépassé dans un crissement de pneus
10. Nom de Dieu !
11. voiture de flic
12. Il y en avait partout.
13. bouquets d'arbres
14. repéré
15. passer par les arrière-cours
16. Il nierait
17. des plaques d'immatriculation
18. L'inverse.
19. Ah, oui, bien sûr

staples[1] left in the kitchen, and he was getting hungry. Then in a couple of days, when the heat was off[2], he'd find a truck[3], hide in the back and get off this damned island.

He shivered as he hurried down the narrow, darkened roads. One good thing: in this shit weather[4], there wasn't any danger of running into[5] people out walking. Hardly any cars on the road, either[6].

But when he rounded a bend in the road, Rob barely had time[7] to jump back into thick hedges[8] to escape being revealed by the headlights of an approaching car. Breathing harshly, he waited till the automobile had screeched past him[9]. Christ.[10] Another cop car[11]. The place was swarming with them.[12] He'd have to get off the road. It couldn't be more than a couple of blocks to the beach now. Moving swiftly along the row of hedges, Rob headed toward the clump of woods[13] that edged the back of the houses near him. Less chance of being spotted[14] there, even if it took longer to wind through backyards[15].

Suppose Nancy had seen him at the lake? She did look in his direction... but maybe not. He'd deny[16] he was there, of course. She was in no state to be a witness about seeing him. Nobody else had. He was sure of that. Except... the driver of that station wagon. Probably a local guy... Massachusetts plates[17]... 8X642.... How did he remember that? The reverse.[18]... oh, sure[19]... 2-4-6-8. He'd noticed that. If Rob did get caught, he could tell the cops about that station wagon. He'd seen it backing out of the dirt road leading from the Eldredge property, and that must have been just around the time the kids disappeared.

But on the other hand, suppose that station wagon was a regular delivery car that they already knew about? Rob hadn't seen the driver at all; hadn't paid attention, really... just noticed he was a big, fat guy. If he did get caught and told about the station wagon, he'd only nail himself[1] as having been Johnny-on-the-spot[2] at the Eldredge house.

No, he wouldn't admit anything if they got him. He'd say he had been planning to visit Nancy. Then he had seen his picture in that story about the Harmon case and decided to get away. The decision made, Rob felt better. Now if he could just get to the beach and into a cottage...

He hurried, careful to stay well in the shadows[3] of the stark[4] trees; stumbled[5]; swore softly and recovered his balance[6]. This sleet was making the whole damn place as slippery as a skating rink[7]. But he couldn't have much farther to go. He had to get indoors somewhere, or[8] someone would be sure to spot him. Steadying himself against the[9] ice-crusted[10] trees, he tried to move faster.

1. il ne ferait que s'incriminer lui-même,
2. en prouvant qu'il était sur place
3. en veillant à bien rester sous la protection
4. dépouillés
5. trébucha
6. retrouva son équilibre
7. patinoire
8. car sinon
9. Se retenant aux
10. couverts de givre

27

Thurston Givens sat quietly in his glassed-in back porch[1], watching the storm in the near dark. An octogenarian, he'd always found nor'easters[2] fascinating and knew that he wouldn't be likely to see them for too many more years[3]. The radio was on very low, and he'd just heard the latest bulletin about the Eldredge children. There was still no trace of them.

Now Thurston sat staring out toward the back, wondering why young people had to know so much misery[4]. His only child had died at five from flu[5] during the epidemic of 1917.

A retired realtor[6], Thurston knew Ray Eldredge well. He'd been a friend of Ray's father and grandfather, too. Ray was a fine fellow, the kind of man the Cape needed. He was a go-getter[7] and a good realtor—not the kind[8] out to turn a fast buck[9] and the public be damned[10]. Damn shame[11] if anything happened to those little children of his. Nancy certainly didn't strike Thurston as the type[12] to get mixed up with murdering anyone[13]. There had to be a better answer than that.[14]

He was drifting into a kind of reverie[15] when some movement in the woods caught his attention. He

1. véranda vitrée à l'arrière de sa maison
2. vents de nord-est
3. encore très longtemps
4. des souffrances pareilles
5. grippe
6. Agent immobilier à la retraite
7. C'était un battant
8. pas du genre à
9. à se faire de l'argent facile
10. tant pis pour les gens
11. Quelle horreur
12. Pour Thurston, Nancy n'était vraiment pas du genre
13. à être impliquée dans un meurtre
14. Il y avait forcément une autre explication.
15. Il était perdu dans ses rêveries

1. scruta l'horizon
2. Il fallait mijoter quelque chose pour être
3. par ce temps
4. cambriolages

leaned forward and peered[1] through narrowed eyes. There was someone out there, sliding along, obviously trying to stay hidden. Nobody up to any good was[2] in those woods in this kind of weather[3], and there'd been a lot of robberies[4] on the Cape, and particularly in this area.

Thurston reached for the phone. He dialed Police Headquarters. Chief Coffin was an old friend, but, of course, the Chief probably wasn't there. He must be out on the Eldredge case.

5. d'un ton brusque
6. Je voudrais signaler
7. un rôdeur
8. chez moi

The phone was answered at the other end, and a voice said, "Adams Port Police Headquarters. Sergeant Poler—"

Thurston interrupted impatiently. "Thurston Givens here," he said crisply[5]. "I want you fellows to know[6] there's a prowler[7] in the woods behind my place[8] and he's heading towards the bay."

28

Nancy sat upright on the couch, staring straight ahead. Ray had lighted the fire, and the flames were beginning to lick at[1] the thick twigs[2] and broken pieces of branches. Yesterday. It was just yesterday, wasn't it? She and Michael had been raking[3] the front lawn[4].

"This is the last time we'll have this job this winter, Mike," she'd said. "I guess just about all the leaves are down[5] now."

He'd nodded soberly.[6] Then, without her telling him[7], he'd picked out the biggest chunks of branch[8] and thick twigs from the pile of leaves. "These are good for fires," he commented. He'd dropped the iron rake[9], and it had fallen with the metal prongs facing upward[10]. But when Missy came running from the driveway, he'd quickly turned over[11] the rake. With an apologetic half-smile[12] he'd said, "Daddy always says it's dangerous to leave a rake like that."

He was so protective of[13] Missy. He was so good. He was so like Ray. Nancy realized that in some incredible way there was comfort in knowing[14] that Mike was with Missy. If there was any way to do it, he'd take care of her. He was such a resourceful[15] little kid. If they were outside somewhere now, he'd make

1. lécher
2. brindilles
3. avaient ratissé
4. pelouse
5. La plupart des feuilles ont dû tomber
6. Il avait hoché la tête avec gravité.
7. sans qu'elle ait eu besoin de le lui demander
8. branches
9. rateau
10. dents métalliques vers le haut
11. retourné
12. petit sourire d'excuse
13. veillait toujours si bien sur
14. il était rassurant de savoir
15. débrouillard

1. bien fermée

2. à voix haute

3. surpris

4. accusait une telle fatigue

5. sans rien donner en contrepartie

6. à distance

7. lui faisant comprendre clairement qu'elle

8. ne devait pas empiéter sur

9. de remplacement

10. à quel point c'était un besoin pour elle

11. impuissants

12. désarmés

13. minuscule lueur d'espoir

14. réfléchit

15. franchise

16. interdisait les faux-fuyants

17. description

18. a été vu, c'est sûr,

sure that her jacket was zipped up[1]. He'd try to cover her. He'd...

"Oh, God."

She didn't know she'd spoken aloud[2] until Ray looked up startled[3]. He was sitting in his big chair. His face looked so strained[4]. He seemed to know that she didn't want him to touch her now—that she needed to assimilate and evaluate. She must not believe that the children were dead. They could not be dead. But they must be found before anything happened.

Dorothy was watching her too. Dorothy, who suddenly looked so much older and so lost. She had taken Dorothy's affection and love without giving in return[5]. She had held Dorothy at arm's length[6], made it clear that Dorothy[7] was not to intrude on[8] their closed family circle. She didn't want the children to have a grandmother substitute[9]. She didn't want anyone to replace Mother.

I have been selfish, Nancy thought. *I have not seen her need*[10]. How odd that it was so clear now. How odd to even think about that now when they were sitting here, so helpless[11], so powerless[12]. Then why was something reassuring her? Why was she feeling some tiny lick of hope[13]? What was the source of her comfort?

"Rob Legler," she said. "I told you that I saw Rob Legler at the lake this morning."

"Yes," Ray said.

"Is it possible I was dreaming? Does the doctor believe that I saw him—that I was telling the truth?"

Ray considered[14], then decided to be honest. There was a strength in Nancy, a directness[15] that wouldn't tolerate evasion[16].

"I believe that the doctor feels that you gave an exact account[17] of what happened. And Nancy, you should know, Rob Legler has definitely been seen[18] near here both last night and this morning."

"Rob Legler would not hurt the children." Nancy's voice was matter-of-fact[1], flatly positive[2]. That was her area of comfort[3]. "If he took them, if he was responsible, he wouldn't hurt them. I know it."

Lendon came back into the room, Jonathan close behind him[4]. Jonathan realized that he inadvertently[5] looked for Dorothy first. Her hands were dug into[6] her pockets. He suspected they were gripped into fists.[7] She had always struck him as a remarkably efficient, self-sufficient[8] person—traits[9] that he admired without finding them necessarily endearing[10] in a woman.

When Jonathan was honest with himself, he realized that an essential part of his relationship with Emily had been his constant awareness[11] of her need for him[12]. She never could unscrew the cap from a jar[13] or find her car keys or balance her checking account[14]. He had basked[15] in his role as the indulgent, able[16], constant fixer, doer, solver[17]. It had taken the past two years to make him begin to realize that he'd never understood the steel shaft of strength[18] at the core of[19] Emily's femininity: the way she'd accepted the doctor's verdict with only a sympathetic glance at him; the way she'd never once admitted to pain[20]. Now, seeing Dorothy with her mute anguish so tangible, he ached somehow to[21] comfort her.

He was diverted[22] by a question from Ray. "What was the phone call?"

"Chief Coffin went out," Jonathan said evasively.

"It's all right. Nancy knows that Rob Legler has been seen near here."

"That's why the Chief left. Legler was chased and left a car he'd stolen two miles down on 6A. But don't worry, he won't get far on foot in this weather."

"How do you feel, Nancy?" Lendon studied her closely[23]. She was more composed than he'd expected[24].

"I'm all right. I talked a lot about Carl, didn't I?"

"Yes."

1. neutre
2. catégorique
3. ce qui était pour elle le point réconfortant
4. sur ses talons
5. sans le vouloir, il
6. enfoncées
7. Et, très certainement, elle serrait les poings.
8. indépendante
9. des traits de caractère
10. séduisants
11. la conscience qu'il avait toujours eue
12. de la dépendance d'Emily à son égard
13. dévisser le couvercle d'un pot
14. tenir son compte bancaire
15. s'était complu
16. compétent
17. toujours capable de réparer, de faire, de résoudre
18. volonté d'acier
19. au cœur de
20. reconnu la douleur
21. brûlait d'envie de
22. Il fut détourné de ses pensées
23. l'examinait attentivement
24. qu'il ne l'aurait imaginé

"There was something I was trying to remember; something important I wanted to tell you."

Lendon kept his voice matter-of-fact. "Several times you said, 'I don't believe... I don't believe....' Do you know why you would say that?"

Nancy shook her head. "No." She got up and walked restlessly to the window. "It's so dark, it would be hard to find anything or anybody now."

Movement was desirable.[1] She wanted to try to clear her head[2] to be able to think. She looked down, realizing for the first time that she was still wearing the fluffy woolen robe. "I'm going to change," she said. "I want to get dressed[3]."

"Do you...?" Dorothy bit her lip. She'd been about to ask if Nancy wanted her to go upstairs with her.

"I'll be all right[4]," Nancy said gently. They were going to find Rob Legler. She was sure of it. When they did[5], she wanted to be dressed. She wanted to go to him wherever they took him[6]. She wanted to say, "Rob, I know you wouldn't hurt the children. Do you want money? What do you need? Tell me where they are and we'll give you anything[7]."

Upstairs in the bedroom, she took off her robe. Mechanically,[8] she walked over to the closet and hung it up[9]. For an instant, she felt lightheaded[10] and leaned her forehead[11] against the coolness[12] of the wall. The bedroom door opened, and she heard Ray cry, "Nancy!" His voice was startled as he hurried over to her, turned her to him and put his arms around her. She felt the scratchy[13] warmth of his sports shirt against her skin and the growing[14] intensity of his grasp[15].

"I'm all right," she said. "Really...."

"Nancy!" He tilted her head up[16]. His mouth closed over hers. As her lips parted[17], she arched her body against his[18].

It had been like this from the beginning. From that first night when he'd come to dinner and afterward they'd walked down to the lake. It had been

1. Elle avait besoin de bouger.
2. clarifier ses idées
3. m'habiller
4. Ça ira
5. Quand ils l'auraient attrapé
6. où qu'ils l'emmènent
7. ce que vous voulez
8. Machinalement,
9. la suspendit
10. ressentit un léger vertige
11. appuya son front
12. fraîcheur
13. rêche
14. croissante
15. étreinte
16. lui releva la tête
17. Au moment où ses lèvres s'écartèrent
18. se cambra contre lui

chilly[1], and she'd shivered. His coat was open, and he'd laughed and pulled her against him, wrapping the coat around[2] so that it covered her too[3]. When he'd kissed her that first time, it had been so inevitable[4]. She'd wanted him so much[5], right from the beginning. Not like Carl.... Poor Carl... she'd only tolerated him[6]; felt guilty about not wanting him, and after Lisa was born, he had never again... not like a husband... Had he sensed[7] her revulsion[8]? She'd always wondered. It was part of her guilt[9].

"I love you." She didn't know she'd said it—words said so often, words she murmured to Ray even in her sleep.

"I love you too. Oh, Nancy. It must have been so bad[10] for you. I thought I understood, but I didn't...."

"Ray, will we get the children back?" Her voice shook[11], and she felt her whole body begin to tremble.

His arms tightened[12]. "I don't know, darling. I don't know. But remember this: No matter what happens, we have each other. Nothing can change that. They've just come by for[13] the Chief. They have Rob Legler at the station house. Dr. Miles went with them, and Jonathan and I are going over too."

"I want to go. Maybe he'll tell me..."

"No. Jonathan has an idea, and I think it could work. We've got to find out. Maybe Rob has an accomplice[14] who has the children. If he sees you, he might refuse to say anything, especially if he was involved[15] last time."

"Ray..." Nancy heard the despair[16] in her voice.

"Darling, hang on[17]. Just a little while longer. Take a hot shower and get dressed. Dorothy will stay with you. She's fixing[18] a sandwich for you now. I'll be back as soon as I can." For an instant he buried[19] his lips in her hair, then was gone.

Mechanically, Nancy walked into the bathroom off the bedroom. She turned on the water in the shower stall[20], then looked into the mirror over the

1. Il faisait froid
2. l'enveloppant de son manteau
3. pour la protéger elle aussi
4. cela avait eu quelque chose d'inéluctable
5. avait tellement envie de lui
6. elle l'avait tout juste supporté
7. perçu
8. dégoût
9. culpabilité
10. dur
11. tremblait
12. Il la serra plus fort
13. Ils viennent de passer prendre
14. complice
15. surtout s'il était impliqué
16. désespoir
17. tiens bon
18. Elle prépare
19. enfouit
20. cabine de douche

1. lavabo
2. voilés
3. tordant ses cheveux en chignon
4. Les jets d'eau chaude lui picotaient le corps
5. et entamaient la tension de ses muscles
6. Avec gratitude
7. Un souvenir lui revint, fulgurant
8. L'insistance de Carl à lui faire prendre des bains
9. se relever
10. il s'était mis à crachoter
11. vacilla
12. tenailler
13. sortit en chancelant de la douche
14. à vomir
15. s'agrippait
16. cuvette des cabinets
17. enrayer
18. la violente succession de spasmes
19. vomissements
20. des frissons glacés
21. la secouaient encore

washbasin[1]. The face she saw looking back at her was pale and drawn, the eyes heavy and clouded[2]. It was the way she had looked all those years with Carl, like the pictures of her in that article.

Quickly she turned away and, twisting her hair into a knot[3], stepped into the shower. The warm needle spray struck her body[4], making a steady assault against the rigid tension of her muscles[5]. It felt good. Gratefully[6] she lifted her face to the spray. A shower felt so clean.

She never, never took a tub bath anymore—not since the years with Carl. She didn't think about those baths anymore. A vivid shaft of recollection came[7] as the water splashed against her face. The tub... Carl's insistence on bathing her[8]... the way he had touched and examined her. Once when she'd tried to push him away, he'd slipped and his face had gone under the water. He'd been so startled that for a moment he couldn't pull up[9]. When he did, he'd begun sputtering[10] and trembling and coughing. He'd been so angry... but mostly so frightened. It had terrified him to have his face covered by the water.

That was it. That was what she had tried to remember: that secret fear of water....

Oh, God. Nancy swayed[11] against the side of the shower stall. She felt nausea rack[12] her stomach and throat, stumbled out of the shower[13] and began retching[14] uncontrollably.

Minutes passed. She clung to[15] the sides of the commode[16], unable to stem[17] the violent waves of illness[18]. Then, even when the vomiting[19] finally stopped, icy chills[20] still shuddered through her body[21].

29

"**Ray, don't count on too much**[1]," Jonathan warned[2].

Ray ignored him. Through the streaked[3] windowpane, he could see the station house. The glow from the gas lamps gave it the look of another century. Quickly parking the car, Ray threw open the door and darted across the macadam into the station. From behind he could hear Jonathan puffing[4] as he tried to keep pace[5].

The desk sergeant looked surprised. "Didn't expect to see you here tonight, Mr. Eldredge. I'm sure sorry[6] about the kids...."

Ray nodded[7] impatiently. "Where are they questioning Rob Legler?"

The sergeant looked alarmed. "You can't have anything to do with that[8], Mr. Eldredge."

"The hell I can't[9]," Ray said evenly[10]. "Go in and tell the Chief that I have to see him now."

The sergeant's protest died on his lips. He turned to a policeman who was coming down the corridor. "Tell the Chief that Ray Eldredge wants to see him," he snapped[11].

1. ne vous faites pas trop d'illusions
2. avertit
3. zébré [de pluie]
4. haleter
5. suivre le rythme
6. Je suis vraiment désolé
7. acquiesça
8. Ça ne vous concerne pas
9. C'est ce qu'on va voir
10. posément
11. lui ordonna-t-il sèchement

Ray turned to Jonathan. With the trace of a wan smile[1], he said, "Suddenly this seems like a far-fetched[2], crazy idea."

"It isn't," Jonathan replied quietly[3].

Ray glanced around the room and realized for the first time that two people were sitting on a small bench near the door. They were just about as old as he and Nancy—a nice-looking[4] couple. He wondered abstractedly[5] what they were doing here. The guy looked embarrassed[6], the woman determined[7]. What would bring anyone out[8] on a night like this? Was it possible they had had a fight[9] and she was pressing charges[10]? The idea was wildly funny[11]. Somewhere outside this room, outside this whole incredible day, people were home with their families; cooking dinner in candlelight[12], telling kids not to be scared of the dark, making love... having fights....

He realized that the woman was staring at him. She started to get up, but the husband pulled her down. Quickly, Ray turned his back to her. The last thing in the world he wanted or needed was sympathy[13].

Footsteps hurried down[14] the corridor. Chief Coffin rushed into the room. "What is it, Ray? Have you heard anything?"

Jonathan answered. "You have Rob Legler here?"

"Yes. Were questioning him. Dr. Miles is with me. Legler's asking for a lawyer. Won't answer any questions."

"I thought as much.[15] That's why we're here." In a low voice, Jonathan outlined[16] his plan.

Chief Coffin shook his head. "Won't work. This guy's a cool one.[17] There's no way you'll get him to place himself[18] at the Eldredge house this morning."

"Well, let us try[19]. Can't you see how important time is? If he had an accomplice who has the children now, that person may panic. God knows what he might do."

1. demi-sourire triste
2. tirée par les cheveux
3. calmement
4. à l'air sympathique
5. vaguement
6. gêné
7. résolue
8. Qu'est-ce qui avait pu les pousser à sortir
9. se soient battus
10. veuille engager des poursuites
11. parfaitement risible
12. à la lueur des bougies
13. de la compassion
14. On entendit des pas pressés dans
15. C'est ce que je pensais.
16. esquissa
17. Ce gars ne perd pas le nord.
18. Il ne reconnaîtra jamais qu'il était
19. laissez-nous essayer

"Well... come in here. Talk to him. But don't count on anything." With a jerk of his head,[1] the Chief nodded to[2] a room halfway down the corridor. As Ray and Jonathan started to follow him, the woman got up from the bench[3].

"Chief Coffin." Her voice was hesitant. "Could I speak to you for just a minute?"

The Chief looked at her appraisingly[4]. "Is it important?"

"Well, probably not. It's just that I felt I wouldn't have any peace unless[5]... It's something my little boy..."

The Chief visibly lost interest. "Just sit down please, ma'am. I'll be back with you as soon as I can."

Ellen Keeney sank down on the bench as she watched the three men leave. The sergeant at the desk sensed her disappointment. "Are you sure I can't help you, ma'am?" he asked.

But Ellen didn't trust the sergeant. When she and Pat had first come in, they had tried to tell him that they thought their little boy might know something about the Eldredge case. The sergeant had looked pained[6]. "Lady, do you know how many calls we've had today? Since the wire services[7] got hold of this[8], we've had nothing but calls[9]. Some jerk[10] from Tucson phoned to say he thought he saw the kids in a playground across the street from his apartment this morning. No way they could have gotten there, even in a supersonic plane. So just take a seat. The Chief'll talk to you when he can."

Pat said, "Ellen, I think we should go home. We're only in the way here.[11]"

Ellen shook her head. She opened her pocket-book and took out the note the stranger had given Neil when he had sent him in for the mail. She had attached the note to her own scribblings[12] about everything[13] Neil had told her. She knew the exact time he had gone in for[14] the letter. She had carefully writ-

1. D'un signe de tête,
2. désigna
3. banc
4. la jaugea du regard
5. ne serais pas tranquille tant que
6. pris un air affligé
7. agences de presse
8. sont sur cette affaire
9. le téléphone n'arrête pas de sonner
10. Un abruti
11. Nous dérangeons, ici.
12. griffonnages
13. retranscrivant tout ce que
14. à laquelle il s'était présenté à la poste pour retirer

ten down his description of the man; his exact words when he'd said the man looked like the picture on television of Nancy Harmon's first husband; the kind of car the man was driving—"a real old station wagon just like Gramp's"—that sounded like[1] a Ford. Last[2], Neil had said that the man had a fishing permit for Adams Port on his windshield.

Ellen was determined to sit here until she got a chance to tell her story. Pat looked so tired. Reaching over, she patted his hand. "Bear with me[3], dear," she whispered. "I suppose it doesn't mean anything[4], but something is making me[5] wait. The Chief did say he'd talk to me soon."

The door to the station house opened. A middle-aged couple came in. The man looked thoroughly annoyed[6]; the woman was visibly nervous. The desk sergeant greeted them[7]. "Hi, Mr. Wiggins... Miz[8] Wiggins. Anything wrong?[9]"

"You won't believe it," Wiggins snapped. "On a night like this, my wife wants to report[10] that somebody pilfered[11] a can of baby powder from the store this morning."

"Baby powder?" The sergeant's voice ranged upward in astonishment.[12]

Mrs. Wiggins looked more upset. "I don't care how stupid it sounds. I want to see Chief Coffin."

"He'll be coming out soon. These people are waiting for him too. Just sit down, won't you?" He pointed to the bench at a right angle to the one where the Keeneys were waiting.

They came over, and as they sat down, the husband muttered[13] angrily, "I still don't know why we're here."

Ellen's ready sympathy made her turn to[14] the couple. She thought that maybe just talking to someone would help the other woman to get over her nervousness[15]. "We don't really know why we're here either,"

1. cela faisait penser à
2. Pour finir
3. Un peu de patience
4. que cela ne veut rien dire
5. me pousse à
6. exaspéré
7. les accueillit
8. Mme
9. Un problème ?
10. signaler
11. a chapardé
12. L'étonnement fit partir le sergent dans les aigus.
13. grommela
14. Toujours compatissante, Ellen se tourna vers
15. surmonter sa nervosité

she said. "But isn't it an awful thing about those missing children...."

Fifty feet away in the office down the corridor, Rob Legler stared through narrowed[1], hostile eyes at Ray Eldredge. The guy had class, he decided. Nancy had certainly done a lot better[2] this time. That Carl Harmon had been some creep[3]. Fear knotted Rob's stomach.[4] The Eldredge kids hadn't been found. If anything had happened to them, they might try to pin something on him[5]. But nobody had seen him near the Eldredge house... nobody except that fat slob[6] who'd been in the old station wagon. Suppose that guy had been a deliveryman or something[7] and called the cops? Suppose he could identify Rob as being around the Eldredge house this morning? What excuse did he have for being there[8]? No one would believe that he had sneaked into the country[9] just to say hello to Nancy.

Mentally, Rob darted around for a story.[10] There was none that made sense.[11] He'd just keep his mouth shut until he got a lawyer—and maybe after that too. The older guy was talking to him.

"You are in a very serious[12] situation," Jonathan was saying. "You are a deserter who has been taken into custody[13]. Shall I remind you of the penalty[14] the law holds[15] for deserters? Your situation is far more serious than that of a man who left the country to avoid conscription[16]. You were a member of the armed forces[17]. No matter what has happened to the Eldredge children or how guilty or innocent you are in their disappearance, you stand right now[18] to spend the better part of[19] the next ten or twenty years in prison."

"We'll see about that[20]," Rob muttered. But he knew Jonathan was right. *Christ!*

"But, of course, even the desertion charge isn't nearly so serious as[21] a murder charge...."

"I never murdered anyone," Rob snarled[22], jumping up from his chair.

1. rétrécis
2. fait un bien meilleur choix
3. était vraiment un sale type
4. Rob avait l'estomac noué de peur.
5. lui faire porter le chapeau, d'une façon ou d'une autre
6. gros lard
7. livreur ou autre
8. pour justifier sa présence
9. repassé la frontière incognito
10. Rob cherchait frénétiquement une histoire qui tienne.
11. Aucune ne tenait la route.
12. grave
13. en garde à vue
14. peine
15. requise par la loi
16. s'éviter le service militaire
17. soldat
18. risquez aujourd'hui
19. de passer quasiment
20. On verra ça
21. n'est rien à côté d'
22. gronda

"Sit down," Chief Coffin ordered.

Ray stood up and leaned across[1] the table until his eyes were on a level with Rob's[2]. "I'm going to lay it out for you[3]," he said evenly. "I think you're a bastard[4]. For two cents, I'd kill you myself. Your testimony almost put my wife in a gas chamber seven years ago, and right now[5] you may know something that could save my children's lives if it isn't already too late. Now, listen, bum[6], and listen hard[7]. My wife doesn't believe that you could or would harm our children. I happen to respect that belief.[8] But she saw you there this morning. So that means you've got to know something about what went on[9]. Trying to stall[10] and say you never got to our house won't help. We'll prove you were there. But if you level with us[11] now, and we get our kids back, we won't prosecute a kidnapping charge[12]. And Mr. Knowles, who happens to be one of the top lawyers[13] in the country, will be your lawyer, to get you off[14] with as light a sentence as possible on the desertion charges. He has pull[15]—plenty of it[16].... Now, which is it, punk[17]? Do you take the deal?[18]" The veins bulged out[19] in Ray's forehead. He moved forward until his eyes were inches away[20] from Rob's. "Because if you don't... and if you know something... and if I find out[21] that you could have helped us get our kids back and didn't[22]... I don't care what jail they throw you in... I'll get to you[23] and I'll kill you. Just remember that, you stinking bastard[24]."

"Ray." Jonathan pulled him back forcibly.

Rob stared from face to face[25]: The Chief... the doctor... Ray Eldredge... that Knowles guy, the lawyer. If he admitted being at the Eldredge house... but what good[26] not to admit it? There was a witness. His instinct told him to take the offer that had been made. Rob knew when he had no cards left to play. At least by taking the offer, he had some leverage on the desertion business[27].

1. se pencha au-dessus de
2. regarder Rob droit dans les yeux
3. t'expliquer où on en est
4. vrai salopard
5. en ce moment même
6. tocard
7. bien
8. Je suis prêt à la suivre là-dessus.
9. sur ce qui s'est passé
10. gagner du temps
11. joues cartes sur table
12. tu ne seras pas poursuivi pour enlèvement
13. un des plus grands avocats
14. de manière à ce que tu t'en sortes
15. le bras long
16. très long
17. qu'est-ce que tu décides, vaurien
18. Tu prends ou tu prends pas ?
19. saillaient
20. soient à quelques centimètres de
21. que je découvre
22. que tu ne l'as pas fait
23. je te retrouverai
24. enfoiré
25. les dévisagea l'un après l'autre
26. quel intérêt
27. sa désertion se présenterait un peu mieux

He shrugged[1] and looked at Jonathan. "You'll defend me."

"Yes."

"I don't want any bum kidnapping rap[2]."

"No one's trying to pin one on you[3]," Jonathan said. "We want the truth—the simple truth, as you know it. And the deal's off[4] unless we get it now[5]."

Rob leaned back. He avoided looking at Ray. "Okay," he said. "This is how it started. My buddy up in Canada[6]..."

They listened intently as he talked. Only occasionally[7] did the Chief or Jonathan ask a question. Rob chose his words carefully when he said he was coming to ask Nancy for money. "See, I never believed she touched a hair on the head of those Harmon kids. She wasn't the type. But I got the word[8] that they were trying to pin the rap on me out there and I'd better[9] just answer questions and keep my opinions out of it[10]. I felt kind of sorry for her[11]; she was a scared kid[12] in a big frame-up[13] as far as I was concerned."

"A frame-up that was your direct responsibility," Ray said.

"Shut up, Ray," Chief Coffin said. "Get to[14] this morning," he ordered Rob. "When did you arrive at the Eldredge home?"

"It was like[15] a couple of minutes before ten," Rob said. "I had been driving real slow[16], looking for that dirt road my friend drew a picture of... and then I realized I'd missed it."

"How did you realize you missed it?"

"Well, this other car... I had to slow down for[17]... Then I realized that the other car had come off[18] that road, so I backed up."

"The other car?" Ray repeated. He jumped up. "*What* other car?"

The door of the interrogation room burst open[19]. The sergeant hurried in. "Chief, I think it's real im-

1. haussa les épaules
2. qu'on m'accuse d'un putain d'enlèvement
3. Personne ne cherche à t'épingler pour ça
4. le marché ne tient plus
5. si tu ne nous la dis pas là tout de suite
6. Mon pote au Canada
7. de temps à autre
8. j'ai appris
9. j'avais intérêt
10. à ne pas la ramener
11. Elle me faisait peine
12. pauvre gosse paniquée
13. coup monté
14. Venons-en à
15. Ça devait être
16. super lentement
17. J'ai dû ralentir pour la laisser passer
18. sortait de
19. s'ouvrit brutalement

portant you talk to the Wigginses and that other couple. I think they have something real important to tell you."

30

Finally[1] **Nancy was able** to get up, wash her face and rinse her mouth. She mustn't let them see that she'd been sick[2]. She mustn't talk about it. They'd think she was crazy. They wouldn't believe or understand. But if the unbelievable[3] was possible... The children. Oh, God, not again, not like that; please, not again.

She rushed into the bedroom and grabbed underwear[4] from the drawer, slacks[5] and a heavy sweater[6] from the closet. She had to go to the station house. She had to see Rob, tell him what she believed, beg him for the truth[7]. What did it matter if[8] everyone thought she was crazy?

With lightning speed[9], she dressed, stuffed her feet into sneakers[10], laced them with trembling fingers and hurried downstairs. Dorothy was waiting for her in the dining room. The table was set with sandwiches and a pot of tea.

"Nancy, sit down.... Just try to have something[11]...."

Nancy cut her off[12]. "I have to see Rob Legler. There's something I have to ask him." She clenched her teeth together[13], having heard the hysteria rising in her voice[14]. She must not be hysterical. She turned

1. Enfin
2. vomi
3. l'incroyable
4. des sous-vêtements
5. un pantalon
6. gros pull
7. le supplier de dire la vérité
8. Qu'importe si
9. En un éclair
10. enfila des baskets
11. Essayez de manger quelque chose
12. l'interrompit
13. serra les dents
14. sentant l'hystérie gagner sa voix

to Bernie Mills, who was standing in the doorway of the kitchen.

"Please call the station," she begged him. "Tell Chief Coffin I insist on coming over... that it has to do with[1] the children."

"Nancy!" Dorothy grabbed her arm. "What are you saying?"

"That I must see Rob. Dorothy, call the station. No, I will."

Nancy ran over to the phone. She was just reaching for it when it rang. Bernie Mills hurried to take it, but she picked it up.

"Hello?" Her voice was quick and impatient.

Then she heard. So low it was a whisper. She had to strain to make out his words[2]. "Mommy. Mommy, please come and get us[3]. Help us, Mommy. Missy is sick. Come and get us...."

"Michael... Michael!" she screamed. "Michael, where are you? Tell me where you are!"

"We're at..." Then his voice faded[4] and the line went dead[5].

Frantically, she jiggled[6] the phone. "Operator[7]," she shrieked, "don't break the connection[8]! Operator..." But it was too late. An instant later, the monotonous dull, buzzing dial tone[9] whined in her ear[10].

"Nancy, what is it? Who was it?" Dorothy was at her side.

"It was Michael. Michael phoned. He said Missy is sick." Nancy could see doubt[11] on Dorothy's face. "In God's name, don't you understand? That was Michael!"

Frantically, she jiggled the phone, then dialed the operator[12] who broke into her perfunctory offer of help when she responded[13] . "Can you tell me about[14] the call that just came here[15]? Who handled it[16]? Where did it come from?"

"I'm sorry, ma'am. We have no way of knowing that[17]. In fact, we're having a lot of trouble generally[18].

1. c'est au sujet des
2. tendre l'oreille pour comprendre ce qu'il disait
3. nous chercher
4. s'éteignit
5. la communication fut interrompue
6. Elle secoua frénétiquement
7. S'il vous plaît
8. ne coupez pas
9. la tonalité lancinante
10. résonnait, plaintive, à son oreille
11. l'incrédulité
12. composa le numéro de la standardiste
13. commença par débiter son offre d'assistance habituelle
14. me renseigner sur
15. que je viens de recevoir
16. Qui a transmis l'appel
17. n'avons aucun moyen de le savoir
18. globalement, la situation est très difficile

Most of the phones in town are out[1] because of the storm. What is the problem?"

"I've got to know where that call came from. I've got to know."

"There is no way we can trace the call[2] once the connection is broken[3], ma'am."

Numbly, Nancy put down the receiver.

"Somebody may have broken that connection," she said. "Whoever has the children."

"Nancy, are you sure?"

"Mrs. Eldredge, you're kind of strung-up[4] and upset[5]."

Bernie Mills tried to make his voice soothing[6].

Nancy ignored him. "Dorothy, Michael said, 'We're at...' He knows where he is. He can't be far away. Don't you see that? And he says Missy's sick."

From far off[7], she was hearing something else. Lisa is sick.... She doesn't feel right. She had said that to Carl long ago.

"What is the number of the police station?" Nancy asked Bernie Mills. She pushed back the waves of weakness[8] that were like clouds of fog[9] inside her head. It would be so easy to lie down... to slip away. Right now someone was with Michael and Missy... someone who was hurting them... maybe was doing to them what had happened before. No... no... she had to find them.... She mustn't get sick.... She had to find them.

She grasped the edge of the table to steady herself[10]. She said quietly, "You may think I'm hysterical, but I am telling you that was my son's voice. What is the number of the police station?"

"Call KL five, three eight hundred," Bernie said reluctantly[11]. *She's really flipped*[12], he thought. And the Chief would have his head[13] for not having gotten to the phone[14]. She imagined it was the kid... but it could have been anybody or even a crank[15].

1. ne marchent plus
2. Il nous est impossible de localiser l'appel
3. une fois la ligne coupée
4. tendue
5. bouleversée
6. apaisante
7. Très, très loin
8. vagues d'épuisement
9. des nappes de brouillard
10. garder l'équilibre
11. à contre-cœur
12. Elle a vraiment perdu la boule
13. allait lui sonner les cloches
14. pour ne pas avoir répondu lui-même au téléphone
15. sinoque

1. nette
2. dans le vide
3. La ligne est coupée.
4. C'est une sacrée tempête.
5. Monsieur l'agent !
6. puisque le téléphone ne marchait plus
7. ne l'avait pas signalé
8. envisagea
9. repoussa
10. bousillerait

The number rang once. A crisp[1] voice said, "Adams Port Police Headquarters. Sergeant... speaking." Nancy started to say, "Chief Coffin" and realized that she was speaking into nothingness[2]. Impatiently, she jiggled the phone. "It's dead," she said. "The phone is dead.[3]"

Bernie Mills took it from her. "It's dead, all right. I'm not surprised. Probably half the houses don't have phones by now. This is some storm.[4]"

"Take me to the police station. No, you go if the phone comes back on and Michael can call again... Please go to the police station, or is someone outside?"

"I don't think so. The television van went to the station house too."

"Then you go. We'll stay here. Tell them Michael phoned. Tell them to bring Rob Legler here. We've got to wait."

"I can't leave you."

"Nancy, how sure are you it was Michael?"

"I'm sure. Dorothy, please believe me. I'm sure. It was Michael. It was. Officer.[5] Please. How far is the station in your car?... Five minutes. You'll be gone ten minutes in all. —But make them bring Rob Legler here. Please."

Bernie Mills thought carefully. The Chief had told him to stay here. But with the phone out[6], there wouldn't be messages. If he brought Nancy with him, the Chief might not like it. If he left and came right back, he'd be gone a total of ten minutes, and if that ever was the kid on the phone and he didn't report it[7]....

He considered[8] asking Dorothy to drive to the station, then discarded[9] the idea. The roads were too icy. She looked so upset that the odds were she'd crack up[10] her car.

"I'll go," he said. "Stay right here."

He didn't take time to look for his coat, but ran out the back door to the patrol car.

Nancy said, "Dorothy, Michael knew where he was. He said, 'We're at...' What does that mean to you[1]? If you're on a street or on a road, you say, 'We're *on* Route 6A[2],' or 'we're *on* the beach,' or 'we're *on* the boat'; but if you're in a house or store, you know you say, 'We're *at* Dorothy's house'; or 'We're *at* Daddy's office.' Do you see what I mean? Oh, Dorothy, there must be some way to know. I keep going over things.[3] There must be something... some way to know.

"And he said that Missy is sick. I almost didn't let her go out this morning. I thought about it. I thought about it. Was it too cold; was it too windy[4]? But I hate to think about them being sick[5] or to baby them about being sick[6], and I know why now. It was because of Carl and the way he examined them... and me. He was sick[7]. I know that now. But that's why I let Missy out. It was damp and too cold for her. But I thought just half an hour. And it was because of that. And I got her red mittens, the ones with the smile faces, and I told her to be sure to keep them on[8] because it was so cold. I remember thinking that for a change[9] she had a matching pair[10]. But she did lose one[11] by the swing. Oh, God, Dorothy, if I hadn't let them out! If I had kept them in because she was getting sick... But I didn't want to think about that.... Dorothy!"

Nancy spun around[12] at Dorothy's strangled cry. Dorothy's face was working convulsively[13]. "What did you say?" she demanded. "What did you say... about the mittens?"

"I don't know. Do you mean—that she lost one—or that they matched? Dorothy, what do you mean?... What do you know?"

With a sob, Dorothy covered her face. "I know where they are. Oh God, I know... and I was so stupid. Oh, Nancy, what have I done? Oh, what have I done?" She reached into her pocket and pulled out the mitten. "It was there... this afternoon on the floor of the garage and I thought I'd kicked it out. And that awful man...

1. Comment vous comprenez ça
2. SUR la 6A
3. Je n'arrête pas de retourner tout ça
4. est-ce qu'il y avait trop de vent
5. les penser malades
6. trop les chouchouter quand ils sont malades
7. un malade
8. de faire attention à ne pas les perdre
9. pour une fois
10. ses moufles étaient assorties
11. en a quand même perdu une
12. se retourna brusquement
13. grimaçait violemment

I knew there was something about him[1]; the way he smelled[2] so sour[3]... so evil[4]... and that baby powder. Oh, my God!"

Nancy grabbed the mitten. "Dorothy, please help me. Where did you find that mitten?"

Dorothy sagged limply[5]. "At The Lookout, when I was showing it[6] today."

"The Lookout... where that Parrish man lives. I don't think I've ever seen him except from a distance. Oh, no!" In an instant of total clarity[7], Nancy saw truth and realized it might be too late. "Dorothy, I'm going to The Lookout. *Now*... the children are there. Maybe. Maybe I'll be in time.[8] You go for[9] Ray and the police. Tell them to come. Can I get into [10] the house?"

Dorothy's shaking stopped. Her voice became as calm as Nancy's. Later—later, for the rest of her life—she could indulge in self-recrimination[11]... but not this minute. "The kitchen door has a bolt. If he put it on, you can't get in. But the front door, the one on the bay side—he never uses it. I never gave him a key. This will open both locks." She dug into her pocket and came out with a set[12]. "This one."

She did not question[13] Nancy's decision to go alone. Together the women raced out the back door toward the cars. Dorothy let Nancy pull out first[14]. She caught her breath[15] as Nancy's car lurched[16], skidded[17] and then righted itself[18].

It was almost impossible to see. The sleet had formed a thick ice shield[19] against the window. Nancy rolled down her side window[20]. Glancing out it, squinting against the pelting sleet[21], she raced the car down the road, across Route 6A and down the street that led to the cutoff[22] for The Lookout.

As she started up the winding incline[23], the car began to slip. She floored the gas pedal[24] and the front wheels skidded, twisting[25] the car on the icy road. Nancy jammed on the brake[26]. The car spun around[27]. Too late, she tried to right it. A tree loomed

1. qu'il avait quelque chose de louche
2. cette odeur qu'il dégageait
3. si aigre
4. si répugnante
5. s'affaissa mollement
6. quand j'en faisais faire la visite
7. clairvoyance
8. J'arriverai peut-être à temps.
9. Allez prévenir
10. Est-ce qu'il y a moyen de rentrer dans
11. pourrait se faire tous les reproches qu'elle voudrait
12. en ressortit un jeu
13. ne discuta pas
14. sortir la première
15. retint son souffle
16. faisait une embardée
17. dérapait
18. se redressait
19. épaisse plaque de glace
20. baissa sa vitre
21. plissant les yeux pour voir malgré le grésil
22. raccourci
23. entamait la montée sinueuse
24. appuya à fond sur l'accélérateur
25. faisant slalomer
26. écrasa la pédale du frein
27. partit en tête à queue

ahead[1]. She managed to yank the wheel in a half circle[2]. The front end of the car pulled to the right and with a grinding crash[3] hit the tree.

Nancy was thrown forward, then snapped back[4]. The wheels were still spinning as she pushed open the door on the driver's side and stepped out into the pelting sleet. She hadn't put on a coat, but she barely felt the sleet go through her sweater and slacks as she tried to run up the precarious hill[5].

At the approach to the driveway, she slipped and fell. Ignoring the sharp pain in her knee, she ran toward the house. *Don't let me be too late.*[6] *Please don't let me be too late.* Like clouds breaking before her vision[7], she could see herself staring down at the slabs at[8] Lisa and Peter... their faces white and bloated from the water[9]... the bits of the plastic bag still sticking to them. *Please*, she prayed. *Please!*

She got to the house and steadied herself against the shingles as she ran around it toward the front entrance. The key in her hand was wet and cold. She grasped it tightly. The house was completely dark except for the top floor. She could see a light coming through the shade[10] on one of the windows. As she rounded[11] the house, she could hear the harsh crashing sounds of the bay[12] as the waves broke against the rocky shore[13]. There was no beach—just piles of rock. The beach was over to the left.

She hadn't realized this property was so high. You could probably see the whole town from the back windows.

Her breath was coming in deep, sobbing gasps.[14] Nancy felt her heart pounding[15]. She couldn't breathe from running in the cold wind.[16] Her numbed fingers fumbled with[17] the key. *Let it turn*[18]*; please, let it turn.* She felt resistance as the rusty lock grabbed at the key[19], then held it[20], and finally the lock turned and Nancy pushed open the door.

1. se profilait droit devant
2. braquer d'un demi-tour
3. dans un fracas épouvantable
4. projetée en avant, puis en arrière
5. pente périlleuse
6. Faites que je n'arrive pas trop tard.
7. Comme si des nuages se déchiraient devant ses yeux
8. fixant, sur les tables de la morgue,
9. bouffis par le séjour dans l'eau
10. store
11. contournait
12. le violent fracas dans la baie
13. rochers de la rive
14. Elle respirait par grands sanglots haletants.
15. cogner son cœur
16. Sa course dans le vent glacé lui avait coupé le souffle.
17. De ses doigts gourds, elle tenta d'introduire
18. Faites qu'elle tourne
19. la serrure rouillée avalait la clef
20. la coinçait

The house was dark—so terribly dark. She couldn't see. There was a musty smell[1], and it was so quiet here. The light had come from the top floor. That was where the apartment was. She'd have to find the stairs. She resisted the impulse to shriek[2] Michael's name.

Dorothy had said something about two staircases in the foyer past the big front room. This was the front room. Uncertainly,[3] Nancy started forward. In the pitch darkness[4], she reached her hands in front of her. She mustn't make noise; mustn't give warning[5]. She tripped[6], fell forward and recovered herself by grabbing something. It was the arm of a couch or chair. She felt her way around it[7]. If only she had matches[8]. She strained to hear[9].... Had she heard something... a cry... or was it just the way the wind howled[10] in the fireplace?

She had to get upstairs... had to find them. Suppose they weren't there?... Suppose she was too late?... Suppose it was like last time?—with those little faces so quiet, so distorted[11].... They had trusted her[12]. Lisa had clung to[13] her that last morning. "Daddy hurt me" was all she would say. Nancy was sure that Carl had spanked her[14] for wetting the bed... had cursed herself[15] for being too tired to wake up. She hadn't dared to criticize[16] Carl... but when she made the bed, it wasn't wet; so Lisa hadn't wet the bed. She should have told them that at the trial, but she couldn't. She couldn't think, and she was too tired... and it didn't matter anymore[17].

The stairs... That was a post under her arm.[18]... The stairs... three flights... Walk on the side... Be quiet. Nancy reached down and yanked off her sneakers[19]. They were so wet they'd make a squishing noise[20].... *Important to be quiet.... Have to get upstairs.... Mustn't be too late again.... Last time too late.... Shouldn't have left children in car.... Should have known...*

1. odeur de renfermé
2. résista à l'envie de crier
3. Hésitante,
4. obscurité totale
5. donner l'éveil
6. trébucha
7. le contourna à tâtons
8. des allumettes
9. tendit l'oreille
10. le hurlement du vent
11. déformés
12. lui avaient fait confiance
13. s'était accrochée à
14. lui avait donné une fessée
15. s'était maudite
16. osé critiquer
17. cela n'avait plus d'importance maintenant
18. C'est un poteau qu'elle sentait sous son bras.
19. enleva vite ses baskets
20. bruit de ventouse

The stairs squeaked[1] under her foot. *Mustn't let him panic.*[2]*... Last time he panicked.... Maybe Michael's call panicked him.... Last time they said the children hadn't been thrown in the water till after they were dead.... But Michael was still alive just a few minutes ago... Twenty minutes ago... and he thought Missy was sick.... Maybe she was sick.... Have to get to her.... The first flight.... Bedrooms on this floor... but no light, no sound....* Upstairs two more flights.... On the third floor there was no sound either[3].

At the base of the last staircase, Nancy stopped to control her harsh breathing. The door at the head of the stairs was open. She could see a shadow against the wall caused by a thin flicker of light. Then she heard it... a voice—Michael's voice... "Don't do that! Don't do that!"

She ran up the stairs blindly[4], furiously. Michael! Missy! She hurried, not caring about the noise, but her thick socks[5] didn't make noise. Her hand grasping the banister[6] was silent. At the top of the stairs she hesitated. The light was coming from down the hall[7]. Silently, swiftly she hurried through the room, the living room probably, that was shadowy[8] and quiet[9], toward the candlelight in the bedroom, toward the gross figure[10] with its back to her[11] that was holding a small struggling[12] figure on the bed with one hand, giggling softly[13] as with the other he pulled a shiny[14] plastic bag over a blond head.

Nancy had an impression[15] of startled blue eyes, of Michael's blond hair matting on[16] his forehead, of the way the plastic clung to his eyelids and nostrils as she cried, "Let go of him[17], Carl!..." She didn't know she'd said "Carl" until she heard the name come from her lips.

The man spun around. Somewhere lurking[18] in that gross mass of flesh[19], she could see eyes that darted and burned[20]. Nancy had an impression of the plastic

1. grinçaient
2. Il ne faut pas qu'il s'affole.
3. on n'entendait rien non plus
4. à l'aveuglette
5. épaisses chaussettes
6. rampe
7. du fond du couloir
8. sombre
9. silencieux
10. silhouette massive
11. qu'elle voyait de dos
12. qui se débattait
13. ricanant
14. brillant
15. image fugace
16. collés à
17. Lâche-le
18. tapis
19. toute cette graisse
20. étincelants

1. ébouriffée
2. son coupe-vent rouge vif en tas
3. un air fourbe
4. Cette voix.
5. d'effacer de sa mémoire
6. se précipita sur elle
7. se dégagea
8. sa grosse main lui enserrer le poignet
9. pesamment
10. coude
11. s'enfoncer dans
12. violente
13. il relâcha sa prise
14. tout près du sien
15. traits bouffis, épaissis
16. odeur de sueur froide
17. mordit
18. flasque
19. envoya un coup
20. violente inspiration
21. faire face à
22. qu'elle arquait le dos sous sa poussée
23. hurler
24. un appel au secours continu, pressant
25. en vain
26. l'étouffait
27. Suffoquant, elle allait perdre conscience
28. relâchèrent
29. s'étrangla
30. gargouillis

clinging, of Missy's tousled[1] figure lying on the bed, her windbreaker a bright red heap[2] beside her.

She saw the look of stupefaction replaced by cunning[3]. "You." The voice was remembered.[4] The voice that over seven years she'd tried to blot out[5]. He started toward her menacingly. She had to get around him. Michael couldn't breathe.

He lunged for her[6]. She pulled away[7], feeling his thick grasp on her wrist[8]. They fell together, clumsily[9], heavily. She felt his elbow[10] dig into[11] her side. The pain was blinding[12], but his grip relaxed[13] for an instant. His face was next to hers[14]. Thick and white, the features bloated and broadened[15], but the sour, dank smell[16]... the same as it had been before.

Blindly, she reached out with all her force and bit[17] the thick, jowly[18] cheek. With a howl of rage, he lashed out[19], but let her go, and she dragged herself up, feeling his hand pulling at her. She threw herself onto the bed, with her fingernails tearing at the tight plastic sheet that was making Michael's eyes bulge, his cheeks become blue. She heard his gasping breath[20] as she twisted around to meet[21] Carl's new attack. His arms pulled her tight against him. She felt the sick warmth of his exposed body.

Oh, God. She pushed back his face with her hands and felt him bend her backward[22]. As she tried to pull away, she could feel Missy's foot under her, touching her, moving. It was moving. Missy was alive. She knew it; she could feel it.

She began to scream[23]—a steady, demanding call for help[24]; and then Carl's hand covered her mouth and nostrils, and futilely[25] she tried to bite the thick palm that was choking out air[26] and causing great black curtains to close in front of her eyes.

She was sinking into gasping unconsciousness[27] when abruptly the hands loosened[28] their pressure. She choked[29]—great gurgling sounds[30]. From somewhere, someone was shouting her name. Ray! It was Ray! She tried to call out, but no sound came.

Struggling up[1] onto one elbow, she shook her head. "Mommy, Mommy, he's taking Missy!" Michael's voice was urgent, his hand shaking her.

She managed to sit up as Carl swooped[2]. His arm passed her and grabbed the small figure that had begun to squirm[3] and cry.

"Put her down, Carl. Don't touch her." Her voice was a croak[4] now, but he looked at her wildly and turned. Holding Missy against him, he ran away, his gait awkward[5]. In the dark of the next room, she heard him bumping into[6] furniture, and she staggered after him[7], trying to shake the dizziness[8]. There were footsteps on the stairs now—hard, racing[9] footsteps coming up. Desperately she listened for Carl, heard him down the hall; saw his dark shadow silhouetted against the window. He was climbing up the stairs to the attic[10]. He was going up to the attic. She followed him, caught up with him[11], tried to grasp[12] his leg. The attic was cavernous, musty-smelling, thick-beamed[13] with a low ceiling[14]. And dark. So dark it was hard to follow him.

"Help!" she screamed. "Help!" At last she could make her voice carry.[15] "Up here. Ray. Up here!" She stumbled blindly after the sound of Carl's footsteps. But where was he? The ladder[16]. He was climbing the thin, rickety[17] ladder that led from the attic straight up to the roof. The widow's walk. He was going onto the widow's walk. She thought of the narrow, perilous balcony[18] that circled[19] the chimney between the turrets[20] of the house.

"Carl, don't go up there. It's too dangerous. Carl, come back, come back!"

She could hear his harsh breathing, the high-pitched[21] sound that was between sob and giggle[22]. She tried to grab his foot as she climbed after him, but he kicked savagely[23] when he felt her hand. The thick

1. Se relevant avec difficulté
2. plongeait
3. se tortiller
4. rauque
5. d'une démarche malaisée
6. se heurter à
7. le poursuivit en titubant
8. surmonter son impression d'étourdissement
9. précipités
10. grenier
11. le rattrapa
12. saisir
13. avec des poutres épaisses
14. et un plafond bas
15. Sa voix portait enfin.
16. échelle
17. branlante
18. périlleuse galerie
19. faisait le tour de
20. tourelles
21. haut perché
22. un sanglot et un rire nerveux
23. donna un furieux coup de pied

sole[1] of his shoe caught the edge of her forehead[2], and she slipped down the ladder. Ignoring the warm, gushing blood that streamed down[3] her face, not feeling the force of the blow, she started up again, crying, "Carl, give her to me. Carl, stop!"

But he was at the top of the ladder, pushing up the door that led onto the roof. Thick sleet pelted down as the door creaked upward[4]. "Carl, you can't get away," she pleaded[5]. "Carl, I'll help you. You're sick. I'll tell them you're sick."

The wind caught the door, pulled it open till it thudded[6] against the side of the house. Missy was crying now—a loud, frightened wail[7]: "Mommmmmmmy!"

Carl thrust his body onto the balcony. Nancy scrambled[8] after him, bracing against[9] the doorframe. It was so narrow. There was barely space for one person between the railing[10] and the chimney.

Frantically[11] she clawed at[12] his clothes—trying to get a grip on him[13], to pull him back from the low railing. If he fell or dropped[14] Missy... "Carl, stop. Stop!"

Sleet beat against him. He turned and tried to kick her again, but stumbled backward, grasping Missy against him. He lurched[15] against the railing and regained his balance[16]. His giggle was now a persistent, hiccuping sound[17].

The walk[18] was covered with a layer of ice. He sat Missy on the railing, holding her with one hand. "Don't come any nearer, little girl," he said to Nancy. "I'll drop her if you do. Tell them they must let me go away. Tell them they must not touch me."

"Carl. I'll help you. Give her to me."

"You won't help. You'll want them to hurt me." He swung one foot over the rail.

"Carl. No. Don't do it. Carl, you hate water. You don't want water to cover your face. You know that. That's why I should have known you didn't commit suicide. You couldn't drown yourself[19]. You know that, Carl." She made her voice calm, deliberate, soothing[20]. She

1. semelle
2. heurta sa tempe
3. le sang tiède qui coulait sur
4. se relevait en grinçant
5. implora
6. la rabatte avec un bruit sourd
7. plainte
8. grimpa
9. prenant appui contre
10. balustrade
11. Désespérément,
12. tenta d'agripper
13. le retenir
14. faisait tomber
15. tangua
16. retrouva son équilibre
17. hoquet
18. passage
19. aller te noyer
20. apaisante

took one step[1] toward the railing. Missy was reaching her arms out, pleading[2].

Then she heard it... a cracking, breaking sound[3]. The railing was breaking! As she watched, the wooden posts[4] gave way[5] under Carl's weight. His head went backward; he swung his arms forward.

As he released his hold on Missy[6], Nancy darted forward and grabbed her baby. Her hands caught in Missy's long hair[7]—caught and twisted[8] and held[9]. She was teetering[10] on the edge of the walk; the rail was crumbling. She felt Carl grab her leg as he fell, screaming.

Then, as she was being dragged forward[11], firm[12] arms came around her waist from behind—arms that held and supported her. A strong hand pulled Missy's head against her neck, pulled them both back, and she collapsed[13] against Ray even as[14], with a last despairing scream, Carl slid off the balcony, across the icy, sloping roof[15] and into the angry, rock-filled surf[16] far below.

1. fit un pas
2. suppliante
3. craquement sec
4. poteaux de bois
5. cédèrent
6. Au moment où il lâchait Missy
7. cramponnèrent la longue chevelure de Missy
8. s'entortillèrent
9. pour ne plus les lâcher
10. chancelait
11. alors qu'il l'entraînait vers l'avant
12. robustes
13. s'effondra
14. en même temps que
15. pente du toit
16. l'écume en fureur parsemée de rochers

31

THE FIRE LICKED HUNGRILY AT[1] the thick logs. The warm hearth smell[2] permeated[3] the room and mingled with[4] the scent of freshly made coffee. The Wigginses had opened the store and brought up cold cuts[5] for sandwiches, and they and Dorothy had prepared a spread[6] while Nancy and Ray were at the hospital with the children.

When they got home, Nancy insisted that[7] the television crews and reporters be fed too[8], and Jonathan had thrown his home open to them[9]. They had taken films of the homecoming[10] of Nancy and Ray, carrying their children in from the car, and had been promised an interview the next day.

"In the meantime[11]," Ray said into the microphones, "we want to thank everyone whose prayers through[12] this day kept our children from harm."

The Keeneys had come back to the house too, wanting to be part of the gladness[13]; frightened that they had waited to come forward with[14] their information; sure that only prayer had made the rescue possible. *We are all so human, so foolish*, Ellen thought. She shuddered thinking that her Neil had talked to that

1. léchait avidement
2. tiédeur de l'âtre
3. se répandait dans
4. se mêlait à
5. de la charcuterie
6. repas froid
7. avait insisté pour que
8. partagent le repas
9. leur avait ouvert sa maison
10. filmé le retour
11. En attendant
12. tout au long de
13. l'allégresse
14. transmettre

1. paisiblement endormie
2. [pommade à base de menthol et de camphre]
3. apaisée
4. la couverture en lambeaux qu'elle appelait son doudou
5. se blottissait
6. un Lendon qui l'interrogeait avec délicatesse
7. pensant à voix haute
8. surexcitée
9. fanfaronne
10. m'a crié de
11. Tu es formidable
12. détacher ses yeux de
13. blafard
14. meurtri
15. d'une beauté si sereine
16. qu'il n'arrivait pas à se débarrasser de la boule qui lui serrait la gorge
17. relut
18. seule
19. se serait opposée à
20. avait bloqué
21. a violemment agressé
22. dans un état grave
23. commotion cérébrale
24. ses jours ne sont pas en danger
25. n'ont pas subi d'agression sexuelle

insane man. Suppose he had asked Neil to get into his car that day...?

Nancy sat on the couch, tightly holding a peacefully sleeping[1] Missy. Missy, smelling of Vicks[2] and soothed[3] with warm milk and aspirin, the ragged blanket she called her "bee"[4] held securely to her face as she nestled[5] against her mother.

Michael was talking to a gently questioning Lendon[6]—telling all about it, thinking it out[7]. His voice, at first excitable[8] and rapid, was calmer now, even a little boastful[9]: "... I didn't want to go away from that house without Missy when the nice man started fighting with the other man and yelled at me[10] to get help. So I ran back up to Missy and called Mommy on the phone. But then the phone stopped working. And I tried to carry Missy down the stairs, but the bad man came...."

Ray's arms were around him. "Good boy. You're quite a guy[11], Mike." Ray couldn't keep his eyes off[12] Nancy and Missy. Nancy's face was discolored[13] and bruised[14], but so serenely beautiful[15] that he had trouble swallowing over the lump in his throat[16].

Chief Coffin put down his coffee cup and reviewed[17] the statement that he would make to the press: "Professor Carl Harmon, alias Courtney Parrish, was pulled out of the water still alive. Before he died, he was able to make a statement, confessing his sole[18] guilt in the murder of his children, Lisa and Peter, seven years ago. He also admitted that he was responsible for the death of Nancy Eldredge's mother. Realizing that she would have prevented[19] his marriage to Nancy, he jammed[20] the steering mechanism of her car while she was in the restaurant with Nancy. Mr. John Kragopoulos, whom Professor Harmon assaulted[21] today, is on the serious list[22] in Cape Cod Hospital with a concussion[23], but is expected to recover[24]. The Eldredge children have been examined and were not sexually molested[25], although the boy,

Michael, suffered a bruise on the side of the face[1] from a violent slap[2]."

The Chief felt fatigue settling into[3] the very marrow[4] of his bones. He'd give the statement and get home himself. Delia would be waiting for him, wanting to know everything about what had happened. This, he reflected, was the kind of day[5] that made police work worthwhile[6]. There was so much grief[7] in this job. There were the times you had to tell parents that their child was dead. Moments like the one in The Lookout when they knew they had found both kids safe were to be cherished[8].

Tomorrow. Jed reflected that tomorrow he would have to judge his own culpability. This morning he had prejudged Nancy[9] because of pique that he hadn't recognized her[10]. By prejudging her, he hadn't let his mind stay open; had ignored what Jonathan and Ray and the doctor and Nancy herself were telling him.

But at least he had driven the car that got Ray to the balcony on the roof of The Lookout in that split second of time[11]. No one else could have gotten up that hill on that ice so fast. When they'd seen Nancy's car crashed into the tree at the bend of the road, Ray had wanted to stop. But Jed had kept going[12]. Some instinct made him feel that Nancy had gotten out of the car and was in the house. His hunch[13] had been right. For that he could defend himself.[14]

Dorothy quietly refilled Lendon's cup at his affirmative nod[15]. Michael would be all right, Lendon thought. He'd come down and see them again soon. He'd talk to the children and to Nancy—try to help her to completely see the past for what it was and then turn her back on it[16]. Nancy wouldn't need too much help. It was a miracle that she'd had the toughness[17] to survive the horror of everything that had happened to her. But she was a strong person and would emerge from this last ordeal[18], able to look forward to[19] a normal life.

1. a un bleu au visage,
2. dû à une gifle très violente
3. pénétrer jusqu'à
4. moelle
5. Voilà le genre de journée, pensa-t-il,
6. pour lequel ça valait la peine d'être dans la police
7. douleur
8. étaient si précieux
9. condamné Nancy d'avance
10. vexé qu'il était de ne pas l'avoir reconnue
11. juste à temps
12. ne s'était pas arrêté
13. intuition
14. Sur ce point, il pouvait se féliciter.
15. quand il fit oui de la tête
16. puis tourner la page
17. solidité
18. se relèverait de cette dernière épreuve
19. prête à entamer

There was peace in Lendon.[1] He had compensated at last for his neglect.[2] If he had gone to Nancy when Priscilla died, so much could have been avoided. He would have realized there was something wrong with Carl Harmon and somehow gotten her away from him. But then she wouldn't be here now with this young man who was her husband. These children would not be in her arms.

Lendon realized how much he wanted now to get home to Allison.

"Coffee?" Jonathan repeated Dorothy's question. "Yes, thank you. I don't usually have any this late[3], but I don't think many of us will have trouble[4] sleeping tonight." He studied Dorothy closely. "How about you? You must be pretty tired."

He watched as an indefinable[5] sadness crept over[6] her face and understood the reason for it. "I think I must tell you," he said firmly, "that any kind of self-recrimination you have is intolerable[7]. We all ignored facts today[8] in a way that might have contributed to disaster[9]. One of the first of these is that every single morning as I walked past this house, I have been annoyed[10] by the glint[11] that hit my eyes. This very morning I considered[12] asking Ray to speak to the tenant at The Lookout about whatever he had[13] in the window. With my legal training[14], I should have remembered that. An investigation[15] would have led us to The Lookout very quickly.

"And one irrevocable[16] fact is that if you had not elected[17] to keep that appointment[18] and bring Mr. Kragopoulos to that house, Carl Harmon would not have been deterred[19] in his evil intent[20]. He would not have had his attention distracted[21] from Missy. Surely you've been listening to Michael's description of what was happening before your call."

Dorothy listened, considered, and in basic honesty agreed[22]. A weight of guilt and remorse[23] dissolved[24], and she felt suddenly lighthearted[25] and glad, able to

1. Lendon se sentait apaisé.
2. Il s'était enfin racheté de sa négligence passée.
3. si tard le soir
4. aurons du mal
5. indéfinissable
6. gagnait
7. que vous n'avez aucun reproche à vous faire
8. Nous avons tous, aujourd'hui, méconnu certains faits
9. et un vrai désastre aurait pu s'ensuivre
10. incommodé
11. reflet
12. j'avais envisagé
13. sur ce qu'il pouvait bien avoir
14. expérience de juriste
15. Des recherches
16. indéniable
17. choisi
18. venir au rendez-vous prévu
19. interrompu
20. projets maléfiques
21. détournée
22. dut admettre la justesse de ses propos
23. de remords
24. s'envola
25. le cœur léger

rejoice fully in the reunion. "Thank you, Jonathan," she said simply. "I did need to hear that."

Unconsciously, she clasped his arm[1]. Consciously, he covered her hand with his own. "The roads are still treacherous," he said. "When you're ready to go home, I'd feel better if I drove you[2]."

It is over[3], Nancy thought. *It is over.* Her arms tightened around her sleeping child. Missy stirred[4], murmured "Mommy," and slipped back into even, soft breathing.

Nancy looked at Michael. He was leaning back against Ray. Nancy watched as Ray gently pulled him down on his lap. "You're getting tired, fellow[5]," Ray said. "I think maybe you kids had better get to bed. It's been quite a day."

Nancy remembered the feeling when those strong arms had grabbed her, held her, kept her and Missy from falling. It would always be like that with Ray. She would always be safe. And today she'd seen and known and been in time[6].

From the wellsprings of her being[7], prayer permeated[8] her mind and heart: *Thank You, thank You, thank You.* You have delivered us from evil.[9]

She realized that the sleet was no longer pelting the windows, that the moaning sound[10] of the wind had died.

"Mommy," Michael said, and now his voice was sleepy. "We didn't even have a birthday party for you, and I didn't get you your present."

"Don't worry, Mike," Ray said. "We'll celebrate Mommy's birthday tomorrow, and I know just the presents to get for her[11]." Miraculously, the strain and fatigue left his expression, and Nancy saw a twinkle begin in his eye[12]. He looked directly at her. "I'll even tell you what they are, honey," he volunteered. "Art lessons from a really good teacher from the kids[13] and a color job[14] at the beauty parlor[15] from me."

1. lui serra le bras
2. je préférerais vous raccompagner
3. C'est fini
4. s'agita
5. bonhomme
6. était arrivée à temps
7. Du tréfonds de son être
8. inonda
9. Vous nous avez délivrés du mal.
10. gémissement
11. je sais exactement ce que nous allons lui offrir
12. son regard pétiller
13. de la part des enfants
14. une coloration
15. salon de coiffure

He stood up, eased Michael back[1] into the chair and came over to her. Standing over her, he studied the part in her hair carefully[2]. "I have a hunch you make a hell of a redhead,[3] honey[4]," he said.

1. replaça Michael
2. il examina avec attention la raie de ses cheveux
3. J'ai dans l'idée que tu ferais une très belle rousse,
4. chérie

La collection Yes you can!

Faux débutants

Ken Follett *The Modigliani Scandal*
Mary Higgins Clark *A Stranger is Watching*
Mary Higgins Clark *Where are the Children?*
Anthony Horowitz *The House of Silk*
Yann Martel *Life of Pi*
Nicholas Sparks *Message in a Bottle*

Intermédiaires

Harlan Coben *Play Dead*
Harlan Coben *Stay Close*
Harlan Coben *Tell No One*
Michael Connelly *The Black Box*
Michael Connelly *The Drop*
Ken Follett *Paper Money*
Mary Higgins Clark *A Cry in the Night*
P.D. James *A Mind to Murder*
Douglas Kennedy *The Big Picture*
John le Carré *A Most Wanted Man*

Avancés

Paul Auster *Oracle Night*
Julian Barnes *The Sense of an Ending*
Michael Cunningham *The Hours*
Elizabeth George *A Great Deliverance*
Stephen King *Misery*

Imprimé en Italie par La Tipografica Varese Srl
Dépôt légal : février 2015
314164-01/11026513-février 2015